VANISHING
HOUR

VANISHING HOUR

~

LISA KING

This is a work of fiction. Names, characters, places, and incidents either are the product of the author's imagination or are used fictitiously. Any resemblance to actual events, locales, organizations, or persons living or dead, is entirely coincidental and beyond the intent of either the author or the publisher.

The Story Plant
Studio Digital CT, LLC
PO Box 4331
Stamford, CT 06907

Copyright © 2019 by Lisa King

Print ISBN-13: 978-1-61188-276-6

Visit our website at www.TheStoryPlant.com

For information, address The Story Plant.

First Story Plant printing: March 2020
Printed in the United States of America

For Mom and Dad, with love

PART 1

◡

35 TREMBLANT STREET WEST

CHAPTER ONE
〜

As it turned out, the downfall of humanity was not a terribly concerning problem for seventy-year-old Matthew Werner—even though it was for six billion others. He was bothered, certainly. But deeply afflicted? Not really. The world, as Matthew knew it, had always been a confusing place. Recently, though, he hardly even recognized it.

For starters, everyone was obsessed with these incessant little computers, orbiting around them like a planet would a sun. No more friendly nods from neighbors. No more handwritten letters. Even smiles nowadays were accomplished by pushing pictures onto screens, as if curving one's real mouth upwards had gotten a little too difficult. Life (for most) appeared to have become no more than a swirl of insensible movements.

People snapping pictures of their hamburgers before taking a bite.

People liking those pictures before sending them along to others.

A *"like."* The word itself made Matthew want to shout, "HA!" As far as he was concerned, the concept was ridiculous. Social mediums—or whatever it was people called them. Just a performance of fake smiles. Then more fake smiles. Push, push, push the tiny screen. Ten thumbs up. One thumb down. People always staring. Down, down, down at those blasted little computers.

Safe to say, Matthew didn't much care for people anymore, with a few exceptions.

Exception One:

His roommate, Sandra. Though, ironically, no one else cared much for Sandra, possibly because she spent most of her time in bed (or at the local bar, drinking herself into a stupor). Also, her voice sounded like a fire of crackling logs. There was a gritty edge to it, which made her very difficult to understand. Oh yes, and her habit of exchanging sexual favors for monetary gains. A frowned upon endeavor, certainly.

But Matthew didn't mind these things overly (or, rather, he preferred not to think about them). Sandra paid him good rent. She was quiet, slow moving, and uninvolved. Plus, she used a *real* telephone when she wanted to talk, one that plugged into the wall and didn't blast crude music when it rang.

Exception Two:

Fran from Fran's Food. Although, if Matthew was being honest, Fran was just *okay*. She was nearly as old as him and every bit as harmless. But mostly she was predictable (and being predictable was important).

For example, every Tuesday when he walked to Fran's Food for groceries, she would say, "Hello, Mr. Werner. How are you today?" And he would say, "Well." Then she would say, "Glad to hear it."

And that was it.

Her voice was soft and clear, the antithesis of Sandra's, and she always smelled of prunes and vitamins. Always.

Exception Three:

Back when Matthew was in eleventh grade, there was a girl named Tabitha Marks who had wild-woman hair. *Matty* is what she called him, which made him tingle in the pit of his stomach.

It was, in fact, one of the only feelings he ever understood.

She'd race around the halls, twirling every so often, always smiling. It wasn't a thin, vapid smile like the other students wore; it was real. And when she'd whoosh by Matthew—her black, curly hair exploding all around her, that silly grin plastered on her face— he'd do something he rarely ever did.

Matthew Werner would smile back.

And he was still smiling on their wedding day, three years later. Smiling through forty-nine years of marriage. Smiling until the day he woke up and Tabitha was gone, at which point there wasn't much reason to smile any longer.

გ

Matthew didn't detest people or anything. They simply presented a number of problems—they always had.

Problem One: *People never stopped moving.*

Shuffling, fidgeting, quibbling, flickering, flouncing. Legs. Arms. Mouths. All together. All at once. Which, to another, might not be so troubling, but to Matthew Werner it went like this:

LOUDNESS! LOUDNESS! LOUDNESS!

So incredibly loud, people were—and they were getting even louder. Now they were shouting by *themselves.* Shouting into—or *at*—those ridiculous little computers they carried around everywhere. Their voices were like a symphony of tambourines, crashing and smashing. Which wouldn't be so bad if not for Problem Two: *People were unpredictable.*

The randomness! How utterly disturbing. But more so, terrifying. How was he supposed to tackle all of that LOUDNESS without a fair warning? He couldn't. Everything appeared brash and sudden, out of sync, each move charging his brain full of chaos. He hated how arbitrary it all felt, people doing this, then that. No method to their madness.

If it was up to him, people would move like a synchrony of wordless robots.

Thousands of flat, unreadable eyes.

Metal torsos, glistening in the sunlight.

That image made him happy, or at least more comfortable. Truthfully, without Tabitha, he felt more like a robot than a human being. Holding in his feelings. Holding in his tears. He often had to wonder: *Am I filled with organs and veins and warm, thick blood, or gears and wires and numbers? Nothing can hurt machines, so that's what I want to be ... so long as I'm not one of those stupid little computer boxes.*

Still, such problems were only pebbles compared to the gigantic mountain that presented itself to Matthew daily.

People. Were. Everywhere.

There was no avoiding them.

Thus, he relied on a precise set of instructions he'd rehearsed for years.

Do not look. Right foot. Left foot. Swing hands back and forth.

In the presence of strangers, he repeated this mentally. Sometimes, he even spoke portions out loud if the noise was overwhelming. "Do not look! Do not look!" And, in such a circumstance, he felt like a human metronome, keeping tempo to the LOUDNESS, which helped. Instead of a thousand pulses, there was only one: his voice, yelling into the chaos.

But still.

Tuesday.

Groceries.

It happened the same way every week: a swell of panic followed by a swirl of dread. But he had no other choice.

"It's good for you to get out of the house," Tabitha used to say. "That's why you're going and not me." And he would nod, even though he suspected there were other reasons why she wasn't going, like the fact she'd started to forget names and faces, and had even gotten lost a time or two on short walks around the block.

Anyway, Matthew hated Tuesdays the most.

At least he used to.

Until the Tuesday that changed everything.

CHAPTER TWO

~

Matthew Werner sat before the clock, his heart racing. The torturous countdown until 3:00 p.m.

Tick. 2:57.

Tick. 2:58.

A cold sweat rose on his neck and slid down his back. He scurried to his room and slipped on a sweater, then returned to the chair.

Tick. 2:59.

No, no, no, no, no, no.

Tick. 3:00.

His knees strained when he stood, like he was fifty pounds overweight. The prospect of seeing people always had this effect, the very knowledge of their existence like a weight on his back (well, that and being seventy).

A grumble escaped his mouth. Like every Tuesday at 3:00 p.m., he wished he'd gotten the whole production over with earlier. But then he remembered why 3:00 p.m. was so important.

Routine.

That word, *routine*, got his heart thumping even faster. There were few things worse than breaking a routine.

He trudged to the door and cracked it open. "Coat?" he grumbled. The sliver of air was fresh and cool. "Yes, coat."

He slipped on a jacket, did up the buttons, bottom to top, careful not to miss any. His palms began to sweat and his knees started to tremble. He slapped on a flat cap and stared at the door. *Do not look. Right foot. Left foot. Swing hands back and forth.*

It was time to face the people.

The first step was always the worst, the store being exactly 152 steps away. He walked quickly, imagining, as he always did, that he was connected to home by an invisible rope. Silly, perhaps, but it gave him a sense of bearing as he faced the outside world.

Do not look. Right foot. Left foot. Swing hands back and forth.

After ten steps, he waited for the noise: people yammering, or the pitter-patter of footsteps, or the whoosh of a bicycle. Or, worst of all, the sound of little computers ringing all around.

But there was nothing, not even the chatter of birds.

When he reached block one, he glanced up. Not a single person in sight. *Strange,* he thought. But also, *wonderful.*

Well, not entirely wonderful. As he peered around, there were several neighborhood details that made his teeth grind together. For example:

Shingles flapping like skirts in the wind. *Those need fixing!*

Lawns overgrown with prickly weeds. *Those need mowing!*

Asphalt cracking like spider veins. *That needs paving!*

By golly, what a mess!—not that he expected otherwise. People didn't care about pride of ownership or doing things correctly anymore. Nowadays, it was all about cutting corners and *cheap, cheap, cheap!*

Lazy.

The whole stinkin' lot of 'em!

His head began to pound just looking at the disarray of his once tidy neighborhood. So on he went, eyes glued to the sidewalk. With every step, he waited for the sounds of people, or, rather, the *symptoms* of people, as if they were some infectious disease. A harsh thought, but he couldn't help it. People crawled through his skin like an illness. They always had—except for Tabitha.

Suddenly, he realized a further absence: the humming of car engines. Yes, the streets were unusually quiet. *Am I missing something?*

But then he shrugged. *Meh.*

When he reached Fran's Food, he peered around.

Still.

No one.

He stared at the sign, Fran's Food, and gave it a nod. He'd always liked that name. It got right to the point, unlike newer stores he'd heard about, like eBay *(probably a boat shop, but who could be sure with a name like that?)*, or Amazon *(something about camping, no doubt, or maybe an umbrella store)*.

But again, *Meh.*

The entrance bell rang with a *ting* as he entered. He sniffed for prunes and vitamins, awaiting Fran's typical greeting, "Hello, Mr. Werner, how are you today?"

Nothing.

"Fran?" he said. Then, assuming Fran was in the washroom or something, he tiptoed inside.

The agenda:

Cheese. Milk. Eggs. Soup. Bread.

Every. Single. Time.

In. That. Order.

He grabbed a plastic shopping basket and walked toward the dairy section. First, he selected the cheddar cheese, followed by a carton of milk and a dozen eggs. He stared into the cooler, noting a few new arrivals.

Almond milk.

Cashew milk.

He scratched his chin. *Nut milk? How the heck do you milk a nut?*

Baffled, he headed toward the soup, still shaking his head. As he passed the junk food aisle, a big, fat, "HA!" shot from his throat. Each time, this section seemed to grow and grow—and it was already the largest and fullest to begin with, filled with candy bits and cheesy puffs and chocolate huffs and all the other crap young people were eating these days.

Young people.

The very thought sent him into a tizzy. *Young people with their baggy pants and underwear puffing from beneath! Young people with hats covering their eyes! Young people saying the first letter of words instead of actual words! BRB! I'll show you a BRB … once I figure out what a BRB is!*

He stomped over to the soup section and selected five cans of chicken noodle, his favorite. Then came the bread: white and fluffy with a golden crust. For a second, he eyed the organic, gluten-free loaf, a new flicker flaming.

Sigh. He simply didn't have the energy.

Back at the counter, he waited for five minutes.

"Fran?" he whispered. Then a little bit louder. "Fran?"

No Fran.

Finally, accepting she was busy elsewhere, he placed twenty dollars and five cents on the counter and left.

∽

The walk back was always better. "Almost there," he'd recite, sometimes out loud if the noise was overwhelming, which usually led to a few odd stares—not that he cared, looking down and all. But today there was still no one.

He kinked his head toward the shops.

Anyone?

Nope, entirely still and vacant.

Well, not exactly *still*—not to Matthew. He stared at their exteriors, LOUDNESS stirring, because *Starbucks!* That building *used* to be Mabel's Cafe, a quaint little shop with homemade biscuits and plain cups of coffee. Now? A chain store filled with mocha-frappa-crappa-whatevers for *young people!* He wandered further, nerves pulsing with each passing shop.

Studio yoga. *People need to pay money nowadays to take a stretch?*

3D printers. *Who the hell needs a 3D printer? The entire world is 3D!*

Neon signs all over. *Sale! Sale! Sale! Shut it!*

A sharp pain drilled into his head, so he resumed staring at the ground.

Almost there! Almost there! Almost there!

Do not look! Do not look! Do not look!

Finally, when the imaginary rope had all but retracted, he rushed inside, safety and silence awaiting.

He poured a glass of milk and sat at the table. How strange the day had been. He'd never been outside without people. Ever.

Perhaps there's some sort of event going on? A festival? People like those sorts of things for some reason.

But then he sipped his milk and thought of something else.

What if there are no more people?

And, with that thought, he felt unimaginably lighter.

CHAPTER THREE

～

Matthew Werner wasn't normal. He'd known this for a very long time. It had, in fact, become a working diagnosis, the asterisk attached to his name.

Not Normal.

Of course, a number of real disorders had been discussed over the years: autism, Asperger's, obsessive compulsive disorder, social anxiety. He had *something*. But no one could say precisely what that something was.

After a while, people lost interest, and Matthew became a dust-covered puzzle—which is how he began to see himself: a collection of pieces put together in a way that others were not. A puzzle no one could solve.

Besides Tabitha.

She never pitied his Not Normal the way others seemed to. Special classes, extra smiles, faces smeared with … *concern*? Matthew could never tell, because how the hell was *he* supposed to know what people were communicating with their *faces*, of all things.

How unreadable they were! For example, he'd noted that the furrow of a single brow could imply confusion, disgust, skepticism, disappointment, sarcasm. Yes, facial expressions reminded him of the alphabet if

A were to also represent B, C, D, and E. Why couldn't people just say their feelings instead of contorting their features so strangely? Not that people needed to communicate *out loud* anymore, thanks to little computers.

At any rate, facial expressions weren't so terrible nowadays, because inside of his house, the only face around was Sandra's (and hers read, more often than not, blankly).

Speaking of Sandra, as Tuesday afternoon became Tuesday evening, Matthew began to wonder what she was doing. Normally, she'd at least call to check in. Then again, it was so quiet without her, probably the quietest he could ever remember. And he couldn't argue with how lovely that was.

∽

For two days, Matthew wandered around his small abode—calm, quiet, everything settled for the first time in, well … ever. He showered and slurped bowls of soup. He dusted off a book he hadn't read in decades: *The Mysterious Life of Bobby Jones*, even though Bobby Jones wasn't really mysterious, but simply solved adventures with friends. It was his childhood favorite.

When it came to *reading* about people, that wasn't so bad. In fact, if real people were narrated to him in a story—their thoughts and hopes and feelings and motives—he'd probably like them as much as Bobby Jones and his crew of amateur detectives.

But the world didn't work like that.

The world expected him to figure it all out on his own. And how was *he* supposed to know what *other* people were thinking and feeling?

What a conundrum.

After a few chapters, Matthew decided to spend the rest of the afternoon *tinkering* (at least that's what Tabitha used to call it). It was the act of taking something apart and putting it back together again. She preferred he abstain from such senselessness, saying things like, "Matty dear, stop *tinkering* with that, will you? What's the point?"

And, in a sense, there was no point.

He just liked it.

The toaster, for example, contained basic elements: sheets of mica wrapped in nichrome wire, grates, the circuit board, a timer, metal, plastic, more wires, screws.

He'd argued (unsuccessfully) that tinkering was a learning experience, that knowing how things worked was important for a husband. But, deep down, he never expected to learn more about the machines he unraveled.

He only hoped to learn more about himself.

And so he grabbed the microwave this time, unplugged it, and set it on the table. He took the Phillips from the drawer and started loosening the screws. He carefully removed the thermal cutout switch with a pair of tweezers, accidentally knocking the turntable shaft. It rolled across the table and landed on the floor.

Just as he leaned down to pick it up, something shuffled outside. He stopped, waited. *What was that? A cat perhaps? Or maybe someone sweeping the sidewalk?*

He crept to the window and pulled back the curtains.

Nothing.

He picked up the turntable shaft and returned it to the table. But then came a rattling in the distance, like thunder. Suddenly, bits and bolts from the microwave began shaking across the table. He ran back to the window and gasped.

People running.

There were hundreds of them, some sprinting down the road with bulging eyes and faces white as sheets, others glancing over their shoulders and falling behind. Except, there was nothing behind them—nothing he could see, at least. One old man, near the back, stumbled and fell across the pavement. Nobody stopped to help. Instead, they trampled him like a herd.

Matthew's heart leaped into his throat. The world was suddenly wild.

Thumping. Banging. Screaming. Hollering.

LOUDNESS!

Sweat stinging his eyes, he closed the curtains and locked the doors. His heart raced even faster as the noises exploded, banging against his skull like a hammer. *Where are they going? Will they try to break in?*

His biggest fear: all those people and all that noise, inside instead of outside, near instead of far, here instead of there.

He raced to the back door and barricaded it with a large wooden cabinet. Next, he sprinted to the front door, a bigger challenge. He considered the dining room chairs—*too flimsy*—then stared into the kitchen. *The island!* He pushed as hard as he could, heaving and straining with all his might. His arms throbbed, sweat pooled along his chest, and, just when he thought he could push no more, the island slid into place.

That will keep them out.

Except:

What about Sandra? What about Tabitha?

The world outside was a great crescendo, growing louder. If they returned, he'd never be able to hear their voices. Unless ...

He stared at the door, knowing he'd have to wait beside the LOUDNESS.

He dropped to the tile, rocked back and forth, back and forth, trying to ignore the commotion. The sounds: growls and shrieks and stretched-out moans, like balloons deflating. He could make out a very weak "help," and then an unforgettable *crunch*.

The doors and windows rattled and shook with such force he feared the old house may very well collapse, crushing him like an insect. He wanted to bury himself in the bottom of a closet or the corner of a room, away from the noises. But he couldn't.

He had to wait.

CHAPTER FOUR

⌒

A s day turned to night and night to day, Matthew dealt with the LOUDNESS the same way he dealt with other unfortunate occurrences: he focused elsewhere. For example, when strange noises came from Sandra's room, as they would on occasion, he'd read a book. Or when Tabitha's voice popped into his head (*Hello, Matty dear! Why aren't you looking for me?*) he'd pace the halls.

But the noises that had been going on outside for over a day were nothing like the grunts and groans from Sandra's room, nor were they like the LOUDNESS from before. Sirens wailed. Horns honked. Children screamed. People talked: "Charles? Charles are you okay? Why do you look so ..." Or, "Did you bring the flashlight? Rebecca? *Rebecca?*" And then there was this sluggish breathing, juxtaposed with a sound that was much more abrupt: the intermittent thump of something heavy hitting the ground.

All Matthew could do was shift his attention. Even though there was very little to focus on in his small world behind the door, he came up with a few activities.

Count the number of watermarks on the ceiling. Bonus points for mold.

Tap the tiles like a drum.

Clench fists. Blink eyes. Alternate for as long as possible.

After a while, though, despite the counting and tapping and clenching and blinking, his stomach growled. He tried to swallow, but couldn't. It was as if a thick coating of plaster had hardened on his tongue.

Still, he fought the urge to leave. What if Sandra needed in?

Or what if Tabitha miraculously found her way home in all of this chaos? What if she banged on the door and shouted, "*I'm finally home, dear!*" in her sweet honeysuckle voice, and he wasn't there to hear it? What if she died outside among the LOUDNESS because he'd left to fetch a drink of water?

The thought destroyed him.

And so.

He waited.

As time pressed on, the noises began to lessen. Every so often, someone—or *something*—shuffled in the distance, or a person's name was muttered from afar. "*Peter? Marjorie?*" But mostly . . . silence. He pressed an ear against the island.

Nothing.

As fast as he could manage, he stumbled to the sink and chugged. He vomited onto the shiny metal sides and then chugged some more. He filled a large pitcher with water, grabbed a loaf of bread, a few cans of soup, a spoon, his book, and a blanket.

Back beside the door, he gobbled a slice of bread, then stuffed another into his mouth before he even had time to swallow the first. He opened a can of soup and slurped it down in less than a minute. Another. The spoon clanked to the floor; *never mind it!* He guzzled the third like a bottle of soda. And when he was full, he stretched his aching back against the island, the silence washing over him. But then came a terrible flashback:

A pile of black ashes, still smoldering.

Tabitha's locket, covered in soot.

For the first time in all his life, Matthew Werner wished he had a little computer screen to stare into.

CHAPTER FIVE

～

In what seemed like no time at all, twelve-year-old Ruby Sterling went from a normal day at Silverlake Junior High to hiding in a shed as the world crumbled around her. It was nighttime now; only a sliver of light peaked in through a crack in the door—which was probably for the better, because spider webs and such.

Or perhaps not.

Because in the darkness of that cold, lonely space, all she could do was think.

Nothing made sense! How was it that one moment she was in the middle of a melting-ice experiment in science class, and the next in a shed? Whose shed? She didn't even know!

It had all happened so fast: her entire class, hiding beneath their desks, eyes ballooning like blimps, legs shaking. Then Mrs. Marconi saying, "It's okay, children. Probably just a drill. Don't be frightened. It's going to be okay."

And just when she'd started to believe her, there was Mom, yanking her from beneath the desk, telling her to move quickly, not to ask questions. Apparently, they needed to leave IMMEDIATELY.

Outside, everything looked normal—even though Mom drove like a maniac to their apartment. It wasn't until she stepped inside the foyer that things began to seem … off. The elevators were packed with their neighbors. Old Mrs. Matheson was running around in circles, her dog in one arm and cat in the other, screaming, "It's okay, boy. It's okay!"

But it wasn't okay—clearly.

Inside their apartment, Mom told her to pack.

"Pack for *what*? What's happening? Where's Dad?"

"No time. We're meeting him."

"But Mom, why is everyone—"

"Ruby, please."

So, she began tossing things into her knapsack: her favorite yellow sweater, chocolate-chip granola bars, water bottles, medication, lip chap, and then Mom snatched her arm so violently a pain shot through her shoulder and a cry escaped her mouth.

Back on the streets, people spilled from their houses, screaming and cursing and running in all directions. To her right, a car slammed into a man. He rolled across the windshield and tumbled onto the pavement, painting it with a streak of red.

To her left, a little girl cried, "MOM! MOM HELP!" But her mom didn't help. Nobody did.

Everywhere, people ran from their vehicles, yelling, shaking their fists. The sidewalks were so crowded there was barely space to move. And then they reached a screaming woman. The child in her arms was limp. It didn't blink.

Ruby stopped.

"Keep moving," Mom said. "Look down." And so she did (even though she didn't want to!), focusing on the space beneath her and nothing else. Regardless, something awful grew inside of her. The world she knew was strong and permanent, full of towers. This world? Delicate, breakable, raging apart. It was very …

Bad.

And then they were on the TTC subway, leaving the city—or trying to. Finally, she had a moment to catch her breath and look around. The people: something about them was off, at least for some. They looked dazed, confused, unreachable, their gaze almost wandering away.

Are they sick? She squinted, trying to get a better look, until the subway jerked to a stop. "Get out!" a man yelled. "Now! Out! Everybody!"

Before she had a chance to grab Mom's hand, people hurled toward the exit. Chaos. More chaos. Seconds later, she was lost in the shuffle, Mom gone. *Stay calm. She's here. She couldn't have gone far.*

"Mom?" Her voice melted into the noise. She yelled louder. "MOM?"

Her heart drummed as she exited the train in a pack of people, stuck in the middle. All she could see were coats and shoulders. "MOM?" she kept yelling. Useless.

Outside on the platform, she waited for a very long time (or so it seemed), searching the crowd. *She will find me,* she repeated over and over, trying not to cry. But there was no Mom, just people looking strange, lost, like something was happening to them. Like they were changing somehow.

Then, finally, Mom *did* find her, except she was different. The same, but different. She didn't say a word. Didn't even take her hand until Ruby reached out. She couldn't make sense of it—not that she had time to. Mom started running, dragging her alongside. They ran until the crowd was behind them, until the tall buildings became condos, then two-story duplexes, then, finally, single homes with small backyards.

"Where's Dad?" she kept asking.

"*Shhh*, not now."

"Mom! Please tell me what's going on!"

But Mom paid no attention. Strangely, she seemed incapable of paying attention, as if she couldn't quite remember what they were doing. One minute they were running in one direction. The next minute, the opposite direction. Others were acting the same. Just running, escaping. To where? Who knew?

Ruby wanted to sit down. She *had* to.

"Please, Mom, my feet hurt! Where are we going?" she cried.

"Somewhere," Mom said. "Somewhere."

So she moved with Mom—unpredictable, confused Mom—until eventually Mom stopped. She turned around and smiled, but it wasn't her usual smile. It was twisted up and strained.

"Honey, it's okay. Everything is going to be okay."

She led Ruby to a nearby shed and opened the door.

"Go inside and stay there."

"But Mom—"

"Please, Ruby, do as I say. Everything is going to be just fine." She passed her a blanket. "Here, wrap yourself in this."

Ruby nodded, even though the wool was scratchy. She sat in the corner of the shed and Mom handed her the duffle bag.

"Take this. Okay? Stay here. I'll only be gone for a while. Don't leave. Do you hear me? Do *not* leave."

Again, she nodded.

"I love you, Ruby. So much."

It was then that Ruby started to cry. It clouded her eyes in a fog, and, when she wiped away her tears, Mom was gone.

A few seconds later, the noises started. Hooting and hollering and shuffling and screaming. People yelling, "Go! Move!" Or names: "Samantha? *Samantha!*" And then there was a terrible crunching noise, like stepping on branches, except Ruby knew it wasn't branches.

All the while, she buried herself in that stupid, scratchy blanket, her heart pounding so hard that tiny specks of light danced before her eyes.

Don't leave, Mom had said. *I'll only be gone for a while.*

By now, though.

It had been a very long while.

CHAPTER SIX

D ays had passed since the LOUDNESS began.
Matthew was certain of it. And in light of this,
an important question arose:
How long should I wait?

Considering he had nothing better to do, he decided he should wait a very long time.

He sat in his uncomfortable nest by the door, trying very hard to ignore the intermittent sounds from outside: the occasional holler, or loud plummet, or, worst of all, the faint but obvious sound of nails scratching against wood. Disturbing, of course, but none of these sounds really mattered, because they weren't Sandra, and they weren't Tabitha.

In many ways, his greatest fear had come true: change and uncertainty, no one around to help. In only a small number of days, the world had become an inaccessible mystery—more inaccessible than ever before. Yet, he'd always wished for the people to go away, because life would be much easier without them and their annoying little computers.

Something he had to consider:
Has my wish come true?
Perhaps.

Finally, when he ran out of food in his cubby by the door and the last drop of water slipped down his throat, he went to the kitchen. For the first few hours, he tiptoed around—if Sandra or Tabitha showed up, he needed to be able to hear them. After a while, though, he stopped, reevaluated. Who was he kidding?

Tabitha wasn't coming back, and neither was Sandra.

He glanced into the living room, an idea arriving. *The television!* Personally, he hated that idiot box and would have chucked it long ago, but Sandra loved her celebrity gossip ("If Brangelina can't stay together, nobody can!"—whatever that meant).

If he turned the thing on, he might discover what was happening outside. Surely, they'd sneak in a few words about the LOUDNESS after those important "Brangelina" headlines, right?

He fetched the remote and pressed the button. Nothing but static.

Sigh.

Wait. *The radio!* He wasn't sure if people even knew what those were anymore, but maybe there was some sort of emergency message being broadcasted? He trotted to the living room and yanked the dust-covered contraption from a shelf. It smelled a bit dingy and weighed a ton, but he plugged it in, straightened the antenna, and fiddled with the knobs.

Nothing. Not even static.

Sigh.

Sigh.

He hoisted it onto the dining room table and began to unravel it piece by piece, remembering how he'd once read a book on radios when he was very young, fascinated by the simple fact that a nine-volt battery and a coin could transmit a radio signal—not very well, of course, but still.

After disassembling the entire device, it appeared the only thing wrong with it was a crack on the metal attached to the antenna. This was an easy enough fix, and there happened to be an antenna on the old TV out back. The metal inside would work fine on a radio, no doubt. He just needed to go—

Outside?

He shivered.

Then again, does the radio really matter?

He had plenty of water and a fair collection of food. If he rationed well, he could survive inside for weeks, perhaps months. Not forever, obviously, but for a while. Plus, an entire bookshelf awaited, and there were many contraptions to tinker with—lots to keep him preoccupied.

Yes, the radio wasn't *that* important; certainly not important enough to venture out into the unknown. He would deal with that when he needed to, and not a moment sooner.

He walked into the kitchen and opened a can of soup.

When he turned on the stove, Tabitha's locket caught his eye. It was sitting on the counter—the same spot it had been for nearly a year.

He'd given her that locket on their wedding day, and he remembered the moment perfectly. Her mouth had parted into a circle. "It's breathtaking, Matty," she'd whispered. Then he'd placed it around her neck, whispering back, "*You're* breathtaking." Because she was. She was the most breathtaking thing in the world, her lace gown flowing all around her, those crazy, wild curls bouncing atop her head.

And much later:

It was the locket that reminded her where she belonged. Even when she'd forgotten where they lived or who she was, one look and her memories returned. For whatever reason, the locket always brought her back.

He dangled the tarnished, silver heart from his pinky finger, one side glistening in the dim light, the other side bent and blackened.

Yes, the locket had always brought her back.

Until it didn't.

CHAPTER SEVEN

I nside the dark, dusty shed, Ruby tried her best to exercise something she'd never been particularly good at:

Being patient.

Now that things were quieter, it had all started to feel like a very bad dream.

Had Mom really left her all alone? And in a *shed*, no less? That didn't sound like Mom …

Whatever. Mom would be back—any second now— then everything would be okay.

Right?

Still, her stomach clenched; she couldn't help but analyze the facts—something Dad had taught her to do—and the fact of the matter was, the people on the subway were acting very strangely. Sort of like … zombies. Not *real* zombies, obviously, but they were zoned out like zombies, their eyes floating off into the distance.

Why would that be? Something *must* have happened to them. Were they sick? And what kind of sickness would make people behave so strangely?

She remembered a sickness Dad once talked about, a parasite called *toxoplasmosis*. Proudly, it was the second biggest word she could spell and recite.

The story of toxoplasmosis went like this: if a mouse was infected, it became less scared of a cat. Then, it would waltz right up to that cat and be eaten, thus passing on the sickness.

Back when Dad had explained this to her, she found it all super neat.

"Not all sicknesses make people sick," he'd said. "Sometimes, a sickness simply changes an animal's behavior."

"Like the mouse," she replied.

"Precisely like the mouse! Sicknesses can be very manipulative of their hosts."

"Hosts? Does that make the sickness a guest?"

Dad chuckled. "I guess you could think of it that way. Just not a very nice guest."

Remembering this moment with Dad made her smile. And then it turned a few gears inside of her. If sickness could change behavior, maybe people on the subway *were* sick. She flashed back to Mom, how strange she'd been, darting all over, a removed look in her eye. And her smile: framed with terror, like she knew something bad was happening; she just wasn't sharing it out loud.

Even though Ruby preferred not to think it, she did.

If all of those people were sick …

Does that mean Mom was sick too?

CHAPTER EIGHT

⟡

T he radio, Matthew decided, was crucial after all. Even though he'd been keeping himself busy (precisely: 149 games of solitaire, a twelve-story house of cards, three entire books, and four completely unbound electronic devices), none of these activities distracted him from the voice of Tabitha, which had started to chirp in his mind.

Matty dear, why aren't you looking for me?

As time passed, the feeling grew heavier, unrelenting, ruthless as hell. It dragged him down and tugged at his skin, and he couldn't make it go away. Because the driving force of this feeling (though he tried his best to repress it) was perfectly clear.

His wife was still missing.

And he was playing cards.

Guilt began to follow him like a shadow—which prompted him to reconsider the possible benefits a working radio might provide. Like, perhaps people had gathered somewhere. He knew this happened in times of crisis, natural disasters and such. Not that he would necessarily *go* to such an area. But if he knew a place like that existed, there might be a possibility—no matter how remote—that Tabitha (and Sandra too; he hadn't forgotten about Sandra) had somehow found their way to that location. And if such a location happened to be the Central Belfort Community Center, for example, it was only a ten- or fifteen-minute walk away. He could surely muster up the courage to investigate.

Plus, the old TV was *barely* outside, stationed on the porch. And, if he remembered correctly (and he was certain he did), he wouldn't even have to leave the house. He could simply reach over, drag the thing inside, close the door, and voila! The entire production would be a piece of cake.

Except, as it turned out, the old TV wasn't the only thing waiting for him on the porch.

∽

Matthew stood before the cabinet that barricaded the rear entrance. His limbs were like jelly, then stiff as winter branches. He considered making a cocoa, or sitting on the sofa instead.

But then he imagined Tabitha and her honeysuckle voice. *Matty, Matty, Matty.* With a single heave, he slid the dresser away from the door and took a deep breath. He was getting far too old for things like this, end of the world or not.

To calm his pounding heart, he imagined what came next as a series of steps. *Open door. Drag in TV. Shut door.* And, when listed as such, there wasn't much to it. What could possibly go wrong?

He forced his shaky fingers to pull back the bolt, and then he pushed open the door before he could change his mind.

Everything stopped.

His heart. His breath. Even time—so it seemed.

There was the TV, yes, except it had been smashed to bits. But this is not what took his breath away. No, what sucked the air straight from his lungs was a shoe … attached to a foot … attached to a leg … attached to a sprawled-out woman, twisted across the porch.

She wasn't moving.

Her beige knit sweater. *Not moving.*

The arch of her spine. *Not moving.*

Her fingers, kinked apart like insect legs. *Also not moving.*

Then came her face, and it too did not move. Her lurching eyes were wide and open, but they never once blinked, and he was sure they hadn't for hours—maybe even days.

He slammed the door. His head began to pound with LOUDNESS and a scream clawed up his throat—a scream he had no choice but to let out.

Precisely because those eyes, wide and bloodshot, were the loudest things he'd ever seen.

CHAPTER NINE

∽

If Matthew were to describe the LOUDNESS (not that anyone had ever asked), he'd describe it as a storm.

A storm in his own mind.

First it came like a gust of wind, blowing around his thoughts, making them a little less accessible. Then, like pellets of hail, the LOUDNESS would pelt him from inside, pinging across his skull, harder and harder, each sting a little longer. Until: lightning. Big, bold streaks of electric current would fry and fizzle until his vision clouded over, at which point there was no stopping it, the worst storm of all: a relentless, swirling tornado of darkness and pain that caused him to close in tightly, unable to think, unable to move.

All of this happened (the wind, the hail, the lightning, the tornado) as he imagined the body of that woman—not that he wanted to. The image had pressed itself into his mind like a stamp.

To make matters worse, the woman kept reminding him of Tabitha, even if the two looked nothing alike. For starters, there were at least three decades between them, not to mention the woman had a common, everyday look about her, while Tabitha had dark eyes nuzzled closely together, prominent eyebrows, and a wild nest of crazy hair atop her head. And then there was the most obvious distinction: the lady on the porch was white, and Tabitha's skin was a deep, chocolate brown.

Unfortunately, these striking differences didn't matter, because every time Tabitha popped into Matthew's head, so did the woman on the porch: kinked apart, not moving, her black eyes cracked with crimson. And if that wasn't terrible enough, every time Matthew saw his own reflection, he also saw Tabitha's.

Brush teeth. *Tabitha.*

Stand at window. *Tabitha.*

Look at blank TV screen. *Tabitha.*

Wherever he went, there she was.

Kinked apart and crimson.

In an attempt to forget such frightful imaginings of his wife, he tried to remember snippets from long ago. Her soft hands, folding into his as they walked down the lane. Her smile: cheeky and toothy and wide as a horizon.

He laughed, remembering the time she burnt their Thanksgiving turkey so profoundly it was unrecognizable: black as coal and crispy all the way through. But he ate it anyway, because he loved her. And she loved him. And together they were all each other ever needed.

These memories always made him smile—for a moment at least, before recent memories elbowed in. Like the first time she asked for their address—they'd lived in the same house for four decades. Or the morning he found her staring into the bathtub, asking what it was for. Or the time she left a coffee mug in the freezer and a thawing pork chop in the cupboard.

Before she went missing, they were becoming parallel people in increasingly parallel worlds.

Tabitha's World:

Distant and unreachable, a place he could only visit on occasion.

Matthew's World:

Removed and complicated and full of sadness.

He missed her terribly, and not being able to find her was like an anchor dragging him to the ground—especially now.

Each time he read a page of his book instead of fixing the radio, the chances of finding her declined. And with all of the madness going on outside? *Impossible.*

Impossible because it was chaos out there.

Impossible because he couldn't face any more LOUDNESS.

So, he stayed indoors, drowning in regret. Tabitha would never know how much he wanted to find her. How truly sorry he was that he hadn't. Yesterday and today.

Now, he grabbed a piece a paper.

I am sorry, he jotted.

If he could, he'd have tossed it outside. And maybe, miraculously, if she *was* out there somewhere, the note would've fluttered in the wind and landed at her feet. And maybe, miraculously, upon reading it, she would remember him and know he was sorry for everything.

But he couldn't bring himself to open the door. So, instead, he slid aside the cabinet, taped it on the window, and continued to wait.

For nothing.

For everything.

CHAPTER TEN

～

Ruby was *so* done waiting. She'd eaten the last granola bar and her knapsack was empty. "*Dang!*" she said.

The water bottles?

Also gone.

It was foolish; she should have rationed better. But what else was she supposed to do besides eat granola bars and drink water?

She'd arranged pieces of gravel into designs and scraped some across the pavement to create roman numerals. She notched the number of days she'd been there in big bold letters: VII.

Now, staring at that number, she could hardly believe it. *Seven days!* If Mom hadn't left her in a shed, there were all kinds of things she would have accomplished in seven days.

One grocery shopping trip with Mom.

Two dinners of takeout food.

Three piano practices with Dad.

Four walks with Mom.

Five whole days of school.

Six nights of television.

Seven sleeps in her own bed.

In the shed, though, she hadn't done much of anything.

Nineteen granola bars, eaten.

Six bottles of water, drunk.

Seven nights of crying.

Surprisingly, nighttime wasn't nearly as terrifying as she expected. Without the barbaric noises, which had stopped days ago, the darkness was sort of ... comforting, a place she could cry into for hours, like a giant pillow. And eventually she'd fall asleep into that pillow, dry and empty and totally exhausted.

Twilight, however, was a different story. Each night, as the brightness of day faded, out came the shadows: razor sharp and menacing. Shovels, pitchforks, gardening supplies—they all came together to produce something quite nightmarish, with claws and fangs and spikes down its back. Pitchfork Monster, was his name. And he was *petrifying*.

Even though Mom had told her to stay in the shed, she couldn't stomach another twilight, couldn't bear to watch the bones of Pitchfork Monster crawling up the wall. The image was practically indigestible, curdling her with fear.

She *had* to get out of there. And, really, she'd waited seven whole days—an impressive accomplishment.

Mom would understand.

She slid the backpack over her shoulder and grabbed Mom's duffle bag. She'd wanted to open that duffle bag a hundred times over, but hadn't. It just didn't feel ... right. Not without Mom. When Mom returned, they'd open it together—soon. Because Mom would be back soon. She just knew it.

She flung open the door and brightness poured in. The glare made her eyes water, everything round and white and glowing. Soon enough, though, the images began to settle. She took a step, then another. The yard was still there, just flattened, like a herd of bison had trampled through. Stuff was everywhere: running shoes and baseball caps and sweaters with giant holes ripped through them, like a few hundred concertgoers had noticed those bison and run for their lives.

Otherwise, things weren't so different. The spring air was crisp. The faint scent of perfume rose from the flowers, pressed against the earth. And the sky was a glorious blue, garnished with the odd puffy cloud. A beautiful day, really. Maybe she'd overreacted, staying inside for as long as she had.

She stepped toward a porch.

And that's when she saw it.

A human-sized lump.

∽

Ruby had never paid much attention to her heart. She'd always been more concerned with other organs in her body, ones that caused her trouble. As Dad had explained to her, organs were much like a long chain of dominos, upheld by nutrients (and other impressive words she could barely remember, like amino acids and electrolytes and pH balances). Problems for one led to problems for another, like falling dominoes. And she was very familiar with this process, because she'd felt the dominoes inside of her falling before—all except for one.

Now, she felt that last domino tumble.

The longest single thump.

Then nothing.

"Mom?" she whispered.

On the window of the door, a sign:

I am sorry.

CHAPTER ELEVEN

~

Matthew sat on the sofa drinking a cocoa. He opened *The Handyman's Guide to Household Appliances*, a text he'd read six times already. *Whatever.* It was excellent.

A quiet gurgle, almost like a drip, caught his attention. *Did I leave the pot on?* Then it came again, a bit louder. *The wind perhaps?*

But it wasn't the wind. He knew exactly what that sound was—a girl, crying—he just didn't like it. He never quite knew what to do with children, and he certainly didn't now.

He started to hum, waiting for her to go away. When she didn't, he opened and closed his book. *Pat. Pat. Pat.* He clicked his tongue against the roof his mouth. *Click. Click. Click.* That helped (at least for a few moments). But when his tongue had done all the clicking it could do for one night and his fingers refused to open the book even one more time—

There was still.

Crying.

The world nowadays was very unforgiving, and Matthew was a careful man.

One minute you're helping your neighbor, the next you're being sued! One minute you're saving a child, the next you're thrown in jail!

What was he supposed to do with a weeping girl anyway? And what was she supposed to do with him? To top it all off, she was sobbing from the worst possible place.

Behind the door.

Beside the woman.

Really, what did the girl think was going to happen here? That he'd open the door? See that woman? Hear the LOUDNESS? Invite her—a stranger—inside? Typical young person, expecting everything to be about *them*! Me. Me. Me.

"Go away," he mumbled. "Find some other house."

He began to pace, praying the girl would move along. But an hour later she was still crying. It seemed impossible that she was *still crying*. On *his porch!*

"This is my property," he said.

Because really, *how dare she! No respect these days!* Perhaps, if he pounded on the door, she would scram. He clenched his fists.

༄

A loud shuffle came from inside. Ruby's muscles tightened. Someone (or something) was moving toward her. She stood back from the door.

Beside her:

The fuzzy blanket.

Beneath that:

Mom.

Her face was wet and cold.

༄

Matthew kinked his ear. The crying had finally stopped, thank goodness. But then came a thought:

What if the same thing that happened to the woman just happened to the girl?

Another body on his porch.

Not moving.

He shuddered.

She's likely fine. But, to be sure, he pressed his face against the door.

Silence.

He knocked three times.

After a moment, a knock came in reply. Another.

The vibrations against his palm were pleasant, soothing, the rhythm easing him (as most rhythms did).

He knocked. Then she knocked.

She knocked. Then he knocked.

And so it went.

Maybe opening the door wasn't such a terrible idea after all.

He cracked it open like a mussel's shell, exposing the tiniest sliver of life. Then he cautioned a glance. The cool night air seeped inside, fresh on his nose. Otherwise, nothing but blackness. He stared into that blackness for quite some time, waiting.

∽

Ruby stared at the door. It was open, barely. She waited and waited for someone to step outside, or at the very least say *something*.

At last, she finally whispered, "Hello?"

LOUD SCRAMBLE. DOOR SLAM.

She jolted. *What the?*

She turned to leave, but then came the knocking. She tapped her knuckles against the wood once more. For some reason, this exchange was making her legs

stronger, her heart less panicked, her jittery jaw a little less jittery. Her knuckles grew sore and tired, but
she kept up with the knocking until finally the door
cracked open, this time a bit wider.

She peered inside, surprised to find a wrinkly old
man. His eyebrows were gray and bushy, and he had
droopy, deep-set eyes, like a basset hound. His face was
so impossibly still she wondered if he was a statue. He
certainly looked like a statue, with his expressionless
features and far-away gaze. But then he blinked.

For many minutes.

Stare. Blink. Stare. Blink.

∾

A dilemma:

It wasn't as though Matthew didn't want to let the
girl in. Well, he didn't *want* to, per se, but he was going
to. He just wasn't sure how. Even though she was quiet
and slight and hardly alarming, she still smelled like
a person and looked like a person and that was more
than he could handle. But she was a child, so maybe
she wasn't a *full* person yet. He could probably deal
with something like that. And although he hadn't the
foggiest of clues what to say to a not-quite-full-person,
there was something soothing in this half-person's
eyes.

∾

With nothing in the way of an introduction, the stat-
ue-man finally moved aside and pointed inward,
which Ruby took as an invitation.

If she had her wits about her—as in, if she hadn't
just cried beside Mom's body for over an hour in the

cold twilight after spending seven days in isolation—
she may have been more hesitant. But she wasn't. She
practically leapt inside, glad to feel some warmth.

Almost instantly, the old man slammed the door
behind her and sealed it with a cabinet. Her nerves
fizzled (there was that last domino again, fluttering
uncontrollably). How could she have been so stupid,
getting herself into a situation like this? Who knew
what the strange old man was capable of?

"Are ... are," she stuttered. "Are you going to hurt
me?"

He scrunched his face and shook his head. His eyes
were saggy—sad. Not regular old sadness, but a special
type of sadness reserved for people who had lost something big, something cherished. In a strange way, staring at the old man was like looking into a mirror. He
seemed, for a moment, a little less like a stranger.

"I'm Ruby," she said. "What's your name?"

But instead of replying, he only winced and walked
away.

She wasn't sure what to do. The old man was weird,
plain and simple, from his wordless stare to his odd
use of knocking. Even his *walk* was strange, rigid and
slow, like he was connected by rusty hinges instead of
joints and limbs. Maybe his body didn't work properly
(which was okay, actually, because neither did hers).

She took a seat on the stiff, crusty sofa—*gross*. Everything about the room was old and worn. The fur-
niture looked like it belonged in a museum! The dim,
mostly vacant space was nothing like her own house.
There weren't any family photos, or colorful paintings,
or knick-knacks sitting on shelves. The air smelled
stale and dusty.

Houses, Mom once told her, *are like stories*. And
she'd always liked this comparison. But as she peered

around the old man's living room, she couldn't find a single story in sight.

A moment later, he returned carrying a glass of water and two boiled eggs on a plate. He handed her the water and she slurped it down. Then came the eggs. Those, she practically swallowed whole.

"Thanks," she said.

He tapped his foot, looking away. "Sure."

After a long stretch of silence, he turned to leave.

"Wait," she said. He stopped. "What am I supposed to do?"

He shrugged. Then he walked away for good.

CHAPTER TWELVE

〰

Ruby jolted awake. "MOM!" she cried. A nightmare lingered: Pitchfork Monster, stomping toward her. She turned over on the sofa. And then it all rushed back, except bigger and bolder this time.

Mom was on the porch.

She ran to the door and yanked the cabinet with all her might. When it didn't budge, she tried again, working herself into an all-out sweat. She punched at the solid wood until her knuckles started to crack. Finally, she slid to the ground, blood trickling from each crevice, her hair tangled and damp.

After wiping her hands on her pants, she began to knock. It had calmed the old man; maybe it would do the same for her? And it worked, at first. She drifted back to sleep, her back pressed against the cabinet—only to awaken a few minutes later.

Pitchfork Monster was back.

"MOM!" she cried once more.

And that's how it went, one nightmare after another, all night long.

CHAPTER THIRTEEN

⁓

Ruby waited, a clock ticking above her. It was
2:00 p.m. and the old man hadn't come out of
his room. She rubbed her eyes, then picked up
The Handyman's Guide to Household Appliances. After reading five pages about toasters, her stomach began to
rumble. *Would it be rude to snoop in the kitchen? Of course it
would.* It would be rude to do anything besides sit and
wait. After all, she was a guest.

She looked at the television, big and black, and
then at the coffee table, with its polka-dotted stains
the size of coffee cups, and then at the curtains, a salm-
on-colored rose that reminded her of old people.

Then she looked at the cabinet.

Mom.

A quick confession:

Ruby had never imagined the end of the world.
Until now. She knew from Dad's teachings that the
world—in a literal sense, meaning planet earth—would
not end easily. Amoeba and bacteria and such: they
were very good at living. She knew when people referred to the end of the world they meant it in a different way. The end of the world *for people.* After all, that
was all most people cared about: people.

She hadn't seen enough of the world to know if
this had happened, or was happening, but that didn't

matter, because she knew that *one* type of world had ended.

Hers.

Before all this, her world was a simple place. She never asked for the sea or the sky, just a tiny shred of wonderful. A forgotten seashell. A silver snowflake. A quiet, happy life was all she wanted.

And so, on that crusty sofa, she remembered her tiny shred of wonderful.

She remembered how Mom used to sing her songs about magical creatures and rainbows knit from yarn, her voice hitting octaves higher than the clouds.

She remembered how those songs would turn into illustrated stories for kids (and how special she'd always felt, hearing them first).

She remembered how the pages of Mom's books smelled like clovers and fresh linen, very unlike the pages of Dad's books (those smelled like chalk and plastic).

She remembered how Dad would tell her different types of stories, factual ones—the type he studied at the university, where he taught. Like, for example, how a new brain connection was formed for each and every memory.

Ruby drifted out of her memories and stared at the cabinet. Was it possible to stop the brain from forming new memories? Like holding two wires apart instead of pushing them together?

She wasn't sure, but wished from the bottom of her heart that it *was* possible. She didn't want any new memories—not without Mom and Dad.

༅

Matthew took a deep breath.

The girl was crying again.

The pain in his head deepened, as though something was digging its way into his skull, hammering through bone and flesh, planting roots. *Why does she insist on crying so much?* It made sense, he supposed, her being a child and all. But still, he couldn't recall crying when he was that age, not even once. In fact, he couldn't remember the last time he physically cried.

Either way, he needed the noise to stop, for her sake as much as his. He tried to imagine things from her perspective, as best as possible. The girl seemed to know the woman on the porch—perhaps they were related? Matthew knew all about crying over a lost loved one. Well, theoretically. He'd never shed any physical tears, but he'd certainly wept.

Inside, he cried every single day.

He opened the door to his bedroom, prepared to pay the girl a visit. On the walk, he breathed from the depths of his belly. *It's okay. She's just a child.* As he entered the living room, her sobbing stopped. He stared at her and she stared back. Her features were soft: cascading curls, bleached-brown eyes, skin so pale and thin it was almost translucent, like a piece of tissue paper.

She was also very still.

"Sorry," he said, shaking his head. "I am not very good with ..." He stopped, cheeks growing hot.

The girl nodded. "It's okay. I understand."

"Would you like some food?" he asked. "Soup?"

"Yes please."

∽

The old man walked back to the kitchen, knees popping with each step. He kept glancing back at her, like she might ambush him, or something. He seemed uncomfortable. And that was *her* fault. He clearly wasn't happy with her being there. It was best if she stayed quiet.

She tiptoed into the kitchen and cleared her throat like, *I'm here*. He shot a glance back like, *I see you*. As he stirred the pot, she took a seat at the table and eyed the variety of items that cluttered its surface. Tangles of wires and tubes snaked out from a broken radio. An iron here. An electric kettle there. What appeared to be a microwave was tilted on its side, half missing. Behind that was something else, possibly from outer space.

Clearly, the old man liked dissecting things. She pulled a tangle of wires toward her, reminded of Dad. He also liked to dissect things, especially brains. Once, she'd even helped him dissect a sheep's brain (well, mostly she just watched). In the process, though, he'd pointed out various structures, few of which she could remember. But one in particular was called the *thalamus*.

She remembered the thalamus because it had to do with pain. That's where pain went (the thalamus) before traveling to other "regions," as Dad had called them. She remembered this conversation crisp as yesterday: Dad's voice, telling her to picture the itty-bitty thalamus when she was sick and full of pain. And it helped, imagining something very small instead of feeling something very large.

Dad was so smart. She wished more than anything she knew where he was.

Tears began to fill her eyes once more.

∽

Matthew stopped stirring the pot of soup.

Don't cry. Don't cry. Don't cry.

He looked into the girl's eyes, at the single tear sliding down her cheek. Somehow, he'd inherited a tiny heartbroken companion, although she was *trying* to hold it together this time, at least.

"I am sorry ... you're ... sad," he said, not used to saying such things (or anything, for that matter).

"Thank you ..."

She stared at him, like she was waiting for something.

"Your name?" she asked.

"Oh, my name is Matthew."

"Well, thank you, Matthew."

He pointed toward the porch and raised an eyebrow. She nodded. "My mom."

He shook his head. *Her mother*. How terrible.

"Where is your father?" he asked, hoping the man might come to collect her at some point.

The girl looked down. "I don't know. He's missing. Are you missing anyone?"

Matthew placed two bowls of soup on the table, careful not to disrupt his tinkering projects. "Yes. My roommate, Sandra. And my wife. She's been missing for a while though."

Ruby's eyes grew wide. "How long?"

"My wife? A year."

"Was she kidnapped?"

He shook his head. "No, she got lost."

"*Lost?* In a forest? In a city?"

"Here. She got lost here."

"In ... *this house?*"

"Not *right* here. Outside, around the neighborhood. I don't know. She was confused. That's why Sandra moved in, to help pay the rent."

The girl bolted to the edge of her chair. "Okay, well, let's go look for her. I can help! I'm pretty good at finding things. Actually, one time, last summer, I—"

He flashed his hand forward like a traffic guard. "I don't want to talk about this anymore."

"But what about your—"

"Never mind."

"I *am* good at finding things ..." the girl mumbled, trailing off as Matthew pressed his fingers to his lips. She'd made him talk about Tabitha, and when it came to talking about Tabitha, it was simply better to refrain.

Lately, he'd been doing his best to store her away in a place that didn't hurt quite as much. In fact, he'd even gone so far as to collect all of their photos, her trinkets (china dolls and cat figurines and other little space fillers), even the locket, and stash them away in a box. Since then, things had been a little easier.

Until now.

The girl's questions stirred up feelings he'd been *trying* to push away. The grief. The guilt. The emptiness. And now the girl wanted to help him *find* her?

He'd tried that. It hadn't worked.

Typical young person, pushing their ideas all over the place. The girl had no clue what it was like to watch the world become unrecognizable, everything replaced, to be Not Normal, and experience true love for the first and only time—only to lose that person, quite literally. Maybe if she understood a single one of these things, she'd be less apt to talk about subjects she didn't understand.

                ~

Matthew was eating his soup so fast that specks of parsley dotted his cheeks. Had she somehow upset him? She was only trying to help.

A second later, he tossed the bowl in the sink and wandered back to his room without a word.

Ruby finished her soup in silence and slipped off to the living room.

The old man didn't seem to like her very much—*that* was obvious. But when it came to other people, she didn't exactly have any she could run to. Dad was somewhere, but that could mean anywhere. She couldn't remember his cell phone number, only that it started with a four. And Mom was ...

Her eyes began to water.

Like it or not, the old man was all she had.

She sat down on the sofa, wondering what to do, when she spotted a box. She knew she was being nosy, but she pulled out a picture frame anyway: a woman standing beside a young, bushy-haired man. His smile was wide and toothy, and it was clearly their wedding day. She had no idea who these people were. But after a few moments, it clicked.

A young Matthew.

And the woman: dark and gorgeous and grinning. She *had* to be his wife. Ruby squinted—there was a heart locket around her neck. How lovely.

She dug a little further: more pictures, trinkets, glass ornaments, lace doilies, the same locket from the photo (except it was a bit filthy). Why were all of these things packed away?

She glanced around.

The empty house.

A packed box.

An idea arrived—one she was *sure* would win the old man's affection.

∽

Matthew stood at the sink, his hands in a froth of bubbles. The girl hadn't bothered him for a while, busy doing who knows what (*thank goodness!*). And in her absence things had begun to feel more ... settled (another *thank goodness!*).

Perhaps, if she simply kept her distance, the whole cohabitation scenario would be tolerable.

Territories.

Yes! Territories. She could have the living room. And he: the kitchen, the bedroom. They could skirt around each other every once in a while (en route to the washroom or pantry). A confrontation here and there would pose no problem. It was the constant hum of interaction he dreaded, the LOUDNESS. But if she could just stay in—

A voice squeaked from behind.

"Matthew?"

He whipped around, opening his eyes as wide as he could. He refused to blink until she got the message: *I want to be alone.*

It didn't seem to work.

"Can you come here please?" she asked.

Before he could respond "NO!" she scurried away.

He stomped behind her, hoping his big, heavy feet slamming against the hardwood would help prepare her for the upcoming discussion about territories— *YOU can stay over HERE, and I will stay over THERE.*

But when he reached the living room—where Ruby stood, arms outstretched and smiling—all of his thoughts scampered away.

Tabitha.

She was everywhere.

Her collectables, trinkets, photos. Things sitting on shelves, hanging from the wall. Everywhere he looked. Something. And the locket: dangling from a window— except only the black, tarnished side was visible.

"What have you done?" he whispered.

"I helped you unpack!"

"I don't need to unpack. I have lived here for forty years."

He stared at the locket, emotions blowing in like a storm. His jaw trembled and his heart dropped, flattened, as though someone had stomped on it—was continuing to stomp on it. Over. And over. And over.

The girl took one step toward him, and he took one step backwards. "I'm sorry," she said. "I didn't—"

"Stop."

"But I said I was—"

"Just ..." He held out his hand. He could feel the tears welling in his eyes, blurring his vision.

"Are ... are you going to cry?" she asked.

"I don't cry!"

He wiped his eyes on the back of his sleeve and stared at the girl, into her soft hazel eyes. Except suddenly they were nothing like that.

Instead:

Two menacing pits of darkness, sucking him in, reminding him of everything he wanted to forget.

His biggest mistake:

Opening the door.

With her possessions all over, he could practically picture Tabitha, in the same spot as Ruby, a lace apron draped around her waist, her crazy curls exploding. And that sweet honeysuckle voice.

Hi, Matty dear. I love you.

The image faded away. It was just the girl.

Tears sloshed in his eyes, threatening to seep. He shook his head and blinked them away.

"Not crying," he stated, just to be clear.

The girl looked unconvinced, so he stood straighter, took a deep breath. *Not crying.* But as the locket caught his eye—its black-as-tar surface—the tears rushed forward like a flood he couldn't damn. A sound blubbered from his lips he didn't recognize, followed by a deep, painful moan.

He had to leave. He had to leave immediately.

He ran to his room and slammed the door, then crumpled onto the bed.

And, for the first time in all his memory, Matthew Werner cried.

CHAPTER FOURTEEN

∽

Five years earlier.

When fifty-nine-year-old Bill Henderson admitted himself to Toronto General Hospital with a mild case of chest pains, it was mostly because his wife, Agatha Henderson, with her permed curls and large mouth, had been nagging at him for weeks.

"Do you have a wife, doc?" he asked, a cold stethoscope pressed upon his chest.

"I do not."

"Ahh, lucky man."

"Sure. Any other symptoms?"

"You mean besides my wife?"

The doctor chuckled.

"Medical problems, sir."

"Lightheadedness sometimes. That's it."

And with that, Bill Henderson was free to leave, diagnosed with a mild case of heartburn.

That is, until he dropped dead two days later.

Destined to investigate, stubborn Agatha Henderson filed an immediate case of medical negligence, and Bill Henderson was shipped off to the Department of Forensics for a proper medical autopsy, diagnosed shortly thereafter with a debilitating case of a heart attack—just as Agatha had suspected. And even though she turned up empty handed in her court case, she still had the self-acclaimed privilege of inscribing upon the tombstone of her husband a very gratifying subheading: *I told you so.*

This, however, was not what made the case of Bill Henderson particularly memorable for Dr. Richard Sterling, who performed the neurological observation.

Instead, it was something very unusual about his brain, a swelling of sorts, characteristic of a viral infection.

As it turned out, the infection was *Rabies encephalitis,* an interesting discovery in itself, though not nearly as interesting as what surfaced in the next wave of testing. That being: Bill Henderson was infected with *Rabies encephalitis twenty-three years ago.*

Yes, while he may have died from a heart attack, Bill Henderson also happened to have a twenty-three-year-old case of rabies—a fascinating and unprecedented finding. As Dr. Sterling went on to articulate in one of his lectures, the former rabies incubation period in humans was typically one to three months, sometimes longer, but not usually. And still, the cause of the death was always rabies (not heart attack with a side of rabies).

Subsequently, "BH" became an infamous example of a *dormant virus,* one that causes few apparent changes to infected cells. A bizarre strain, perhaps. But then the whole thing blew over, replaced by another infamous example, and BH became a line in a textbook, seldom thought about.

Until, much later on a sunny afternoon in July, Richard Sterling explained viruses to his seven-year-old daughter, Ruby.

"Viruses are remarkable," he'd said afterwards, thinking of BH for the first time in years.

Ruby nodded.

And that was all.

Except.

What Richard Sterling did not know was that hidden inside his cells at that very moment was the same dormant virus. He'd acquired it that morning when a waitress spat in his soda. (She'd had a hard day.)

In fact, Dr. Sterling was one of 983,564,221 infected others—and counting.

Not that it really mattered.

Because the virus was dormant.

CHAPTER FIFTEEN

~

Ruby sat up from the crusty couch and stretched.
The sun peeked through the space between
each blind. *Good morning.* Except it wasn't a good
morning at all.

Would *good* and *morning* ever belong together again?

She wandered into the bathroom and swirled her
mouth with toothpaste—*one Mississippi, two Mississippi,
three Mississippi*—then she looked around the kitchen.

Matthew?

No Matthew.

One full day had passed; he still hadn't come out of
his room. She slurped down half a can of soup, trying
to be quiet, then returned to the living room.

She'd spent the remainder of yesterday packing up
the box she *definitely* shouldn't have opened, her chest
as heavy as a boulder. Now everything was packed
away, but the heaviness remained. She'd wanted to pay
Matthew back for letting her in. She'd wanted to help
him organize his things. She'd wanted, ultimately, to
become friends.

What a mistake. Maybe she should have just stayed
in that dark, lonely shed.

She plopped onto the crusty couch, *again*, and eyed
her belongings: Mom's duffle bag, her favorite yellow

sweater, lip chap, pills. She snuggled into the sweater, then stared at the duffle bag, still unopened.

It was time.

She unzipped the zipper and peaked inside. The first layer was pretty boring: more granola bars, a flashlight, batteries, Mom's cell phone. She pressed on the power button. Dead.

Next came bandages, one exploded pen, hand sanitizer, a deck of cards, a tin of cashews (which she pried open and began to nibble at). Then, buried at the bottom, were two items that belonged to Dad: his Book of Smart Stuff (or "idea book," according to Dad) and a tape player.

She flipped through the Book of Smart Stuff.

Inside: a bunch of smart stuff.

If only she knew what all the diagrams and formulas and notations meant. But she didn't, so she set down the notebook and picked up the tape player. Dad used to murmur into that machine all day long.

Something about cells.

Something about brains.

Then she remembered, specifically: *I'm speaking into this machine to see if my daughter is paying attention, because very shortly she is about to become the victim of some intense tickling.*

She could almost hear his booming voice as those big hands closed in on her belly, laughter climbing up her throat.

She pressed play. The tape was empty.

She leaned back against the stiff, crusty cushions.

Everything was wrong.

Everything being Mom and Dad, of course.

But also, Matthew. Not only had she made the old man cry (and he *never* cried, apparently), but there she was, spread out on his couch, unpacked, using his toothpaste, sneaking cans of soup, clearly overstaying her welcome—not that she'd been given a welcome. It wasn't nice. And it wasn't fair.

But what else was she supposed to do? Leave? All by herself? She'd already run through the city—her home—as it fell apart, lived with Pitchfork Monster for seven days in a cramped shed, and found Mom lying on the porch. Dead. She had no idea what awaited beyond the house, and, even though she'd checked all the windows, all she could see were hedges, nothing more.

What next? She couldn't face any more terror. Her last domino couldn't handle it!

She had to do *something*, though—something to make the old man feel better. She owed him that, for letting her in, and for letting her stay. So she hummed and hawed, pacing around the living room until she found an idea—a *good* idea this time.

She snatched up the tape player and skipped over to the cabinet. She knelt, finding a comfy spot, and then polished her knuckles like an apple, warming them up. After a few practice knocks—*knock, knock, knock*—she pressed "record."

At first, it was pretty annoying, all of that knocking. Then it was just boring. *Knock, knock, knock.* More like *blah, blah, blah.* But a while later, the knocking rhythm became almost soothing, like the songs Mom used to sing to her. And, just like those songs, it was as if her mind had been taken somewhere else, to nowhere in particular. And she liked it there.

Much later, when the light between blinds had disappeared, she stopped, rewound the tape, took a much needed pee, and plugged in a pair of headphones. She walked over to Matthew's room and knocked on the door with a very sore wrist.

～

Matthew's eyes shot open. Something had woken him.

Of course.

The girl.

"No thank you," he said. "Please leave."

He rubbed his swollen eyes, thoughts coming together. He'd cried himself to sleep (*ridiculous!*) some time ago. And now, though the tears were long gone, a tightness pinched his stomach—and his chest. *Odd.* He checked his pulse. Normal. But his hands were clammy and his cheeks were practically aflame.

Hmm.

A feeling surfaced. Embarrassment? *No, obviously not.* Embarrassment was for sissies and little girls, not grown men. He stood, remembering the locket. He leaned on the bed post, lightheaded. *Tabitha.* A groan escaped, then another. So many sensations sloshing around inside, he couldn't keep track of them.

Messy.

Too messy.

This was all because of the girl.

She'd infected him.

Infected him with feelings.

Knock. Knock. Knock.

Just as he was about to yell, "Go away!" the door opened. *No thanks! No more feelings!* He waited, prepared to holler, or point his finger very sternly; one of the two. But the girl didn't enter. Instead, she placed something inside the door and disappeared.

He edged toward it and shrugged. He didn't care what it was. What could she have possibly brought to him that would make a difference? Then—his stomach prepared to begin consuming itself—he moved in closer. *Soup?*

But it wasn't soup.

It was a tape player.

A tape player? What the dickens am I supposed to do with this?

He turned it around, gave it a shake. *Take it apart?* He liked to tinker, obviously, but that couldn't be right. Stumped, he set it down, picked it back up again. *Unless ...* He pushed the headphones into his ears and pressed play.

Knock. Knock. Knock.

Instantly, it was as if he was swimming in the sound instead of just listening to it. The tightness everywhere eased, inviting something new, something familiar, like:

A balloon inflating with warm breath.

Being wobbly then stable.

Drowning—if drowning were a good thing.

For a moment, he couldn't put his finger on it, and then he remembered.

Tabitha.

Specifically, whenever they held hands, her pinky finger would stroke his palm, over and over, reminding him: *It's okay. I'm right here.* And in those moments, hand in hand, they were one instead of two. The continuous motion of her soft finger against his palm edged out the LOUDNESS and made the world tolerable. It was like floating and falling, being lost and being found. And even though he couldn't understand all of those opposites happening inside of him, she made him feel like nothing else ever did, or ever could.

And while the knocking wasn't like *that* exactly, in a way it was a bit like her soft pinky finger, or her voice saying *Matty*, over and over again.

∽

Ruby couldn't help but grin when she saw him. Not only was Matthew wearing the headphones, but his shoulders looked straighter, and his eyes were a little less sunken into his face like craters.

"Does it help?" she asked.

"I suppose."

"Well good! I saw the tape recorder and thought, *you know, he really liked all that knocking the other night, I wonder if—*"

He raised his hand. "Not *that* helpful."

"Okay. Gotcha."

He pointed at the objects scattered around her, the contents of Mom's duffle bag.

"What's all this?" he asked.

She explained (in as few words as possible, because "not *that* helpful") that the objects were in a duffle bag, and the duffle bag belonged to Mom. Surprisingly, she managed to say all of this without her lip quivering, particularly at the word Mom. Then she offered the can of cashews.

"Want some?"

He stared at it for a moment, his eyes getting wide.

"Here." She pushed the can toward him. "Help yourself."

Silence.

"Are you okay?"

"The radio," he whispered.

"What?"

"The radio."

CHAPTER SIXTEEN

～

Cashews spilled across the table as Matthew cut the can into one long coil. Next, he flattened it with a knife and carefully affixed the strip to the radio, securing it over the broken metal. Meanwhile, the girl—*Ruby*; he'd actually begun to think of her as *Ruby*, and not just "the girl"—chomped on the cashews, silent (for once).

The can, he'd realized in a moment of eureka, would serve as a fine replacement part, thanks to *Practical Electronics: Devices and Techniques*. Or, more specifically, thanks to good old-fashioned books. Ones with real covers and real pages. Ones that smelled a bit damp, like history. Ones he could flip through with his fingers, unlike e-readers or text messages or Wikipods or whatever they were—

"Matthew?"

"Yes?"

"Are you done?"

He'd gotten lost in thought. "Oh, yes. I'm done."

"So what's next?"

He flicked on the power switch. A wave of intermittent crackling spilled forth. "That."

"Whoa! It works!" Her eyeballs were practically outside of their sockets.

He slipped off the headphones and put a finger to his lips. *Shhh*. Time to concentrate. But a few moments later, still nothing from the device save a drawn out *hiss*. Ruby tapped him on the shoulder.

He swiveled around. "Yes?"

"Is this all it does?"

"*This*? Of course not. It's not a static-making machine. What would the point of that be?"

She looked away. And for some reason, his stomach tugged.

"It will do more, hopefully. We just have to wait."

Ruby nodded.

He curled around the speaker, trying to pay attention to the smallest blip in the static.

Except:

"Matthew?"

His eye twitched. "Yes?"

"How long will we have to wait?"

"I'm not sure."

"Okay."

Exactly eighteen seconds later:

"Should I get us something to eat? Soup?"

"Yes! Go to do that."

He returned to the static, waiting for even the quietest pulse of sound, but, soon enough, Ruby was back with two bowls of soup.

"Is soup your favorite food?" she asked.

His muscles tensed, followed by a sigh. Conversation was going to happen sooner or later, whether he liked it or not.

"Yes, it is. Always has been."

Wide, spacious eyes. It appeared she was waiting for something.

"Would you like to know what my favorite food is?" she asked.

"No."

"Cake!"

Junk food—typical young person.

"Well, I don't have any cake."

"That's fine."

Ruby leaned into the radio, inspecting the device like it was some sort of ancient robot she couldn't make sense of without a screen to tell her or a keyboard to type into. But, as her face puckered in concentration, a few new details came into view.

Her eyebrows were virtually nonexistent.

Beneath her curls were a number of bald spots.

Her extremely pale skin was also a bit purple.

"Are you okay?" he asked.

She sat up straight. "What do you mean?"

"Well, you look a bit … sick."

She stared into her soup, not making eye contact, which probably meant she was … *Upset? Confused? Angry?*

He took a deep breath. "I'm sorry if that was rude. I'm not so good with these conversa—"

"I have a brain tumor. It's full of cancer."

His stomach dropped. *Brain tumor full of cancer?* Little girls weren't supposed to have brain tumors full of cancer.

He searched for something to say—anything—but before he could respond, Ruby grinned and shook her head.

"It's okay. Just don't be weird about it like everyone else, all right?"

He nodded, unsure what *being weird about it* meant, exactly. But he would try.

"Good. Now what's all this stuff?" She pointed toward the half-tinkered objects scattered across the table.

"Oh, nothing."

"It doesn't look like nothing."

Wide, spacious eyes again. Those eyes were hard to ignore, for some reason.

"I call it tinkering. My wife never liked it."

"*Hmm, tinkering.* Interesting."

"Yes. Very."

He picked up a telephone receiver, a wire dangling from its side. Then suddenly, hardly realizing it, he found himself describing the history of the telephone, how it was probably one of the simplest devices a person owned, considering its basic structure and functionality hadn't changed since the 1920s.

On he went, Ruby staring back wide-eyed, like no one had ever told her that those annoying little computers were once something different. Typical of young people, to think the world began when they were born, no histories attached to anything, just *me and mine and me and mine.*

But Ruby seemed interested, so he wouldn't hold it against her. In fact, maybe he could teach her a thing or two. He handed her the telephone receiver and paused. "Any questions?"

She swallowed. "Yes, actually. How is a radio different from a telephone? Is a radio like an iPad? Why is it so big? Is there a part to speak into like a telephone? Does it—"

He held out his hand.

Maybe he could teach her a thing or two.

Then again, maybe not.

But right as he was about to say "never mind," a woman's voice rose above the static. "Hello?"

"Hello!" Ruby yelled into the speaker.

He shook his head. "That's not how it works." He turned up the volume.

On the other end, the woman began coughing. "Hello? HELLO?"

Other voices tumbled in the background, hard to make out. For sure, there was a "This is dumb," and "Everyone's dead," and "Come on, let's go already." But then came a loud shuffle, more coughing, and a few grunts.

"Just wait," the main voice said. "I'm almost done. Okay, if there's anyone out there, if you can hear me, please come to the Horizon. That's where we're going. And there are others, too. The Horizon; come as soon as you can."

A blip.

Then static.

Matthew didn't move until it was obvious there was nothing more to be heard. He leaned back, repositioned his headphones, turned up the volume, and shrugged. None of that was of interest to him.

Ruby, on the other hand, started squirming like a colony of ants had crawled into her drawers. "The Horizon. Do you know what that is?" she asked.

He nodded. "Of course, the break between earth and sky."

"No, I mean a place *called* the Horizon. It has to be a place. We should go find it!"

Find it? Why on earth would they do something like that? For all he knew, the voice from the radio was trying to draw them into some experimental ploy, their bodies to be studied with scalpels and tweezers. Or shipped off to a different planet. Or preserved in foul-smelling liquids like human pickles. Who knew what people were capable of these days? Which he was about to say, when, abruptly, everything stopped—the *hum* of the fridge, the *hiss* of static—enveloped by instant darkness.

The power was out.

Matthew gripped the table.

In the moments that followed, everything became suddenly legitimate.

Real.

Actual.

Inescapable.

Up until a few seconds ago, he could make a cocoa or boil a soup, read or tinker beneath the soft yellow lamp. He could easily forget that anything terrible had happened, because inside his tiny house life was no different, really.

But now?

Change.

A shiver rattled through him.

He hated change.

CHAPTER SEVENTEEN

‿

Ruby stood before the open fridge. It was dark and empty, save a few bottles of warm, sticky condiments. The pantry too was bare—only two cans of soup left. She shone a flashlight directly onto Matthew, who stood behind her.

"We can't stay here much longer," she said.

The sun was rising. Thin waves of light trickled through the blinds.

"Well, I'm not leaving."

She rolled her eyes. Getting the old man out of his house was going to be a problem. "But we're running out of food. And maybe there are people out there who can help us—at the Horizon."

Matthew let out a huff. He didn't seem to like the idea of finding the Horizon. What was it he said? Oh yes, "I don't give two licks about the Horizon; not even *one* lick!" She'd said nothing in response, because what did licking have to do with anything?

But the Horizon was important. She just knew it. What else were they supposed to do? Where else were they supposed to go?

She crossed her arms. "We need to find it."

"No we don't."

"Yes we do."

He shook his head.

"Well, maybe I'll just go by myself then."

Matthew's eyebrow went jagged. "Be my guest."

Her mouth slid open. *Really?* After all they'd been through—the crying and headphones and living together for days—that's all he had to say about her leaving? She tried to breathe, but the air seemed thick, like putty. Her cheeks bloomed with heat.

"Fine!" She stomped her foot, then thundered off to the couch and dove beneath the covers.

ა

Matthew wasn't quite sure what to make of it all. She was angry. *That* was obvious. But what did she expect? Outside? Not for him; never was. And the Horizon? Why would he care about something like that? For all he knew, it was some technology-filled spaceship carting people off to Mars. Or some underground dungeon where vegetables grew in tubes and people had to wear helmets. Or, equally as bad, a world exactly like it was before, full of ringing computers and BRB and everything else he didn't understand.

Regardless, there would be people. So, *no thanks!*

He plopped onto a chair, staring into the almost-bare cupboard. On the other hand, Ruby *had* made a good point. Eventually he would have to leave.

Or maybe not.

Maybe this would be the end of him. He'd starve to death, sitting alone on a chair, surrounded by broken-apart appliances and empty cans of soup.

It wouldn't be a great death, but did he deserve a great death? Not really.

He'd lost the only thing that ever mattered to him.

He didn't understand the world, and didn't care to try anymore.

He left young girls crying on porches.

All things considered, he was okay dying in that very chair. Might as well.

Then again:

Ruby.

What would happen to her out there? Her small, pale body drifting through the world like a sheet of paper, all by herself. *No mom. Missing dad. Cancer.* What would she do? Where would she go? Would she survive?

He'd never know.

And that, for some reason, made him sick to his stomach.

∽

Even though Ruby was curled beneath the covers, she could tell Matthew was standing above her, grunting.

"Okay," he said finally. "I'll come."

She popped right up and tossed the blanket aside. "You will?"

"Yes, but on one condition."

"What's that?"

"We're only going to Fran's Food for groceries and supplies. Then we're coming straight back. Do you understand?"

"Straight back?"

"Yes, enough of this Horizon nonsense."

She thought for a moment, assuming Fran's Food was a grocery store. They could definitely use one of those. In the short term, it was a good idea (and then, of course, they'd find the Horizon next time).

Matthew tapped his foot. "Do we have a deal?"

"All right," she replied. "But we leave first thing to-morrow."

He nodded. "Fine. Now come eat."

At the table, they sat across from each other in silence, even though Ruby very much wanted to say something—especially after storming off. That was childish behavior, as Mom would have called it. And truly, she wanted to be friends with the old man, not enemies.

Unfortunately, making friends was never one of her strengths.

In school, she'd been just sort of there, like the wind. Other kids passed her by—even when she used words like *biodiversity* and *prognosis* to impress them (though she hadn't the slightest clue what either of those meant). Whatever, Dad used words like that, and they'd always impressed her. But, instead, the other kids only squinted and walked away.

"You're a bright girl," Dad had said. "They're probably just intimidated."

After that, she stopped using impressive words. But then came the cancer, and *that* was a far worse friend repellant than any impressive word she knew—even though she'd learned many more, like *chemotherapy* and *angiogram* and *anesthesia*. Mind you, based on the reactions from before, she kept *those* to herself.

But later that night, as she sat beside Matthew in the living room, the silence between them still ongoing, she remembered for the first time in a very long while her personal collection of impressive words. Since Matthew was older, wiser, and far different than any of the kids from school, she decided to give some a try.

"Hey, have you ever heard of the word *angiogram*?"

His eyebrows closed together. "Yes."

"Okay. Well has anyone ever told you that before babies become babies they're called *zygotes*?"

"Indeed."

"Do you know about *anesthesia, amoeba,* or *ampersand?*"

"Medication. Organism. Punctuation."

"*Chemother—*"

"Ruby, are you just saying words?"

She nodded.

"Please stop."

She sank into the couch, out of ideas—until Matthew picked up *The Handyman's Guide to Household Appliances.* She cleared her throat until he looked up, then she smiled as wide as possible. "Will you read to me?"

"*Read* to you?"

"Yes, please."

He seemed to consider it.

"Will you be silent while I read?"

"Yes! Promise!"

After a few seconds of staring, he finally nodded.

Unable to help herself, she squealed and scooted in closer. He reached over to the cassette base and cranked up the volume button for some reason, then flipped over the page and cleared his throat.

"Refrigerators are comprised of five main parts. A fluid refrigerant, a compressor, which controls the flow of the refrigerant, condenser coils, which are visible on the side exterior of the unit ..."

As he droned on, she tried hard to pay attention. But the detailed mechanics of refrigeration wasn't her favorite topic, exactly, and soon her eyes began to wander over to the bookshelf, landing upon *The Mysterious Life of Bobby Jones.*

That title seemed far more interesting.

She tapped Matthew on the shoulder and he stiffened. "Can we read the *Mysterious Life of Bobby Jones* instead?"

His eyes went very narrow. "What's wrong with this?"

"Well, it's not really a story."

"But it's important."

"Not to me."

"Well, it *should* be important to you," he said. Then he began to mumble, only some of which she could make out. Something about "Typical young person," and "Story instead of practical knowledge," and "No one's willing to get their hands dirty anymore."

"Please?" she whispered.

He glared for a while longer, then grunted, stood, and stomped over to the bookshelf. His fists were clenched and his cheeks were dark red, but she could tell he wasn't *really* mad, just pretending.

Back on the couch, she snuggled in beside him. After the first page, though, he shuffled over a little, so she shuffled too.

Page two.

Shuffle.

Page three.

Shuffle.

Page four.

He went to shuffle, but was flat against the armrest. Nowhere left to shuffle. His fluffy eyebrows moved up and down like feather dusters, then his mouth cracked open as though he was going say something. But, instead, he only sighed, continuing on with page four.

Even though the book was great, Ruby's eyes grew heavy. She tried to keep up with the words, but by the time page twenty arrived, they were floating in and out. By page thirty, her eyes were only half open—and even that was a struggle. Finally, giving in, she coiled up beside Matthew and shut them fully. She expected the old man to be stiff and cold, a bit jagged around the edges, but he wasn't. He was surprisingly soft and warm.

She hadn't felt a soft, warm thing in a long time.

A moment later, the world began to fade and the emptiness in her gut—an emptiness that had been there since finding Mom on the porch—seemed to disappear as she slipped away into the darkness.

CHAPTER EIGHTEEN

～

Matthew woke with a jolt. It took a moment for everything to register. Candles flickered all around him. He was huddled on the mildewed sofa. A book lay open on his lap.

Oh yes. The Mysterious Life of Bobby Jones.

Something warm stirred beside him.

Ruby.

Normally, human warmth was a sensation he detested, much different than mechanical warmth, like that emitted by a radiator, for example (which he liked). Unlike the pleasant heat of mechanical warmth, human warmth was stuffy and suffocating (well, human warmth emitted by all humans except for Tabitha. Her human warmth was like a toasty marshmallow melting in his mouth. It was the most beautiful sensation of all).

In general, though, when it came to human warmth, *no thank you.*

For whatever reason, Ruby had wanted to be close to him—scooting up beside him, curling into him—which he'd been prepared to combat with a firm, "Move over!" But, unexpectedly, her warmth was … okay, a bit like sunshine appearing after months of frost. It wasn't Tabitha's warmth, obviously, but it was neither stuffy nor suffocating. And when he'd looked into her soft amber eyes (thick as molasses and almost jiggling, like Jell-O) he couldn't say, "Move over!" He couldn't say anything.

Now, in the middle of the night, he could feel her warmth again, hot against his side. He thought about his uninhabited bedroom, pitch black and full of loneliness. He expected that to appeal to him, but it didn't.

He rested his head on Ruby's soft, tangled curls and closed his eyes. Then, what seemed like only a second later, his neck jerked forward from the backrest. Sunlight blared into his eyes, hot and piercing.

There was Ruby, standing before him, a knapsack slung around her shoulder.

"Time to go."

CHAPTER NINETEEN

～

R uby's heart flapped against her chest as they prepared to leave. She rested her hand on the island. Behind that: the door. To think, they were about to go outside, a place she hadn't been since leaving the shed. Even still, those moments were a blur, a small ray of sunshine before finding Mom.

"Where are we exactly?" she asked, turning back toward Matthew.

"We're in Scarborough," he replied. "Thirty-five Tremblant Street West."

"Scarborough. Interesting." She didn't know where that was, but liked the word *Scarborough*, how it sounded rough and smooth at the same time. "And where is Fran's Food?"

"Two blocks, straight ahead."

She nodded. "Are you ready?"

He shrugged. His face was saggy, like it was falling somehow.

"It's okay. It's not like we're leaving forever. We'll come back!"

"People don't always come back when they leave," he said, staring at the floor. Then he turned up the volume to his headphones. "Okay, let's get this over with."

Ruby tightened the straps on her backpack—their "just-in-case" supplies: a flashlight, an umbrella (it was spring, after all), batteries, her favorite yellow sweater, two bottles of water, and her medication.

Matthew heaved aside the island and motioned toward the door.

"After you," he said.

She cupped her hand around the door handle, overcome by a tugging sensation; she was definitely missing something.

"Wait!" she said, rushing back to the living room. She returned with Dad's Book of Smart Stuff, barely able to catch her breath. "Almost forgot *this*."

"Why do you need that?"

She remembered an impressive word that seemed appropriate. "It's *sentimental*."

"Oh," he said. "Well, just a second then."

He returned a few moments later with something tucked under his shirt. *The locket.* She stared at him and smiled. How could she not smile? The old man was wearing a heart locket around his neck—the same one his wife wore in their wedding photo.

"Okay, okay," Matthew said. "Enough smiling; let's get a move on."

With a gust of courage, Ruby flung open the door, her heart practically beating in her eyes. She expected there to be bodies, or body parts, or Pitchfork Monster, but there was only a small fenced-in veranda. And a shoe. She looked back at Matthew.

"Is that yours?"

He shook his head.

Venturing a little further, the sky became visible, glorious and blue, but nothing else, just overgrown shrubs and tangled-up bushes. The air smelled so fresh she couldn't stop taking deep, gutful breaths.

A flashback zoomed across her eyes: trampled flowers and trampled garbage and puffy white clouds.

And Mom, lying dead on the porch.

It was like a brick had been dropped down her throat. But she kept going, trying not to think about it—which wasn't hard, because just up ahead the whole world was waiting. A horror so large it was scarcely believable.

Only footsteps away, a man and a girl lay jagged on the sidewalk. They barely even looked like people. Their bodies were old, stiff, decomposing. Blue and purple veins spiraled around them like roads on a map. They were covered in maggots.

Upon closer inspection, parts of their skin had burst like tiny volcanos.

Ruby clutched her stomach as vomit splashed up her throat. The smell was overwhelming: worse than garbage, worse than formaldehyde in science class. It burned her nostrils like a chemical.

Behind them, more bodies were tossed about like seeds for birds, one here, a few there. Contorted and flattened and stiff. Some were missing parts—a hand, a foot—picked away by wild animals or ... who knew? Tufts of hair blew in the breeze.

Red. Black. Blonde.

It was the only movement.

Around the bodies, cars had stopped at random angles, some smashed to pieces with their drivers slumped around the wheel. Others were intact, vacant, but posted up on lawns. Doors to houses had been left wide open, like howling mouths, frozen into a gape. *People didn't even have time to shut their doors?* And then, one entire section of the street had burnt to a crisp. There was nothing left—nothing but posts curving from the earth. They looked like rib cages.

It was almost too much to take in, and, even though there was no sound, the silence was just as loud. Ruby's ears started ringing. Her stomach felt like it had been squeezed by a giant hand, which choked the air right out of her lungs.

Breathe.

Except she couldn't. The world was a nightmare—a real, permanent nightmare. There would be no waking, no moment of relief. And there was nothing she could do to change that.

She looked back at Matthew, who was staring off into the distance. His eyes were cloudier than a foggy day.

"Matthew?"

He didn't move a muscle.

"Matthew?"

∽

Matthew wasn't sure what was happening to him.

At first, he'd fixated on a small slice of everything— one body—and, while terrible, his heart only thumped a bit faster (*aka*, the LOUDNESS only clicked against his skull—hardly a storm). He listened to the knocking (*knock, knock, knock*) and breathed very deeply.

But then he stood back, widening his view, and the body began to multiply. It became *bodies.*

One, two, three, fifteen, twenty-eight, forty-five, ninety-nine ... until he reached the burnt section of street, ashes everywhere. He clutched the locket beneath his shirt, staring at the ashes until they began to smolder, like magic.

Huh?

He squinted, trying to make sense of it.

Suddenly, he was standing directly above the ashes, smelling that burnt, familiar smell. And there was the locket, no longer around his neck, but lying in the soot. A man's voice began talking, except the voice was distant—or it sounded distant.

"Mr. Werner? Did that locket belong to your wife? Hello? Mr. Werner?"

His teeth clenched, because the man had asked whether the locket *did* belong to his wife, instead of *does*. And who was he to draw such a conclusion?

"Matthew?"

He swiveled around. It was Ruby.

Normally, the LOUDNESS followed a certain progression: wind, hail, lightning, thunder. But this time, it did not.

One second, he was staring at Ruby. The next, he was swallowed up, twisted, the biggest tornado of all blasting through his thoughts.

CHAPTER TWENTY

〜

"See you in a jiffy!" Tabitha had said. A *jiffy*: precisely the type of confusing, subjective language Matthew despised. Because *how long was a jiffy*? Five minutes? Thirty minutes? An hour? Two?

He looked at the clock.

Three hours.

That definitely seemed like more than a *jiffy*.

He slung on a coat and opened the door. *Tabitha?* No one. He checked the back. No Tabitha. He stepped outside onto the veranda. His heart began to pound. *She couldn't have gone far.*

He paused.

Right?

He hustled down the street, nerves starting to drum. LOUDNESS was coming. It knocked against his temples, drilled against his skull. But he shook his head. He simply didn't have time for it. Not today.

"Tabitha?" he said, then louder. "TABITHA?"

"Sir," a woman tapped him on the shoulder. "Are you okay?"

"My wife, Tabitha. I can't find her. She's—"

A little computer began ringing. The woman glanced down.

"Sorry, one second …"

"Oh never mind."

He ducked into a bookstore, forcing down some air. Bookstores were Tabitha's favorite. She was probably just reading a novel, or drinking a peppermint tea.

He paced down the aisles, through the reading section, past the back counter. "Tabitha?" he said, over and over.

No Tabitha.

His heartbeat tripled; heat scampered up his spine.

Beside the cash register, he waved at the attendant, whose name tag read *Brad*.

"Brad!"

Brad swept his dramatically parted hair to one side. "Yeah?"

"Have you seen my wife?"

"I don't know who your wife is, man."

"Her name is Tabitha … and she's missing … and I don't know what to do." He was running out of breath. His throat was lodged with something.

"Look, I think you've got the wrong guy, I'm just—" The phone rang and Brad quickly answered it. "Hello, Pages on Main Street, Brad speaking. What can I do for you today?"

"Brad!" Matthew said. "I need your help!"

But Brad only turned his shoulder.

Outside, everything seemed brighter and hotter, like he was standing under a spotlight. His palms were so sweaty they were practically dripping. He focused on the ground and started pacing. LOUDNESS stomped across his brain cells, popping them like bubble wrap. But, *no time! Not today!*

"Tabitha? TABITHA?"

A group chuckled to his right—young people. They were practically indistinguishable with their puffy

hoodies and giant tuques, big stomping boots and pur-
ple-streaked hair. One of them was holding up a little
computer, pointing it at him for some reason.

"TABITHA! HAVE YOU SEEN HER?" (He had to
yell to hear himself over the LOUDNESS.)

"Seen who? I can't hear you."

"TABITHA!"

"Are you getting this?" one of them whispered.

"Huh?" another one asked him. "Who are you looking for again?"

"TABITHA!!!!"

The one with the little computer moved in closer,
shoving it in his face. The others started howling.

At this point, Matthew ran—or he thought he was
running. Everything was moving so fast, up then down
then left then right. His pulse was beating so quickly
he felt detonated, combustible, about to blow up—or
throw up. Acid burned his throat; he forced it down
with a swallow.

"TABITHA!" He could barely hear himself.
"TABITHA WHERE ARE YOU?"

∽

An hour later, he was sitting in a chair—his chair—
with a blue-suited man in front of him.

"My wife, Tabitha, I can't find her," he told the police
officer. "She has Alzheimer's! I'm afraid she's gotten lost!"

The man held out his hand like, *stop*, then he flipped
open a notepad. "Okay, how about you tell me exactly
what happened."

And so he did.

Afterwards, the man reviewed his notes, a kink in
his eye. "So you're telling me your wife with Alzheimer's proceeded to leave, and you just *let her*?"

He wasn't very skilled at this type of thing, but Matthew swore the way the officer said "let her" was meant to imply something.

"She's a grown woman," he said.

The man scrunched up his mustache. "And you didn't even ask her where she *was going?*"

There it was again, an implication of some sort.

"I didn't, no."

The man looked at him like police officers looked at criminals, like he'd done something terrible. His stomach clenched.

Had he done something terrible?

The officer stood. "Well, I think I have all that I need."

"You're going to find her, right?"

"I don't know, Mr. Werner. I'll try."

As the man walked away, Matthew tried to stand, but his legs were too wobbly.

"Wait! What do I do?"

The man wiggled his mustache. "I think you just answered your own question. You *wait.*"

∽

Waiting felt a lot like the word *jiffy*. There was nothing substantial attached to it. And just like *jiffy*, Matthew wasn't sure what to do with *waiting*—which was precisely the problem. He couldn't *do* anything with waiting. Waiting was the opposite of doing.

Waiting was sitting in a chair, thoughts replaying over and over. *You just let her? You didn't even ask her where she was going?*

Staring out all of the windows, hoping she might be there.

Lying in bed, beside an empty space, wishing it wasn't empty.

Mostly, waiting was like standing in quicksand. As each hour passed, he sank deeper and deeper. No one to pull him out. He couldn't eat. He couldn't sleep. He couldn't even think, his mind preoccupied with one stream of thought.

You just let her? You didn't even ask her where she was going?

Then eventually, what seemed like forever later, the police officer called. Something about a building, something about needing him to answer a few questions—he didn't provide many details. But that didn't matter, because *Tabitha!* They must have found her. He couldn't wait to run his fingers through her fuzzy curls, rest his palm against her dark, warm cheek.

On the way there, he rode quietly in the back of the police car, scripting their perfect reunion. He had so many things to say.

Act 1:

I'm so sorry. I'm sorry I let you leave. I'm sorry I didn't ask where you were going.

Act 2:

I'll take care of you, like you take care of me. We'll take care of each other. I promise.

Act 3:

I love you. I love you more than anything.

He was so preoccupied by these thoughts (holding her in his arms, whispering into her ear: *I love you more than anything*) that he hardly noticed the cruiser come to a stop. It wasn't until the man opened the door and said, "Mr. Werner, I need you to step out now," that he looked around. No Tabitha, just an abandoned building.

Burned to the ground.

Where is Tabitha? Why would she be here?

He looked around—*Tabitha?*—as the man led him to a pile of ashes, still smoldering. The whole world smelled charred, nothing like Tabitha. It made no sense.

Then he saw it—a locket—lying in the soot.

"Mr. Werner, we have reason to believe your wife may have been seeking refuge in this building. We've found some human remains, but they're burned beyond our capacity to personally identify—" The man's voice lapsed away, and it was just the locket—her locket—at the center of everything.

"Mr. Werner? Did that locket belong to your wife? Mr. Werner?"

Upon hearing that word—*did*—he considered punching the man.

"That locket *does* belong to my wife, but she's not here. She's somewhere else. Keep looking!"

Stupid police officer and his thick, prickly mustache! Everyone thinks they know everything these days! Well, what do they know? Nothing! They know nothing!

"Mr. Werner, I know this is difficult for you, but—"

"I said keep looking! You're wasting time with this burned-up old building. Maybe she was here, but she's not here now. So let's go already!"

The police officer frowned.

"Okay, Mr. Werner. We'll keep looking."

Except they didn't keep looking.

No one did.

CHAPTER TWENTY-ONE

୰

As Ruby stood above Matthew, who had curled himself into a human ball, she remembered the day she was first diagnosed with cancer. She was eight, almost nine, sitting in an office that smelled like hand sanitizer. The doctor spoke to her parents mostly, saying words she didn't understand at the time, like *medulloblastoma* (now the biggest word she knew). Regardless of what it meant, she knew right away it referred to something terrible, not because Mom started crying (because she cried when Ruby so much as stubbed her toe). Rather, she could tell by the look in Dad's eyes. Normally, he was strong, sturdy. But after hearing this word, his eyes became glossy and he looked away.

"Dad?" she asked.

He held up his hand for a moment. Then he turned to her, eyes dripping, and smiled.

"It's okay, Ruby. Everything is going to be okay."

It amazed her how quickly Dad had pulled himself together that day in the doctor's office. She'd always wondered how he did that, figuring it must be a grown-up thing. But now she understood, because as she crouched beside Matthew—curled in a ball, deep moans coming from inside—everything else faded away. Suddenly she felt ... okay—not because she *was* okay, but because she needed to be, for Matthew.

She circled her hand on his back.

"It's okay. Everything is going to be okay."

He stared at her, eyes bloodshot.

"No it's not. Nothing is ever going to be okay. Tabitha's gone."

"Maybe she's gone for now. But we'll find her. Don't worry. I'll help you look!"

He wiped his eyes. "No use." And then he just kept repeating it. "No use. No use. No use ..."

She scooted even closer. "Why is it no use?"

"Oh, you wouldn't understand. You're just a *young person!*"

Young person? Was she supposed to be offended by that? "Yeah, I'm a young person. You're an old person. So what?"

"So ... so ..." But he didn't say anything else. He pulled out the locket from under his shirt and cupped it in his palm.

﹏

Before he knew it (and against his better judgment), he'd told Ruby everything, from the *jiffy* to the police officer to the smoldering pile of soot. And then he waited—waited for her to confirm what he'd been denying for years.

Tabitha's gone. And it was his fault.

But for a long while, Ruby was quiet. It seemed she had nothing to say (how unusual). Then her mouth cracked into a smile. *A smile?*

"So ... there's a chance she could still be alive?" she asked.

"Well, I suppose. But the point is she's probably—"

"Yeah, I understand that, but you can't give up!"

"But I just told you—"

"You just told me they never found her. Not for sure."

He opened his mouth and then closed it. No words at the moment. Because really, looking for Tabitha was certainly useless. Deep down, he'd known so all along. He just preferred not to think about it. It was easier that way.

But Ruby didn't believe so. In the face of ninety-nine percent certainty, she'd sided with the one percent. And part of him wanted to say something about that, about living with your head in the clouds. Because life wasn't all rainbows and unicorns and lollies—especially not *now*. Life was change, and fear, and never fully understanding everything (no matter how old you got), and having everything taken from you—love, safety, silence—and breaking down, and never finding what you're looking for.

The sooner she understood this about life, the better. But as he looked into her big, amber eyes, staring at him so wide, he knew he wouldn't say a word—he couldn't. He wished (a warmth spreading through his chest) that she could stay inside that one percent for all eternity, like a time capsule. If only he could join her in there.

"Okay, let's go," she said suddenly.

Before he could respond, she was pulling him upwards, into a rotten-smelling world so chaotic he couldn't focus his eyes in a single direction.

"Wait," he said.

But she didn't wait. She just kept pulling him along.

With each step, LOUDNESS crept forward, pressing into his temples. To make matters worse, he'd forgotten all about the invisible rope that typically connected him to home—he'd never deployed it. In light of this, the world started spinning and spinning. He couldn't do it; he couldn't take another step, not without crashing back to the ground.

"We have to stop," he said. "Right now."

Ruby stroked his hand, just like Tabitha used to, and there was that warmth again, spreading through his chest.

"It's okay; you can do this," she said.

For a moment, he forced his focus onto her alone. And suddenly she seemed less like a small, clueless young person, and more like a tiny hero, pulling him from the wreckage.

Maybe she understood more than he thought.

And so, with her hand curved around his, anchoring him to the world, and the knocking from his headphones, giving him something to hold onto, he stared directly into the LOUDNESS, at the bodies and smashed-up vehicles and dark soot all over.

And so it came:

The Storm.

He gritted his teeth and fought against it, like swimming up a current—if that current also contained piranhas, and was being constantly zapped with electricity, and was louder than a vacuum pressed to one's ear. When things got especially bad, he squeezed Ruby's hand.

"It's okay," she said. "Just one thing at a time."

He paused.

One thing at a time.

He said it out loud—"One thing at a time"—something clicking.

෴

An expression Matthew never understood:

Seeing the whole picture.

Metaphorically, it made no sense (like most metaphors), but even literally. How could someone *not* see the whole picture? He always did. If there were a thousand things to see, he saw each and every one, everything happening all at once: movements and colors and textures and sounds, people staring, talking, moving, squawking. The world was basically a blaring orchestra—one he was powerless to conduct.

It had always been like this, ever since he was a boy, though he never considered it a problem, not even a symptom of his Not Normal. No one told him otherwise. The world was simply an overwhelming mess of everything. That's just the way it was.

But as he stared out into the world *one thing at a time,* it presented a bit differently. He forced himself to focus on one part, instead of everything.

Like sand flowing through a strainer.

Like one knock, and then another knock, instead of a hundred banging fists.

As a result, air traveled into his lungs—not tiny sips of air, either, but real, full breaths. And with air in his lungs, the world wasn't spinning as much, so he wasn't at risk of toppling over. And with his bearings about him, he could see more clearly, focus better. And, most wonderfully, the LOUDNESS only pressed against his skull, instead of blasting it to smithereens.

It wasn't perfect, but it was better.

On he went, with the knocking from his headphones, and the *one thing at a time,* and the girl beside him.

If he was being honest, he joined her on this quest because he worried for her safety. He thought she needed him.

But maybe he needed her just as much.

Maybe they needed each other.

CHAPTER TWENTY-TWO

R uby stood at the entrance to Fran's Food, her hand still wrapped in Matthew's. It was hard to believe they'd only traveled two measly blocks. It seemed more like a ten-mile journey!

"We made it," she said. "Good job."

"Thank you," he replied, then he pulled away (like he'd just realized they were holding hands) and wiped his palm on his trousers. "Do you really think Tabitha's still … out there?" She nodded. *Why wouldn't she be?* Those burnt human remains could have belonged to anyone. The locket could have easily been dropped, or stolen. Such was the problem with adults. Always jumping to conclusions.

Matthew made a *hmm* sound, like he was somewhat convinced, then he began fiddling with the door to Fran's Food, which appeared to be stuck.

While she waited, she stared out into the place called Scarborough, at the bodies that looked more like manikins, or props from horror movies—too inhuman to have ever been real humans. But they *were* real humans. And this time, she wasn't distracted by the old man. This time, their faces were crystal clear.

Dried-out eyes, stuck in a gaze.

Sagging skin, collapsed like a tent.

Open mouths, screaming at her.

Except, they *weren't* screaming. And that was the weirdest part.

Everything was so ... still. Sirens stopped mid spin, houses flared wide open, vehicles screeched to a halt, people everywhere. All of this should have been loud—was loud at one time (she remembered all those sounds from the shed). But now, it was only quiet and haunting.

It made her gut ache.

She remembered something Dad had told her years ago called *fight or flight*

"You see," he'd said. "The human body is prepared to deal with threat via neural mechanisms that instinctively guide one to *fight* or run away—*flight*."

"Why?" she'd asked.

"Survival. If something threatens you, you'll want to defend yourself or escape."

"Got it."

Dad smiled. "Okay, now that you understand, I'm going to let you pick one. What will it be, fight or flight?"

She thought for a moment. "Fight!"

And with that, Dad tackled her into the covers.

Now, though, *fight or flight* didn't seem right at all. Was there a third thing Dad had forgotten to tell her? Was there something else people's brains did if the threat was invisible? What were people supposed to do when the world was silent instead of loud?

It was all backwards.

"Ruby?"

Matthew was suddenly crouched in front of her; their hands were interlocked again.

"It's okay," he said. "Everything is going to be okay."

"Is it though?"

His mouth moved slightly, almost a grin. "Yes, because you told me so."

≈

Ruby expected Fran's Food to be totally trashed—or, at least, that's what happened in movies and books when the world ended over aliens or Jesus or war or zombies. Food was always a priority when something terrible happened. And there was no question about it: something *very* terrible had happened.

But, surprisingly, Fran's Food was fairly neat and tidy. A few cans were scattered on the ground, some were missing from the shelves. People had been here recently, but not many.

They walked past the produce section. The smell was a bit off. Certain foods had started to rot without refrigeration: meat, dairy. Still, she'd just smelled far, *far* worse.

A while later, after she'd filled a basket with all kinds of food her parents wouldn't approve of (cookies with sprinkles in the center, green and yellow gumballs, chips the flavor of French fries *with gravy!*) she met Matthew back at the front. Of course, his basket was full of one thing: chicken noodle soup.

"Probably enough for now," he said. "Time to go home."

She looked at the floor. Going back to that cramped little house was the last thing she wanted—especially with a place called the Horizon out there somewhere. And not that she didn't like the old man, but what about Dad? Shouldn't she be looking for him? Was he looking for her?

Matthew stomped his foot. "Remember, we made a deal."

"I know."

"We're going back home."

"I know."

"But you're not moving."

"I know."

Technically yes, she'd made a deal, but her gut was tugging in a different direction—especially now that she knew there were others around. Were those others the voices from the radio? The people going to the Horizon?

Plus, the old man was kind of … a problem. All the work it took to get him out of his house and walk *two* blocks—and he'd barely managed. Whatever he had, there was no fixing it. He was old, set in his ways, and grumbly. He didn't like people, or talking, or doing anything, really. A word popped into her head, one only cruel people thought.

Burden.

She hated that word, but did she *have* to stay with Matthew? In that tiny house? Eating soup and tinkering? Forever? Even if it meant never finding the Horizon? Or Dad?

She didn't have forever.

"Ruby." He pointed at the door. "It's time to go home."

∿

Matthew crossed his arms as Ruby whipped around with her bucket of junk food and marched straight out the door. She was mad (*probably?*). But what did she expect? Fran's Food, then home: those were the terms of their arrangement. He'd made them perfectly clear.

And she had her mountain of junk food from the big, wide junk food aisle (he'd almost shouted "HA!"

when he saw her prancing down there). What more could she possibly want?

He followed along, trying to focus on the knocking and breathing and *one thing at a time,* just as he had before, but Ruby was distracting. She kept turning and glaring, turning and glaring. Every so often, she stomped her foot a little harder, or let out a huff.

Still angry?

As if to answer that question, she whipped around and flared her nostrils like a bull. Quite possibly, she was about to charge him like a bull, too.

But then she asked, "How are you doing?" It was clear she didn't *want* to ask, since she barely opened her mouth and her teeth gritted together as she said it, but she asked.

"I'm okay," he replied.

"Do you want me to hold your hand or something?" Again, mouth barely opened, teeth gritted together.

"No, it's fine. We're almost home."

She tossed her chin in the air and kept marching.

He wanted to say something about all of this. Mostly, that her hissy fitting was unwarranted—she'd agreed to the terms, fair and square!—and that he didn't appreciate her grumbling, stomping, teeth gritting, glaring, and so forth. But as he stared at her tiny body (still stomping, still huffing) he didn't care about any of this. If she was mad, so be it.

She cared about how he was doing—even though she was clearly upset.

She'd taught him *one thing at a time.*

She'd given him hope about finding Tabitha (a little bit, anyway, for the moment).

Even if Ruby had a proclivity for talking he didn't share, she was sort of ... nice to have around. Tolerable, at least. Besides, in a few minutes, they'd return home.

She'd surely settle down. Maybe they'd even have a nice evening together. He turned up the volume to his headphones and imagined it.

The agenda:

· Unpack groceries.
· Tinker for a bit.
· Make dinner (chicken noodle soup).
· Read *The Mysterious Life of Bobby Jones* out loud on the sofa.
· Allow her warmth to trickle beside him.

Just then, he realized there wasn't any LOUD-NESS. Not a tick against his skull, or burning down his neck, or even pressure behind his eyes. For the first time in a very long while, he was *actually* okay.

Until:

Out of nowhere, a cluster of people turned onto the sidewalk.

He barely had time to register the man at the front. He was carrying a large object, which he rotated, until a barrel was pointing straight at Matthew's chest.

Ruby stumbled back, her mouth wide.

"Run!" she screamed.

CHAPTER TWENTY-THREE

Three years earlier.

Thanks to Global Warming, for the first time in eleven thousand years, the Siberian permafrost had started to thaw. Consequently, what was formerly a barren expanse of frozen tundra had begun to resemble a muddied-up pond, which excited a very small portion of people (and a very small portion only).

Geologists.

They came running by the flock, eager to study that which had been frozen away for so very long. Things like extinct Eurasian cave lions with bodies so perfectly preserved by frost that their blood was still liquid. In some cases, the meat on their bones was fresh enough to eat. Simply remarkable.

And then there were less dramatic discoveries, routine findings like amoebas and plants and viruses, harbored in test tubes then quietly placed beneath microscopes, still and inert.

Or *most* of them were still and inert.

There happened to be one small virus, termed *Mollivirus sibericum* (or, more informally, the Frankenvirus), that, in the process of thawing, literally surged back to life.

To be accurate, the Frankenvirus wasn't small, exactly; it was the largest virus ever discovered. But, unlike other things that died and stayed that way, it revived after thirty thousand years of stillness—a troubling discovery (even though, as it turned out, the only entity it could infect was a lowly amoeba).

What else lurked far beneath the frozen tundra? No one knew. But one thing was clear: climate change could awaken dangerous microscopic entities—a headline quickly embraced (at least, until something new took its place).

But the scientific community took note, for the Frankenvirus was one example of a small but growing handful of other notable phenomena. Like, how the presence of a parasitic worm was recently discovered to reactivate a popular dormant virus (herpes) via an immune response. Or how the same process had been demonstrated in mice: *viral reactivation.* Except not from a parasite, but stress. Specifically, a type of stress called *chaos stress,* or extreme change in social order.

The Frankenvirus was one example of a small but growing handful demonstrating that dormant viruses didn't always stay that way.

CHAPTER TWENTY-FOUR

✆

Cans of soup rolled across the pavement as Matthew bolted. A deep voice behind him thundered.

"Stop! That's an order!"

But he didn't stop, not even for a second, which no doubt upset the group, the deep voice in particular.

"Come on! Get them!" it said, after which came shuffling and panting and *stomp, stomp, stomp.*

He forced his feet to keep moving, even though his teeth were chattering and his eyes were blinking so fast he could barely see. Ruby was up ahead, fast as a rocket. At the rate she was moving, they'd never catch her.

He, on the other hand, was falling behind. His old limbs weren't cut out for this caliber of escape. Within seconds, his legs started to drag, then came the knee cramps. He needed to slow down and stretch.

Then again.

Gun.

Ruby looked back over her shoulder.

"Come on, Matthew, faster!"

He pushed himself as hard as he could, leaning into it, every single muscle burning. Still, no use. He couldn't keep up with Ruby—not even close. The gap between them only widened by the second.

"I'm trying," he said.

"Well try harder!"

But he couldn't try any harder. This was as hard as he could try, being old, out of shape, and not a particularly fast runner.

A loud gunshot pulsed through the air, then another.

He swore a bullet whizzed right past him. And even though his chest felt like a game of ping pong was being played inside of it, he simply couldn't go any faster.

Suddenly, his knee buckled, and before he knew it he was tumbling across the pavement. The whole world was spinning and, for a second, everything went black. Then, just as quickly, the world snapped back into focus and he scrambled to his knees, pulling himself together. Except something was wrong, missing.

The knocking.

Where is the knocking?

"Come on, Matthew! Get up!"

Ruby was so far away he could barely hear her—could barely hear anything. LOUDNESS was coming, and it was coming fast.

But he couldn't get up—not yet. He pawed across the gravel, nicking his fingers across crumbles of rocks. *Where is the tape player? The headphones?*

"What are you doing? Come on! Get up!"

"Tape player," he said.

"What?"

His thoughts were whirling so rapidly he could barely think them—except one. He was costing Ruby precious time.

"Go on without me!"

∽

Go on without him? She threw her hands in the air.

"No! I'm not going to leave you!"

Or ... *Am I?*

Her skin tightened. For a moment, she couldn't believe that thought came from her own head. It left a bitter taste in her mouth. She wasn't a traitor. She was a nice girl, a friendly girl.

Then again, none of that seemed to matter.

Not anymore.

Now, it was about survival, about *fight or flight,* and, for a slice of a second, she stood there, practically paralyzed, the old man behind her. Time appeared to slow.

It all came down to a choice.

To stay or to go?

She'd have to make it sooner or later. And yes, it wasn't who she was—or the person Mom and Dad raised her to be—to leave an old man lying in the dust. But what if she *did* leave him? She could finally start looking for the Horizon—and Dad. Sure, it would be lonely for a while, but she'd find other people.

A vision beamed into her head, one in which she and Dad were safe at the Horizon, surrounded by others, the world starting anew.

Her future wavered like a mirage, and she took one step toward it—one step away from Matthew. But then she remembered her time in the hospital. Specifically, she remembered the concept of regret.

Dying people seemed to have a lot of regrets, and she'd certainly seen her fair share of dying people. They had all kinds of advice for her—*Do what you want! Always believe in yourself! Don't take things too seriously! Tequila!*—but anchored to these strings of advice was always a wish: *I wish I had,* or *I wish I hadn't.*

Ruby hadn't thought much about her own death, only that she didn't want any of *those* wishes—of that, she was certain. She considered what she was about to do as a regret.

I wish I had stayed.

I wish I hadn't left him.

And those both sounded like very real thoughts.

She felt like herself again, instead of a stranger living in her own skin. *Leave him?* She couldn't leave him. Matthew was all she had now—even if he was old and strange and slowed her down.

She raced to his side and knelt beside him. "Are you okay?"

He nodded, connecting the headphones. His lip quivered as he stumbled to his feet.

She tugged at his arm. "Let's go."

But it was too late.

The others were already there.

CHAPTER TWENTY-FIVE

～

Matthew whispered to Ruby, "I'm sorry," as the man lowered his gun and flashed them a humongous smile—which was odd, considering he'd just chased them down at gunpoint and all.

"Sorry about the shots," the man said. "Just wanted to talk to you folks!"

He was wearing a pair of orange hospital scrubs, except they were smeared with something. *Vomit? Blood?* Matthew didn't want to know. Over the top, the man sported a fancy black blazer—which looked very out of place, especially considering his hair: tangled as a tumbleweed and peppered with bits of ... *leaves?* His teeth were piss yellow and pointed, as if someone had filed them into daggers.

Despite all of this, the man kept smiling as though he was the most ordinary fella in the world, just stopping to make small chat.

"So, I'm Jud. This here is my crew."

A few others cowered behind him: an old woman with sagging eyes and a boy whose features were flat and stretched. Behind them, a middle-aged man and a girl in a wheelchair were just catching up.

"What's your name, sir?" Jud asked, staring at Matthew with drifty eyes.

His throat went pasty. He couldn't seem to find any words.

"Hello?" Jud pretended to knock on a door. "Anyone home?"

～

Ruby stepped forward, even though her stomach tumbled like a dryer full of marbles. She glanced back at Matthew, who was looking straight at the ground, arms crossed, swaying a little. The volume on his headphones was turned up to the max.

"His name is Matthew," she said.

"I see. Well, what's up with him?" Jud asked.

"Just been a long day. We'd like to go home."

He inched closer. "Whoa, not so fast, girl. You haven't even heard what I have to say yet. In fact, it's your lucky day! We happen to be recruiting."

"Recruiting?" She glanced at the people behind him. They were all looking away.

"Yeah, me and Sam here." He tapped the gun. "We're going to save humanity. Like I said, it's your lucky day."

Ruby stared at the large, shiny rifle. "Did you just say your gun's name is Sam?"

"Sure did. So whaddya think? Would you like to be saved?"

His eyes bulged. Ruby shivered.

"Thanks, but we're not interested. We just want to go home, if you don't mind."

The man's smile disappeared. "Well yeah, I *do* mind, actually. I probably should have mentioned this earlier: *recruitment isn't optional.*"

The faces behind him turned a ghastly shade of white. Every single pair of eyes was glued to the concrete. Ruby's cheeks prickled with coldness. This wasn't a "crew." This was a crazy man and his captives: a bunch of sick people with no other choice but to follow.

She reached back and grabbed Matthew's hand.

"It's okay," he whispered. "It's going to be okay."

"Huh? What was that?" Jud asked, pointing the gun at Matthew.

"Nothing," Ruby said, pulling Matthew in closer. "We'll come with you. Just please, put that thing down!"

His face twisted into a crooked grin. "You mean … you want to join us?"

"Umm, you said we didn't have a choice."

"I *said* . . ." He cleared his throat. "That we have a wonderful opportunity for you, and you'd be ill-advised not to take it."

Was she missing something? He wasn't making any sense. She stared into his eyes and shivered. His pupils were practically specks. "Actually, that's not what you said. But if that's what you *mean*, then we'd like to go home."

Suddenly, the gun was inches from her face.

"Sam says no!"

Her heart stopped, but before she had time to register anything else, Matthew slapped the gun away and scowled. A *hiss* came from his throat, a bit like a cat, and then his entire face puckered.

"Don't touch her!" he snapped.

She gripped onto Matthew's arm and shut her eyes, prepared for the worst. But Jud didn't seem upset. Instead, he let out a slow clap.

"Bravo! You've got spunk, old man. Congratulations, you're hired. Welcome to the team! Now, if you touch Sam again, I'll shoot you in the head." He slung Sam across his back. "You two can follow me—or don't. But like I said. Shooting. Head. You know. Let's try and keep this all amicable, shall we?"

CHAPTER TWENTY-SIX

~

Ruby picked up her bottle of pills, followed by the package of cookies with sprinkles in the center. Above her: the barrel of a gun. Or rather, *Sam*.

"Waste not, want not!" Jud said.

He propped a hand on his hip. "You know, the infrastructure is critical, in my opinion. Sam is always like No! *Shooting! Blood!*—which I get. I mean, of course that's what he says. He's a gun. That's his job, his role. But my role is much greater. These people aren't going to save themselves, am I right? I can tell you get it, whatever your name is."

He nudged her with his foot.

"Ruby," she said between her teeth.

"Right. Well, Ruby, you understand. You're hangin' out with Tape Recorder over there. You guys related or something?"

She shook her head.

"Then what are you doing with an old bag like that, huh Ruby? My point exactly! You're *helping* him, just like I'm helping all of you. You'll see. I'm one of the good guys."

Somehow, she doubted this.

When they'd finished collecting the items on the pavement, they began to walk. Up front, Jud was singing—*singing*—something about marching and artillery and soldiers. He stomped his boots and waved Sam in the air.

Everyone else hung their heads.

Ruby did the same, trying not to stare at the gruesomeness everywhere.

So. Many. Bodies.

Unfortunately, not all of those bodies were dead.

As they marched on, some began to twitch, or thrash, or call out. "Help me! I need my medication! Please."

Ruby couldn't bear to watch these poor suffering people. Couldn't they do something—anything?

"Hey!" she yelled at Jud. "You want to help people? Let's help *these* people!"

But he only yelled back, "Lost causes!" Then resumed singing.

∽

Matthew had no clue what was happening. He lagged at the back of the line beside Ruby, the order in which they were collected, as Jud had insisted. Order was important, or something. He'd stopped listening. It was like every time the man—Jud—opened his mouth, a bunch of nonsense fell out. *Infrastructure? Roles? Saving humanity? Providing human names to artillery?* He was Not Normal, sure, but *this* man? Especially Not Normal.

Ruby leaned in and whispered, "You doing okay?"

He shot her a stare. *Okay?* Of course he wasn't okay. He was supposed to be home, slurping soup and tinkering with the refrigerator. Instead, he was farther from home than he'd been in decades. Not to mention everything else: decaying bodies all over, people dying, the crazy man, strangers. The expansive stretch of world he'd spent his entire life avoiding was now unavoidable. He was smack dab in the middle of it.

Not a single thing was okay.

He fixated on the ground and held the locket beneath his shirt.

Yet another thing that wasn't okay.

After a while, they veered from the road and entered a park. He gazed up at the trees, finally starting to turn green again. But then he was ... *sinking?* He looked down. Indeed, he was sinking into the mud like quicksand—and so was everyone else. The earth was terribly damp, practically impossible to walk through.

Collectively, they trudged through the mud, save the girl in the wheelchair, whose wheels spun in vain but did not move. The man behind her pushed with all his might. He grunted and pushed, grunted and pushed, but after a few minutes he stood back and leaned over. Sweat dripped down his rosy cheeks.

The entire chair was basically a giant clump of dirt.

"You two," Matthew said to the old woman and the flat-faced boy. "Over there." He pointed to the opposite side of the chair.

"And you," he said to Ruby. "You're with me."

When everyone was in place, he looked at the man, who'd started shaking, and gave him a nod.

"Lift!" he said.

And they did. But the weight of the wheelchair only pressed them all in deeper, like a sinking ship in an ocean of putty. Useless.

"It's okay, thank you," the man said. "I will carry her." He lifted the girl from the chair; all of her limbs dangled. She was clearly paralyzed from the neck down. The man was shaking even harder now: shoulders, arms, legs. He looked like he might well collapse. Just as Matthew moved in to help, Jud stepped forward from the sidelines.

"Drop her."

Matthew froze. The man let out a whimper, pulling the girl in closer.

"I *said*, drop her."

"Sir," the man said, placing the girl back in the wheelchair. "Let me carry her. I won't slow us down. I promise."

"*Ugh!*" Jud grunted. He began to pace. "I don't think you quite understand me ... name?"

"Clark."

"Cool. As I was saying, I don't think you quite understand me, *Clark*."

Clark was shaking so hard he was practically seizing, at which point Matthew realized the shaking wasn't because of fear or exhaustion, as he originally thought, but some sort of illness.

Jud circled the man like a vulture. "You see, *Clark*, what we have here—me, you, Ruby, Tape Recorder, etcetera—is a bit of an organization. Have you ever worked for an organization before?"

Clark nodded.

"Great, so you're familiar with how they operate. *Organizations*, as you know, require a certain level of contribution from each party. Now, if one member were to, say, stop working, what would happen to the organization?"

"I ... I don't ..."

"It's a rhetorical question, Clark. The organization wouldn't function. That's pretty obvious, right?"

Jud looked around. No one seemed to be making eye contact.

"What I'm trying to say—politely—is that *she stays*."

Matthew couldn't help it, a loud gasp escaped his lungs. They were just supposed to leave the paralyzed girl behind? Leave her to die all alone? *How* ... There was hardly a word to describe such a thing. The others seemed to agree. Ruby buried her face into his side, like she couldn't watch another minute of it. The old woman and the flat-faced boy began to sob. And the man, Clark, clutched his gut and started to wail.

"No, sir, please!" he cried. "I'm begging you! We can't leave her. She's my niece. She won't survive by herself."

Jud appeared to consider this for a second. He stared at the sky, and Matthew's jaw unbuckled. Maybe everything would be okay after all.

But finally Jud shook his head. "How about I make this a little easier for you, Clark?"

He lifted Sam, perfectly level with the man's head.

A shot bled through the air, followed by a thump.

"Anyone else?"

All was silent.

Matthew looked down. Clark was now a heap in the mud. Blood leaked from his face like a river siphoning into streams, flowing through the dirt. The girl in the wheelchair began to cry. And then came a noise like nothing he'd ever heard before. Almost like a squeal, but softer. Like an animal succumbing to a predator.

Ruby unlatched from Matthew's side and began to scream. It was long and loud and relentless. And when she was done, she marched up to Jud and pulled back her shoulders.

"Come back," Matthew said, grasping at her hand, but it was too late.

She stopped before Jud and crossed her arms. Behind them, the girl in the wheelchair let out a howl. The sound was deep and gutted and echoed amongst the trees.

"You're sick!" Ruby said. "Do you hear me? SICK!"

Jud only huffed, calmly resting his hand on her shoulder. "Oh Ruby, take a look around, sweetheart. We're all fuckin' sick."

CHAPTER TWENTY-SEVEN

～

Three weeks before Matthew's *Not so Terrible Tuesday*, a new type of parasite sprang into existence—thanks to the process of genetic mutation. It was a member of the *Lethacotyle* family (aquatic parasites that survive on the gills of fish). This particular strain, however, was smaller and preferred skin, which it was very accomplished at securing onto, thanks to a set of clamps characteristic of all lethacotyles.

Lethacotyle cutis, cutis meaning skin. Or, *L. cutis*, for short. That would have most likely been its formal name.

That is, if scientists would've had a chance to name it.

And so it began. In Lincoln, New Hampshire, one tiny L. cutis, one microscopic blob, fastened securely to the underbelly of a mink frog. Except it didn't like it there, really. Thanks to the genetic shuffle, it preferred things hot and dry versus cold and wet. And seven-year-old Franklin Wellington, who spotted the mink frog from two feet away, was about to become that hot, dry thing.

The boy slinked up to the creature, catching it with a giant splash. "Gotcha!" he said, inspecting the frog carefully. Meanwhile, the tiny L. cutis, resting on the underbelly, was delighted (or comfortable, rather, it being a parasite). The surface of the boy was warm, desirable—a lovely little feast. So as Franklin held that mink frog for eight whole minutes, the microscopic parasite released and attached to the boy instead.

As it turned out, Franklin was an exceptional place to live. So exceptional, in fact, that the parasite grew a family of other parasites, who moved from Franklin to Franklin's mother, Belinda. And from Belinda to her neighbor, Fran. And from Fran to her co-worker, Dave. Skin-to-skin transfer was all it took. And, lucky for L. cutis, there were a great many humans, which meant a great many houses.

Yes, the real estate market was certainly booming.

L. cutis wasn't problematic—at least, not intentionally. It was only a small, humble parasite, looking to settle down, to survive comfortably and plentifully, as all parasites desire. Unfortunately, the human body never much liked invaders. Upon sensing the intruder, each human infected with L. cutis released a unique protein as part of an immune response, a protein intended to send L. cutis on its way. Well … *intended.*

Meanwhile, the dormant strain of rabies waited patiently inside the cells of nearly everyone, waiting for something very specific to activate it, much like a lock and a key.

The key?

The specific immune protein intended for L. cutis. (Whoops.)

It was a great unfortunate coincidence—arguably the greatest and most unfortunate in all of human history. Because, once activated, the virus got to work quickly, causing, at first, flu-like symptoms: some weakness in the limbs, a slight fever, possibly a headache that wouldn't abate. Next came abnormal behavior, hallucinations, delirium, a sense of complete and utter detachment. Words became hardly speakable, thoughts hardly graspable. Like losing one's mind, except worse. Because the brain was hot, enflamed, and that sensation, that burning from within, could be very much felt, like a fire without water, until, finally, death.

Parasite + Immune Response + Viral Reactivation.

All in all, the formula occurred in 38% of people infected with the dormant strain of rabies. Of those, some died quietly, some died loudly, but they died, and they continued to die, from a once-harmless virus that, when enlivened, caused a fatal case of fast-acting rabies.

Of course, it didn't make sense, not to anyone. People were dropping dead everywhere, infected with something like rabies, but airborne?

The headlines were bold and vague.

PEOPLE ARE DYING.

RABIES?

WE DON'T KNOW MUCH.

Stress escalated among the people, television screens and Facebook updates and Twitter feeds and text messages, each producing a swirl of panic.

THERE IS SOMETHING WRONG!

THE END IS UPON US!

THE WORLD AS WE KNOW IT IS OVER!

Mothers called their sons and fathers called their mothers and grandparents called their grandchildren, all of them babbling. *Are you okay? Have you heard?* The stress it caused was unique, rare, and catastrophic.

Something scientists had already discovered.

Chaos stress. (Also known to reactivate dormant viruses.)

In its defense, the human body believed it was doing something good, when in fact it was doing something very bad. Streets flooded with people, some sick, some not sick—at least not yet. Many walked straight into their demise, huffing and puffing. *The world is changing. The world is ending.* And then: *My head hurts. I feel chilly. Are my cheeks warm?*

No one deciphered what was happening. No one had time. And perhaps no one suspected such a complicated series of biological reactions. Wasn't it supposed to be a single decipherable cause? The Avian Flu? Mad Cow Disease? SARS? An asteroid? Biological warfare? Chemical warfare? World War Three?

A prediction no one heard: a parasitic infestation, as well as chaos stress, both released a specific immune protein capable of reactivating a dormant strain of rabies.

Three weeks.

Six billion people.

Dead.

Well, everyone except …

෴

Prior to all of this ruckus, Dr. Richard Sterling and his seven-year-old daughter, Ruby, shared an ice cream cone in a park. They licked the edges of a strawberry-lime lump, sharing a moment—and also a virus. It was the first of many instances in which Ruby would contract a dormant strain of Rabies encephalitis.

"Dad," she said, staring at the melting treat. "Where does the color pink come from?"

Richard smiled, and then he began discussing light spectrums and wavelengths and color-receptor cells called cones. Meanwhile, the virus traveled deep inside Ruby's brain and searched for a proper place to integrate: a nice fat neuron.

But something was wrong. Yes, the virus remarkably sensed the wrongness inside of Ruby, the early stages of brain cancer. For the lowly virus, its only goal in life was to find a suitable nervous system, which Ruby did not have. And so, it did nothing. It didn't integrate, it didn't multiply, and, eventually, it was destroyed, exiting Ruby as a pale, yellow tinkle.

Alas, the cycle occurred again and again. It occurred inside of Ruby and it occurred inside of everyone. Inside of people with sick brains, the virus said, "No thank you," and inside of people with healthy ones, the virus said, "Yes please." Meanwhile, the sick got sicker, cursing the diseases that would one day, ironically, save their lives.

And of all the crazy things to predict, who would have thought there would be such a day when weakness meant strength and sickness meant survival?

Well, actually, there was one mentally ill person who just so happened to believe that one day sickness would save them all. His thoughts were alive with psychosis. And his name was Jud.

PART 2:

∽

CENTER ONE

CHAPTER TWENTY-EIGHT

*M*atthew had no idea where he was. Nothing looked familiar—not that he expected it to. He'd never been so far away from home before. He turned up the volume on his headphones and began to count. He needed a distraction.

One, two, three, four, five …

No matter, awful memories arose regardless.

That terrible park. How everyone was slipping in the muck as they tried to free the paralyzed girl.

And the man, Clark. Shaking uncontrollably as he lifted the girl from the chair. He'd tried to help. But it hadn't worked. Because now Clark was dead.

And Clark's blood. How he'd just watched it flowing through the dirt—everyone had. Because that's what people did now. They watched. And that's all they *could* do. Watch or get shot by Sam.

And the paralyzed girl. That sound she'd made afterwards, her face contorted in agony: shrill, primal, like an animal expiring. Slowly. Painfully. It had made his hair stand on end. Heck, it *still* made his hair stand on end knowing she was back there, probably making that same sound, waiting in the mud beside Dead Clark. No hope. Not even one.

He tried to shake away the images.

Six, seven, eight, nine, ten …

Great, now he was dizzy. He stopped, leaned over for a second, hoping to catch his breath. They'd been walking for hours—aimlessly, as far as he could tell. Not knowing their whereabouts was starting to take a toll. His mind was all over the place. Were they headed north? South? Were they even in Scarborough anymore? So many twists and turns. Home could be anywhere.

He glanced at Ruby, who'd also stopped walking. She gazed around like she was memorizing their location. An excellent sign.

∽

Ruby looked to the left, then to the right. *Where the heck are we?* She hadn't been paying attention. It was the first time she'd stopped thinking about the paralyzed girl in hours.

Oh no.

The paralyzed girl.

The image of her sitting in that wheelchair—staring up with dark, watery eyes, like they were reaching out toward her—made her want to hurl.

And then there was this heaviness dragging down her chest.

The Horizon.

To think, she'd been looking forward to it, whatever it was, and finding Dad along the way. She'd even pictured their reunion: him calling out her name—*Ruby? Ruby?*—and her running toward him, jumping into his big arms, smelling his woodsy scent. He would tell her what happened to the world because he knew everything, always, and then they would go live at the Horizon.

Happily. Ever. After.

Now, she felt silly thinking about all that. There would be no Horizon. No Dad. Instead, she was a prisoner, just like all these other people.

From the front, Jud turned around.

"How's everyone doing?"

The old woman, who'd said nothing except, "That poor girl, still waiting," every few seconds, continued to say, "That poor girl, still waiting." Every time she said this, the flat-faced boy began to cry.

Beside her, Matthew carried on like he had for the past hour: silent, almost dragging himself forward.

When Jud made eye contact, she glared as hard as she could, like her eyes were made of ray guns.

"Okay, okay," he said. "I get it. You're all pissed. Look, I liked Clark too. I really did. And nothing against the girl in the chair, but they were never going to make it. You *must* know that. I did them a favor—I did us all a favor. Besides, you're going to LOVE what we're putting together. You hear me? *Love* it. Got that, Tape Recorder?"

Silence.

"What are you listening to anyways?"

Silence.

"Oh *come on*, people! Cut me some slack. You've just been saved! S-A-V-E-D! Sure, we had to make a tough choice, but that's why I'm here, to make the tough choices. Me and Sam."

"Whatever," Ruby mumbled.

"Hey, I heard that! Look, let me sing you a little melody about—"

Suddenly, a sound stirred behind him and Jud whipped around, pointing Sam straight at it. He moved out of the way to reveal a young boy carrying a cane. He lowered the gun.

"Well, what do we have here?"

The boy's skin and eyes were about the same shade of gray. He was probably the skinniest person Ruby had ever seen. He went to speak, but instead his whole face started shaking, followed by a strange, rhythmic flaring, like he was trying to fly.

"Hi," he said finally, after the movement had stopped. "Can I join?"

Ruby wanted to shout, "No! What are you doing?" Then again, Sam.

Jud circled around the boy like a vulture.

"Whatcha got, kid?"

The boy's shoulders shimmied up and down. "Chorea."

"*Hmm*. Haven't heard of that one."

"Basically my body jerks around a lot. Can't help it."

"Gotcha. What's your name?"

The boy smiled. "Joshua Maximilian Campbell."

"Well, Joshua Maximilian Campbell, it's your lucky day. We happen to be in the process of recruiting. Let me tell you a little something about infrastructure ..."

Ruby shook her head. Poor Joshua, out looking for some friends and he'd wandered straight into a hostage situation. But, as Jud continued, Joshua looked far less frightened than she'd imagined. Instead, he was nodding more than a bobble-head—and it wasn't because of the chorea, either.

"Well that sounds great," Joshua said when Jud had finished yammering. "I'm happy to join."

Ruby's cheeks went hot. "Well you *shouldn't* be happy to join," she said, unable to hold it in. "Because he just killed someone!"

Jud whipped around and glared at her. He tapped Sam with his fingernail.

Click, click, click.

She latched onto Matthew's arm and shut her eyes.

"Is that true?" Joshua asked.

She opened one eye as Jud rested his hand on the boy's shoulder.

"Son, I'm going to be honest with you, because that's the type of fella I am. I did kill a man. I killed him straight up, point blank. But I killed him for a *reason*. Would you like to know that reason?"

Nodding like a bobble-head again.

"It was to make room for you, comrade! To give boys like you an opportunity. I have something in the works that will knock your socks off. And when it comes to *that*, you're either with me, or against me. So, what do you say, Joshua, you with me?"

After a bit more flapping, Joshua went completely still. For a second, Ruby swore he glared straight at her, but then he turned toward Jud and smiled.

"Yes, sir!"

"Good, now how about you walk up here with me and we'll talk business. You know, Josh, I can already see you as one of my right-hand men ..."

He trailed off and Ruby slunk back beside Matthew.

She wanted to punch something. But, instead, she leaned into Matthew and lowered her voice. "You know, this is *so* dumb, this new society or whatever. It'll never work. No one's going to listen to him. He's crazy!"

But then she looked at Joshua up ahead—*skipping!*—and she suddenly wasn't so sure about that.

CHAPTER TWENTY-NINE

Matthew stood at the back of the group, not exactly sure what to make of the ... *thing* before him. Everyone seemed just as uncertain. The old woman kept gasping every few seconds, as if she'd forgotten how to speak, and flat-faced boy was squinting so intensely his eyes were invisible.

Ruby turned to him. "What *is* it?"

He shrugged. He'd never seen anything like this place—surely *none* of them had. The large rectangular building, an old community center, was so bright with glaring graffiti that it appeared physically alive.

Everywhere he looked: neon. Brazen red skulls and brash purple crosses. Yellow circles brighter than the sun. Names in fancy cursive or big block letter. Not a single section of the original building was visible. Even the sign itself had been replaced with bright green scribbling.

Welcome to Center One, it read.

Out front, gadgets and gizmos cluttered the parking lot: old kitchen appliances, car motors with wires distending, piles of little computers, a few other electrical items he assumed were medical devices. Stuff was everywhere—glorious stuff. He stared at a metal coil, reaching up toward him, begging to be touched. His hands shook. He wanted so badly to grasp it.

The entire parking lot was like a large-scale version of his dining room table. An exercise in tinkering.

Jud pranced around the group. "Welcome home!"

Joshua went to say something, but only a yelp squeaked out. He was like a child in a toy store, too excited to even speak.

Ruby looked at Matthew and shook her head. "*Pfff!*"

She clearly wasn't impressed. Judging by the way she rolled her eyes, the place might as well have been a dump owned by hipsters (*Hopsters? Hipstars?* Whatever they were called).

Jud strutted around, flapping his arms, whooping like a baboon. "All right, everyone," he said. "Let's get a tour started, shall we? First stop, our department of innovation!"

He walked through the crowded parking lot, pointing Sam to the left, then to the right, shaking his hips.

"Repurposing, that's what this department is all about. Creative opportunities. For example, just yesterday one of our members made this!" He pointed at hundreds of little computers, their screens broken and switchboards showing through. Someone had arranged them into a flower.

Matthew gasped. It was, in all of his years, the most beautiful piece of artwork he'd ever seen. All those little computers reduced to a silly flower. *Fantastic!*

Ruby didn't seem to agree. She took a step forward, pointing at the display with her eyebrows folded. "What does it even *do?*"

Jud lifted his chin in the air. "It's art, kid. It doesn't need to *do* anything."

"Yeah, but,what's the point of it? The phones don't even work!"

"I'm sorry. I'm sort of in the middle of a tour here, okay? If you don't mind, please shut the hell up. Now where were we … Ahh yes, follow me."

The tour continued. Ruby stomped along beside Matthew.

"Can you even *believe* him?" she whispered into his shoulder. "Who does he think he is?"

Matthew shrugged. He didn't fully understand what was going on between Ruby and Jud, but wished she'd be more careful, on account of Sam.

Jud led them to the back of the building, where he stopped beside a large hole and extended his hand like a game-show co-host. Matthew stared down into the blackness. *Deep.*

"This, my friends, will be a garden in due time, which I'm sure you all agree serves a very important *point*." Jud seemed to look specifically at Ruby. "Fresh produce will be plentiful: potatoes, tomatoes, onions, carrots—you name it. And one day *that*—" he pointed toward a shed— "will be a chicken coop. Yet another development here at Center One with a *point*."

He looked again at Ruby. Something unspoken transpired between them—something that made Matthew's stomach twirl. Then Jud whipped around and kept walking.

"All right, folks, let's go inside, shall we?"

They continued to the back entrance where a large, brutish man waited. Half human, half wildebeest, possibly. His muscles were bigger than Matthew's head. The only thing about the man that *wasn't* ginormous were his pin-prick eyes.

Jud tapped him on the shoulder. "This here is Lance, our Head of Security."

The introduction was unnecessary, because the man wore a label on his right breast pocket: HEAD

OF SECURITY. Then beneath that: DEVELOPMEN-
TALLY DISABLED.

Matthew squinted. Was he reading that right? *Developmentally disabled?*

"Don't worry, recruits," Jud said. "You'll all get your
very own label, part of the formal orientation process."

"Formal orientation process?" Ruby whispered.
"Labels? What a joke!"

"I don't think he's joking," Matthew said.

She rolled her eyes. "I know. I just mean it's dumb."

But it wasn't *that* dumb, not really. Labels seemed
like a straightforward and sensible idea to Matthew.
He couldn't argue against it.

"Now, now," Jud said. "I know what you're all
thinking. You look at Lance here, our fine head of security, then you see *developmentally disabled* and think, *well
isn't that cruel, to make a person wear that like a label*—literally on a label, I guess. But what's new, really? We've
been labeled our entire lives, haven't we?"

He pointed to the flat-faced boy, and then the one
with the cane.

"Oh hey, there's Down Syndrome! What's up Chorea? Whatcha listening to—" he looked at Matthew
and stopped. "Dementia? On the spectrum? Whatever. The point is this: you don't have to hide anymore.
We here at Center One believe disease is something to
be celebrated. It's the reason we're still alive, after all.
Isn't that right?" He slapped Lance on the back.

Lance nodded, his beady eyes unreadable. "Jud
predicted all this, yah know."

Jud smiled. "Some people around here like to call me
a prophet, but I'm not about all that—who was right, who
was wrong, who foresaw what, who didn't. *Blah blah blah.*
I want you to think of me as your pal. And I want Center
One to be your home as much as it is mine."

Matthew looked around the group. Joshua was practically cooing like an infant. The old woman cracked a grin. The flat-faced boy clapped.

The others seemed to like the idea of celebrating sickness—whatever that meant. Not that he could dispute it, exactly. He'd been an outcast his entire life. What he had—his Not Normal—had never been celebrated. Not once.

Ruby, on the other hand, seemed to have a lot of objections about Center One. She crossed her arms and stomped her foot.

"All right," she said. "If we all have to wear labels, where's yours then?"

Jud flashed a crooked smile. "Well, aren't you the observant one around here? Thanks for pointing that out. Mine's right here."

He smacked it on his blazer: PRESIDENT, CEO. Beneath that: SCHIZOPHRENIA, BIPOLAR DIS-ORDER, BORDERLINE PERSONALITY DISOR-DER.

"Now, I'd say those are quite the credentials. Wouldn't you, guys?"

CHAPTER THIRTY

～

Inside Center One, Matthew tried hard to practice *one thing at a time*, even though it seemed impossible. There was so much going on.

First, and unfortunately: more people. At least forty of them mingled in the large space, now separated into smaller sections with room dividers. Conversations piled on top of each other: "Where are you from?" and "Multiple sclerosis, eh?" and "Yeah, I heard he predicted this whole thing."

At least none of them had little computers.

Still, noises were everywhere. A generator rumbled in the background; dishes clanged together in a kitchen he couldn't see. Plus those constant voices popping up: "Where are we supposed to sleep?" and "How long have you been here?" and "Why is everyone sick?" And then the spray paint—*more* spray paint, plastered just as thickly inside as it was outside, like the place was some sort of coloring book for young people and hipsters, because who else would be spraying paint all over like that?

LOUDNESS! A whole tidal wave of it.

He took a deep breath. Another.

A woman with a name tag labeled COORDINATOR OF ORIENTATION, MAJOR DEPRESSIVE

DISORDER looked up at him. A pair of thick-rimmed glasses sat halfway down her nose.

"Hi," she said.

It wasn't a friendly "hi." The woman yawned, sighed, then picked up a piece of paper and began to read. Her voice sounded like it belonged on an answering machine.

"Congratulations. Welcome to Center One. You have been saved. We are thrilled to have you. I am the coordinator of orientation. Please take this information packet. Read it carefully. When you are finished, form a line. Jud will speak with you directly."

She handed him two pieces of paper (though it was really more of a thrust). He passed one over to Ruby.

She flapped it back and forth. "What's this?"

"It's a brochure," the woman said, like that was obvious.

Matthew glanced at it. There was a paragraph or two, a map, then a series of ... *numbered rules?* He pushed down a grin. He rather enjoyed numbered rules. And, frankly, it had been a while since he'd seen some. Nobody came up with numbered rules anymore. It was just do as you please, to each their own, *don't want to hurt any feelings!*

Suddenly, there was a tug on his hand, followed by another.

∽

Ruby stomped over to Jud, dragging Matthew behind her. She'd had enough.

"Wait, I haven't finished reading—"

"Doesn't matter," she said. Sure, everyone else was studying the paper in detail, but that was *their* problem. She wasn't going to waste another minute on that nonsense. And neither was Matthew.

Once they reached Jud, now sitting at a desk off to the side, she stopped and handed him the paper.

"Done!"

"Well I wasn't—" Matthew began, until she nudged him in the hip.

Jud picked up the paper and crumpled it into a ball, all the while staring at her with dagger eyes.

Her skin went prickly. Maybe she should have just read the thing.

"Sit down," he said. "If there's one thing I loathe, it's being mocked. And I'm well aware that's what you're doing. You know, you've been given a wonderful opportunity here, kid. It would be a shame for you to get fired on your first day."

"Fired?"

He gave Sam a tap. "We don't know each other well, but trust me when I tell you: you do *not* want to get fired."

Her whole body tensed.

"Anyhoo, now that we've gotten that out of the way, what ails yah?"

"What?"

"What do you *have*?"

"Oh. Medulloblastoma."

"Huh?"

"Cancerous brain tumor."

He pulled out a label and wrote CANCER in big, bold letters. "Cancer. Classic. Any specific medications you need?"

"I have something for pain. But I haven't needed it for a while."

"Noted." He scribbled into a binder. "Now hand it over."

"But—"

"Sorry, strict protocol. Can't have a bunch of un-regulated drugs floating around. Safety first!"

She reached into the knapsack of supplies and grabbed the pills. A big "UGH" dragged from her mouth.

Jud huffed. "Don't be so dramatic. If you need medication, just go to the pharmacy."

"The pharmacy?"

He pointed at the crumple of paper. "That's why I gave you a map! Now, hand over the meds, kid."

She handed him two bottles.

He looked over at Matthew. "All right, your turn, old fella. Whatcha got?"

Silence. Matthew was looking straight at the ground, bobbing a little.

Jud poked him on the shoulder. "I said whatcha got?"

Matthew glanced up, his eyes swelling from their sockets like an animal caught in headlights. Numbers flew from his mouth. "Thirty-seven! Thirty-eight! Thirty-nine!"

"Oh, for Christ's sakes. Ruby, what's he got?"

She shrugged. How was she supposed to know?

"Fine." He scribbled HEINZ 57 across a label. "Any meds?"

Matthew was staring at the ground again, numbers still bubbling from his lips.

"You know what, never mind. We'll deal with that later. But I do need to know what you folks want to do here at Center One. I'll assign you both the same position because, well … *him*."

Ruby slunk down in her seat. What did she want to do at Center One? Nothing. Absolutely nothing—not that she could say this out loud, to Jud, especially after he'd brought up *firing* her.

"Come on, kid. I'm trying to give you fulfilling and purposeful employment. You must have some sort of interest. What do you want to be when you grow up? Or what *did* you want to be, rather?"

Did.

Her mind drifted from Center One as she remembered the assignment from kindergarten. *What do you want to be when you grow up?*

She'd been sitting at the kitchen table for over an hour, thinking. *Come on! Pick something!* Dad was there waiting.

Finally, it came to her.

"I'd like to be in the sky."

"Like a pilot?"

"No, space. I want to be in space."

"Ahh, an astronaut!" Dad rustled her hair. "That's a wonderful aspiration. I will help you spell it."

And he had. A-S-T-R-O-N-A-U-T. He told her about the stars and the planets and a cool thing called black holes. She liked black holes so much she drew them all over the assignment, except she used purple instead of black, because even if they were *black* holes, they felt very purple to her at the time.

Being an astronaut. Flying through space. Purple black holes.

Thinking those thoughts made her whole body tingle. She couldn't wait to one day be higher than the clouds, surrounded by all of those cool, purple things.

But then came the cancer.

"I can still be an astronaut, right?" she'd asked Dad. And he'd replied "yes," but the *yes* sounded like a *no*, kind of, like it was empty inside. Maybe she wouldn't be higher than the clouds after all—that is, until a nurse named Agatha told her about a place called Heaven.

"Not everyone grows up," Agatha had said. "But that's okay, because their souls float into the sky and become angels in Heaven."

Angel in Heaven? That sounded like something she could easily become.

The next day, she'd waltzed right up to Dad. She couldn't wait to tell him.

"I'm not going to be an astronaut. I'm going to be an angel in Heaven! What do you think?"

He looked away. It wasn't the reaction she expected.

"Dad?"

But he didn't answer. Instead, he walked to his office and shut the door. From the other side, Ruby could hear him sobbing.

Jud clapped his hands in front of her face and the memory dissolved.

"Hey! Earth to Ruby! What do you want to do here at Center One?"

She looked down. "I don't know."

"Fine then." He scribbled JANITOR on some labels and tossed them over. "Congratulations! Now, go sit over there and wait."

As she turned to leave, he threw the crumpled "information packet" at her.

"And take that with you!"

Slumped against the wall with Matthew beside her, she uncrumpled it. First, there was a ridiculous paragraph written by Jud, clearly.

"*Hi!*" it read. "*Welcome to Center One! Not to toot my own horn, but I saw all of this coming. And now I'm here to save us, because I'm connected to something greater, obviously. You get it. You're welcome. Now, please make yourself at home!*"

Next, came a bunch of numbered rules, vague and mostly dumb, like:

1. Always listen to Jud (and Sam).
2. Accept one another (YAY sickness!)

What kind of place was this with its rules and labels and *YAY sickness*? And what was she supposed to do here exactly? Clean all day? Make flowers out of broken cell phones? *Accept one another?*

She tried to remember that tingly feeling from years ago. How excited she'd been to become an astronaut.

But then she looked at her label.

JANITOR. CANCER.

She ripped the paper to shreds instead.

CHAPTER THIRTY-ONE

～

L ater that night, Ruby tried to fall asleep but couldn't. There were people everywhere, tucked away in sleeping bags, breathing into her space. Snoring and sucking and slobbering. How was she supposed to sleep with all that noise?

Not to mention her brain wouldn't stop thinking. The events after "formal orientation" kept zipping through her thoughts.

First, she and Matthew had been taken to a place called "customs" where she'd been touched during a so-called "random search"—even though Jud had pointed straight at her. She could practically feel the hands of the customs officer slithering across her skin. She'd screamed, but he didn't stop. He kept feeling his way over her shoulders and up her thighs, until Matthew ran over and shoved him away. She was certain the old man was about to strangle the guy. She'd never seen a person's face so tight and red. But he hadn't, and eventually the customs officer waved them onward.

Their supplies: all confiscated, besides some "personal items." Matthew was allowed to keep his tape player and Tabitha's locket, and she still had her favorite yellow sweater and Dad's Book of Smart Stuff—thankfully.

After formal orientation, they'd missed "formal dinner" (whatever *that* was) and were taken to a section called "the hospital" instead. There were more people in this section than anywhere else in Center One. Stuff was everywhere: stretchers and equipment; liquids hanging from posts; deep-red blood sloshing in packets. And it smelled exactly like sickness: hot and sour and stuffy. The people in this section looked at her like, *You're next.* Or maybe not. Maybe she'd just imagined that.

And then it was suddenly late. She and Matthew were guided to a corner, given a sleeping bag and pillow, and told to stay quiet. She curled up beside Matthew, which was okay, until *others* came along, with their hot breath and snoring.

~

Matthew rolled over, wondering where he was for a moment.

Oh right. Center One.

He waited for that to register, via a loop in his stomach, or tightness in his chest, or straight up LOUDNESS. But nothing happened. *Strange.*

He didn't *like* this place, that's for sure. But he liked that people in Center One didn't look at him differently. For the first time in his life, there were people behaving just like him. People with heads down, and eyes closed, and fists clenched, and bodies rocking back and forth. People with missing legs and eyes and hair and teeth. In Center One, no one looked at him differently, because *everyone* was different.

Plus, being in Center One was better than being outside. Unlike the world, Center One was a finite space. There was a beginning and an end. Even though it was cluttered and full of people, it was also organized and structured. In fact, it reminded him of a place he toured not long ago: Memory Lane, a residence for elders with Alzheimer's and dementia.

Tabitha had insisted he join her.

"*Matty dear, the time will come.*" He'd huffed and puffed for a while—because what idiot decided to name a place for people who are forgetting things *Memory Lane?*—but ultimately he'd agreed.

He expected the building to be cold and sterile, like a hospital. But instead the *home* (as people insisted on calling it) was quite comfortable. There was *breakfast time* and *stretch time* and *snack time* and *card time*, name tags with *Beatrice* and *Philippe* and *Nurse Belinda*. No one looked at him strangely, and everyone was polite, respectful—even the young people (but mostly, there weren't very many young people).

It had been like traveling back in time to a place in his memory with very little LOUDNESS.

"You can come with me!" Tabitha had suggested, and he'd agreed. Because what else would he do without her? Sit around all day being lonely? That was never the plan.

Of course, Center One wasn't Memory Lane, but there were structural similarities that reminded him of potted plants sitting on windowsills and the sweet smell of applesauce, of *Nurse Belinda* and *hello sir!* and friendly games of bridge. But mostly of Tabitha, of her soft hands and honeysuckle voice.

To his left, Ruby flipped over, dragging him back to reality. The impression of Tabitha slipped away and his chest began to ache.

"How did you sleep?" she asked.

"Well, and you?"

She let out a grunt. "I haven't!"

Others were also awakening, grunting and yawning and moaning. There was a bit of crying, somewhere. Then everyone sat up straight, becoming very quiet.

Out trotted Jud, again wearing a pair of scrubs, blue this time, but still the ridiculous suit jacket.

He stopped at a podium and cleared his throat.

"Good morning, fellow comrades! I hope you all slept well. Another *glorious* day in Center One is upon us. Can I get an amen?"

Mostly mumbles—except that boy with the cane, Joshua, who shouted "AMEN!"

"Still early. I get it. Now, first and foremost, I would like to welcome some new faces to our family. I'm delighted to introduce two new janitors, a washroom attendee, and two dishwashers! Please give them a warm embrace."

Some weak clapping.

"As we prepare for formal breakfast, I'd like to reiterate the values of Center One, if I may. As you know, we've all been given a second chance, spared from a terrible illness—one I've been predicting for years, mind you. But who's keeping score? Because hallelujah! We've been saved, folks! Can I get an amen?"

There was Joshua again, squealing like a pig. He seemed to be the only one who cared about the crazy man's speech.

"Alrighty then, on that note, all cooks to the kitchen!"

Jud left the podium as a number of others stood. Ruby, who'd miraculously grown dark circles under her eyes since a moment ago, curled back into her sleeping bag. "Good night," she mumbled.

"But it's not—"

Too late. The girl was already snoring.

He turned the other way. A woman with stubbly hair was taking a stretch. Her label read PARKIN-

SON'S DISEASE and then JANITOR. *Good,* another Janitor.

Unlike Ruby, who seemed to think being a janitor was about as terrible as hunting puppies for a living, Matthew was fine with the arrangement. He'd been a janitor before, and quite liked it. Granted, that was back in the day before people had *swiffers* and *swaffers,* or tiny robots that hovered across the floor like some sort of spaceship. Those corner-cutting gadgets and gizmos couldn't be trusted to get the job done, not like good old-fashioned elbow grease. Of course, people didn't appreciate good old-fashioned elbow grease anymore, being allergic to hard work and all …

He shook his head, staring out at all the people. *People with their silly little … people with their lazy old …* but it stopped there. Because the people before him had labels and roles and problems just like him.

And that left very little to complain about.

"Hello," he said to the woman with Parkinson's disease, who in return gave him a good stare down. He tried not to look at her left hand, which appeared to have a mind of its own, jerking here and there and up and down. At one point, she tried to contain it in the pocket of her jeans, then she gave up and carried on with her staring.

"So, you're one of the new janitors, huh?" she said eventually. "Welcome to hell. It's a riot. You from around here?"

"Yes, sort of. You?"

"Naw. Philadelphia. Was in town for a family reunion. *That* didn't go well." She slapped her knee and let out a crackly, high-pitched laugh, then she stared off into the distance.

"Is it really *that* bad around here?"

Crackly, high-pitched laugh again.

"Well, yes and no. I mean, I'm not sure what you've seen of the world, but it's sort of bad everywhere. As far as I can tell, there's nowhere else out there for a declining gal like me. I'm like most of us. This is the best of a bad situation."

She opened a small bag of toiletries and removed a toothbrush. Matthew caught a glimpse of a photograph, a boy in a school picture. His smile was big and wide, no front teeth.

"Is that your grandson?" Matthew asked.

"Yes. His name was Ralphie." She closed the bag. "He's dead."

"I'm sorry to hear that."

She nodded, looked away for a minute, then turned back toward him. "Anyway, let me show you the ropes, Mister … ?"

"Werner. Matthew Werner. And your name?"

"Ester Lamont."

He nudged the sleeping bag with his foot. "This down here is Ruby."

Out came a grunt.

He nudged a little harder and she poked her head out like a gopher. "Yeah. I'm Ruby."

"Great," Ester said. "Well, Ruby and Matthew, we best get going or we'll be late."

CHAPTER THIRTY-TWO

~

Inside "the shop," which was really just a heap of supplies and rickety old shelves partitioned with a room divider, Ester selected two toothbrushes wrapped in plastic. She looked at Ruby, then at Matthew, then back at Ruby.

"We're going to need some clean clothes," she mumbled to the STROKE-VICTIM, ATTENDANT who sat behind a desk.

Ruby glanced down, realizing she'd been wearing the same outfit (a pair of black jogging pants and a white T-shirt) for *way* too long. There were still bits of shed on her pants! She stretched and took a quick sniff.

Yep, she could definitely use a shower.

The attendant, who was about the size of a dump truck, waddled past a pile of clothing, half-folded. His face partly sagged and his eyebrows were stuck at unusual angles. It seemed he was heading toward a shelf at the other end of the shop, but then he stopped, wheezed a little, and turned around. Instead, he pulled some clothing from the half-folded pile and tossed them toward Ester.

"Those'll do. Anything else?"

"No, that's fine. Thank you," she replied.

He sat back down and opened a binder. "The tooth-brushes and clothing: they for Cancer and Heinz 57?"

Ester nodded.

He recorded the information and gave them a hand wave. "Go on now."

And so they did, heading next to the pharmacy.

"That's Big Mike," Ester said as they walked. "He runs the shop, as I'm sure you've gathered. If you need anything, go see him. They don't have much right now, but y'all are welcome to put in requests. Probably won't happen, but y'all can try."

Ruby looked back at the binder. "Are the items we took being tracked or something?"

Ester shrugged. "Who knows? Jud talks a lot of nonsense. You'll hear him toss around words like *audit* and *control* and *inventory*, but, in my opinion, it's all smoke and mirrors. Delusions of grandeur."

They stopped at the end of a very long line.

"Which isn't to say *he's* all smoke and mirrors. He's scary as hell. But I'll give you a piece of advice, dear. If you're ever in a pinch, just play along."

Ruby wasn't exactly sure what she meant by this, but nodded anyway.

When they finally reached the end of the line, a PHARMACIST with ALZHEIMER'S DISEASE prepared Ester a cup of pills. Ruby edged closer to make sure she was reading his label correctly. *Alzheimer's?* Isn't that what Matthew's wife had? The disease that made her forget where she lived?

She leaned into Ester and whispered, "Should he *really* be a pharmacist?"

"Actually, he *is* a pharmacist," she replied. "Or *was* a pharmacist, before all of this. Only early-onset Alzheimer's, thankfully. He's one of our gems. Like Dr. Harrington." She pointed in the direction of the hospital.

"Got lucky with Dr. Harrington. Waltzed in here, free will and all. Just wants to help people."

"What does Dr. Harrington have?" Ruby asked, glad to learn that not everyone's job title was a made-up lie.

"Cancer, just like you."

"Oh."

Next, they headed to the washroom, where another long line awaited. At the front stood Joshua, handing out towels and greeting people as they arrived. He seemed to have a permanent smile on his face—until he saw Ruby, at which point his smile cracked. She was sure of it.

"When it's your turn," Ester said, "the washroom attendant will give you a squeeze of toothpaste, then you'll brush your teeth and shower in there." She pointed to a door. Both men and women were coming in and out of it.

"We take off our clothes ... *in front of people?*" Ruby asked.

"Well you can't very well shower with your clothing on, can you girl?"

Ruby tried to swallow; a lump had formed in her throat.

Ester rested a hand on her shoulder. "Don't worry, they're fairly private. You'll be fine."

On the other side, Matthew leaned into her ear.

"Yes," he said. "I'll make sure of it."

When they reached the front of the line, Joshua handed over a towel. Then, just as he went to squeeze a pinch of toothpaste onto her toothbrush, his hand flared dramatically, launching the paste onto her wrist instead.

"Hey!" she said.

His eyes narrowed. "Whoops." He pointed to his name tag. "My bad. Can't help it."

She huffed. *Sure.*

He then passed over the smallest bit of soap she'd ever seen, like a fleck of dandruff shaved from a scalp.

"That's it?"

He didn't reply, just kept on smiling. That stupid, toothy smile made her want to kick him in the shins.

"You guys need any toilet paper?" he asked.

Ester stepped up from behind. "Please, for all."

He handed them each a square.

"Oh come on!" Ruby said. "One stinkin' square?"

"Strict orders."

Toothy smile again.

She wanted to say something, but Matthew shooed her along before she had a chance.

The washroom was spacious but sour smelling, like a community pool with too many people in it. Ruby knew exactly what era it was from: the sixties. Not that she knew much about the sixties, only that women burned their bras and people went crazy (*clearly!*). Almost everything in the room was turquoise: walls, tiles, sinks, trim. Different shades of turquoise, but turquoise nonetheless. Except for the countertops. Those were a shade of yellow positioned somewhere between morning pee and stomach bile. Her stomach grew queasy looking it.

"And *this* is the place they chose not to cover in spray paint?" she said to Matthew. "That was a mistake."

༌

Matthew forced his mouth closed. The girl didn't know what she was talking about, obviously. Or her taste in decorating hadn't yet developed. One of the two. Frankly, he hadn't seen a yellow like that in ages.

Turquoise, either. Such colors reminded him of being a young man. The colors of his youth: assertive, bold, a bit reckless. Unlike colors nowadays, all gray and beige and *greige*, no personalities to them, every room the same color as every other room.

What a yawn!

He walked up to one of the turquoise sinks and inspected it—a fine piece of porcelain. Beside him, a slight woman with hair resembling peach fuzz brushed her teeth while another woman with thick, healthy locks combed her hair. Woman A appeared to scowl at Woman B, until Woman B dropped her towel. In place of breasts were two blistering scars, at which point Matthew looked away. So did Woman A.

All around him, people were dressing themselves, doing up buttons and zipping zippers. He didn't mean to stare, but everywhere he looked there was pale, saggy skin or popping, purple veins. One man had a scar that orbited his entire scalp.

"This room," Ester said, "is the main dressing area, as you've probably gathered. Individual showers are to the right, washroom stalls are to the left, and if you feel uncomfortable dressing in the open, there are some private stalls at the end. I'll meet you both outside when you're finished."

After the whole customs officer incident, Matthew didn't trust leaving Ruby alone for one second. It was best they stick together. He grabbed her hand and brought her to a free shower.

"Here, you first," he said.

He covered her with a towel until she disappeared behind the curtains. And then he waited, on guard. He avoided all eye contact—not that he needed to. People seemed unconcerned with his presence. A man to his left removed a prosthetic leg and stepped inside a stall.

Another man collected his dirty laundry and exited the room. No one seemed to care about him and his Not Normal.

In the past, seldom had he looked into the world without it staring back—*people* staring back. He knew exactly what they were asking themselves: *Is there something wrong with that man? What does he have?*

Now, though, his Not Normal was a moot point. *No one* was normal.

When Ruby had finished, he handed her the tape player and entered the stall. After removing his clothing and tossing them outside, hot water flowed over his body, soothing his aching muscles. Honestly, life had become so different lately he'd almost forgotten about washing and brushing and dressing, about hot water and clean clothing.

Routine.

That's the word he was looking for. He whispered it out loud, and everything felt a bit sturdier.

CHAPTER THIRTY-THREE

～

Inside one of the private stalls, Ruby dressed her-self, trying to avoid contact with the slimy tile floor. *What a dump!* Everything, it seemed, was old or worn, outdated or questionable—not to mention filthy. Mildew had sprouted up in every crevice.

If there was one thing she knew for certain, they couldn't stay. Not only was the place being run by a cra-zy man, but it was practically falling apart. To think, they had the entire world to explore, and they were being housed in a junky old community center with pee-colored countertops and sleeping bags for beds. Dad had told her stories about scientists replacing body parts with robots, brains growing in test tubes, and rockets soaring into outer space.

Suddenly *this* was the future?

No way! They needed to get out of Center One as soon as possible.

She followed Matthew out of the washroom, eager to start planning an escape. Ester continued the tour. "All days follow the exact same structure," she said. "We tend to hygiene early, followed by formal break-fast, then formal lunch, then formal dinner."

Ruby rolled her eyes.

Ester stopped.

"Be careful where you roll those eyes, girl. Eye-rolling is one of Jud's biggest pet peeves."

Great, another thing to be careful of.

Ester carried on. "Between meals, people perform their roles—which, for a janitor, is a typical list of cleaning duties. Dusting, mopping, sweeping—you know. About five hours of the day in total, probably less now that I have some help. As long as the place is clean, Jud is happy."

She described other processes too, like how dirty clothes were put in a barrel by the front door and washed. Not by the janitors, thankfully. Clean clothes could be picked up at the shop, which Ruby already knew.

Most of it was pretty straightforward. If you wanted medication, go to the pharmacy. If you were sick, go to the hospital. Free time could be spent however a person pleased—as long as they didn't leave. Ester was quick to add that a number of security guards were in place to ensure this didn't happen. She pointed to a humongous man with a barbed-wire tattoo across his neck.

Ruby gulped.

"What happens if you try to escape?" she asked.

"Nothing good, I can tell you that."

As they walked back into the main area, Jud approached the podium once more.

The place looked different than before. Instead of sleeping bags, several rectangular wooden tables had been pushed together to form one large table with a bunch of fake flowers heaped in the center.

"Those look like they belong on a casket," Ruby whispered to Matthew.

Around the casket flowers, spindly gold candles were being lit by a heavily eye-shadowed TABLE DEC-

ORATOR with EPILEPSY. The woman was wearing a floppy-brimmed hat, the type country club women wore to fancy brunches. She looked at Ruby and blew her a kiss.

Ruby was about to roll her eyes when Jud flashed her a stare. She looked at the ground instead.

As Ester led them to their chairs, she noticed the crowd was a bit sparse. A number of seats were empty, despite having place holders—which everyone had, apparently. She pointed to one gold-rimmed card in particular labeled LAUNDRY FACILITATOR, ALS.

"Why are there so many people missing?" she asked Ester.

Ester pointed toward the hospital with a shaky finger. Ruby looked away; a chill fluttered through her.

"Another *glorious* breakfast in Center One," Jud began. "All thanks to the power of infrastructure, the power of organization, and the power of *you*. Yes, *you* fine folks. You're to thank for the abundance of today."

He stepped down from the podium and began to wander.

"Look, I know I can be hard on you sometimes, and I apologize. Part of it has to do with my credentials." He pointed to his label. "But we're cut from the same cloth, me and you. We've been dealt a bad hand. AND YET ..." He pounded his fist on the table. "Here we are! The world belongs to us now. To me, and to you."

He rested his hand on Joshua's shoulder, who smiled, of course.

"Bring out the champagne!"

Three women in chef's uniforms exited the kitchen. They handed out plastic cups of bubbly liquid. From the hospital located at the other side of the center, someone cried out in pain. The women stopped—everyone stopped.

"As I was saying," Jud said. "Please join me for a toast. To Center One!"

A few people cheered their neighbors. Ruby grazed her cup against Matthew's, feeling obligated, then she turned toward Ester.

"Do we do this every morning?"

"Every few days."

As the cooks brought out breakfast, Jud wandered over. His mouth burst into a smile.

"Hi!"

Zero replies.

"Just wanted to check in. See how things are going."

"Fine," Ruby said.

He frowned. "Just fine?"

She nodded.

His face turned a bit purple, like he was holding in his breath. Eventually, though, he shook his head and smiled.

"Great! Great. So, I wanted to personally apologize to you for yesterday. I'm sorry you had to see that, with Clark and the girl. Eventually, I think—*hope*—you'll understand. Tough choices need to be made. For the greater good."

Tough choices for the greater good? He'd shot an innocent man and left a paralyzed girl to die all alone. There'd be no forgiving him for that. And *no*, she'd never "understand." But she nodded nonetheless until he walked away.

She took a bite of her breakfast: oatmeal swirled with apples and candied pecans. All around, people were raving about the "flavors!" and "textures!" and "exceptionally talented cooks!" Which was exactly what she'd been waiting for. Once the room was loud enough and Jud was out of sight, she leaned over to Ester.

"Have you ever heard of the Horizon?"

"Like where the sky and the ground meet?"

"No, like an actual place called the Horizon."

Ester shook her head. "I'm sorry, girl. I have no clue what you're talking about."

CHAPTER THIRTY-FOUR

A lthough Matthew hated to admit it, formal breakfast was *almost* as good as chicken noodle soup. Of course, chicken noodle soup was still superior, but it was nice to get a home-cooked meal every once in a while. Hot oatmeal with swirls of cinnamon and sweet pecans: that was something Tabitha would have made him. And, with each bite, he could almost feel her, somehow.

Her soft, dark hands wrapping around his shoulders, pressing into his chest. Her locket, cool against his back. Her honeysuckle voice, whispering into his ear.

Matty dear, would you like a cup of coffee with that?

Matty dear, would you like a second helping?

Matty dear, I love you.

Even though formal breakfast was over, and they'd moved on to janitorial duties, he could still feel her presence, like those memories weren't as far away as they used to be. And maybe that's why time seemed to pass more quickly. In what felt like only a few minutes, he'd already swept and mopped the floor, dusted off some tables, and polished the wood with oil.

"You're good," Ester said.

He almost cracked a grin. "I know."

This was precisely the type of task he excelled at—straightforward, independent, *good honest work*. On he went, sweeping and dusting and polishing, every so often providing his coworkers with a bit of commentary.

"Smell that? That's good old-fashioned soap that smells like soap! No mango-pineapple mumbo jumbo."

"Now that's elbow grease, ladies!"

"No floor robots here. Not today."

They seemed to ignore him.

Fair enough.

After their cleaning duties were complete and he'd gobbled down a delectable formal lunch (homemade pasta with mushroom sauce and fresh bread) he asked Ruby whether she'd like to join him in the department of innovation.

She replied, "Whatever."

That'll do.

Outside, he stood before the mountain of everything with a jittery stomach. He was drawn to those objects like a magnet, an endless expanse of projects to tinker with. More than he could tackle in his lifetime, surely. There were machines he'd never even heard of, let alone seen. Wires and buttons and knobs and tubes and levers and cranks and—his hands began to tremble. He couldn't wait to unravel it all.

Plus, something about seeing all those blasted little computers, broken and unusable, was unduly satisfying, like he'd won something grand.

The losers?

Society.

And young people!

A moment later, he was elbow deep in a pit of those little computers, throwing them into the air like confetti.

∽

Ruby considered marching back inside. The old man was practically leaping with delight. Is this what he wanted? To clean all day and play with a bunch of junk afterwards? Why on earth would anyone want to play with a bunch of junk?

Instead, she sat on the sidelines, an unpleasant, jittery sensation buzzing through her. She needed to find the Horizon. She needed to find Dad. She needed to get the *hell* out of there.

Except when it came to *that*, she hadn't a single good idea. Everywhere she looked, security guards were lurking with their big bold shoulders and constant pacing. Not to mention Sam.

Roadblock. Roadblock. Roadblock.

Which is why she'd brought Dad's Book of Smart Stuff with her, for inspiration.

She whipped it out from under her shirt and began flipping through the pages: formulas, diagrams, super-impressive words. *Hippocampus?* Still, looking at those pages made her tummy flutter, even if she didn't understand a single thing. If Dad could figure out the human brain, *surely* she could escape from Center One.

She glanced at Matthew, still tinkering in the afternoon sun. He was prying apart a cell phone and ... *smiling?* Not exactly, but it was the closest thing she'd seen to a smile yet. Her cheeks went warm and prickly.

Did Matthew even *want* to escape? It didn't seem so.

Just then, two stretchers wheeled through the front door accompanied by three men, one for each stretcher, and the last with a shovel. Two of the men were security guards; the third was simply a DIGGER. On each stretcher there was a sheet, thinly veiling a ...

Body.

Gasp. Her stomach dropped to her toes. The security guards wheeled past her, heading around the side of the building. For a moment, she couldn't help but picture herself lying under one of those sheets. Eyes closed. Body stiff as steel.

She turned back to Dad's Book of Smart Stuff, trying to forget about it. *Except ...* why were they headed around the side of the building? Where were they going? She had to find out.

She tiptoed around the corner. The men had stopped beside the giant hole (the *supposed* garden) and were staring. Down. Down. Down. The digger wheeled up a body.

Her mouth fell open.

A grave?

No, she couldn't believe it.

Maybe she'd made a mistake? Then one of the security guards tilted a stretcher. A body tumbled, landing with a *thud.*

"Miss?" a voice called out from behind her.

She whipped around.

It was Lance, the head of security, beastly as ever. "What are you doing here?"

"I ..." She could barely speak her mouth was so dry. "I ... thought this hole was supposed to be a garden."

She glanced at his name tag, specifically at DEVELOPMENTALLY DISABLED. Lance seemed to notice her noticing. He hung his head, covering his eyes from view, like he was ashamed.

She knew that feeling well.

"Don't be ashamed," she said, before she could think better of it. "It doesn't matter what's up here." She tapped her head. "It only matters what's in here." She pointed to his heart, and, for a moment, Lance's pin-prick eyes softened. Then, just as abruptly, he huffed. "You isn't supposed to be here. Jud said."

"Well *Jud* also said this hole was going to be a garden. But it looks like the only thing being planted here is bodies."

"It ain't what it looks like," Lance replied.

"Is that so." She propped her hand on her hip, waiting for an answer. Lance kicked the dust at his feet, and then he got this *look* about him—the same look Dad gave her when she asked questions like, "How are babies made?" or "Am I going to die?"

Finally, Lance whispered, "We got a bunch of sick people here that ain't gunna live forever."

Now, he was staring at *her* name tag—at the word CANCER. The blood drained from her face, leaving it cold.

Lance kinked his head to one side, staring at her with eyebrows so low she could barely see his speckle eyes. "I wouldn't tell nobody about this," he said. "Jud didn't wanna dampen spirits, or something."

Ruby nodded. "Okay." If she could go back to thinking the grave was a garden, she would in a heartbeat.

She headed back toward Matthew, wishing she could go back in time.

She should have played with the pile of junk instead.

CHAPTER THIRTY-FIVE

～

Matthew was fairly impressed with himself these days. He'd slid into the routine of Center One without much effort, and there were a lot of things about that routine he happened to like.

A steamy morning shower.

Walking among the people like a ghost.

Knowing there was formal breakfast, then formal lunch, then formal dinner.

If his mind was a series of gears, those gears were finally starting to rotate in synch. And he loved being a janitor. Loved the feeling of his hand scrubbing in a circle, the shiny surface afterwards, so spotless a person could see their own reflection. He could clean the entire building in approximately three hours—single handedly, too. Ester was hardly effective with her uncontrollable tremors, and Ruby just stared off into space the whole time. That or *talk, talk, talk.* Except she only had one thing to talk about.

Escaping.

They needed to escape because of her father, and the Horizon, and "Jud will eventually kill us all," and "Don't you want to find Tabitha?" On and on she went, at which point his mind floated elsewhere. Even if he tried to pay attention, he soon found himself thinking about the department of innovation: the sea of little computers, or the crank of a bicycle, or the beautiful mess of wires to be found within a heart monitor. Which isn't to say he wanted to stay at Center One. Though he didn't exactly want to leave, either.

Even if the place *was* being run by a maniac, the days themselves were more than tolerable, filled with structure and tinkering and delicious home-cooked meals. Plus, when it came to Tabitha, staying at Center One was probably the best chance he had at finding her, oddly enough.

Ruby had suggested they look for her out in the world, like some sort of expedition. The idea was cute, but what exactly did the girl expect? That they'd wander the globe, calling out "Tabitha," as he'd done long ago? What good would that do? He was old, Not Normal, and so very tired. He'd be dead in less than a week, just like the rest of them.

Meanwhile, at Center One, day after day recruiters traveled near and far in search of survivors. It was a long shot, but if Tabitha *was* out there, did they not have a better chance at finding her, with their young bodies and sharp-seeing eyes?

This considered, wasn't staying put the better option?

He held Tabitha's locket close to his chest and imagined her voice on his headphones: *Matty, Matty, Matty,* instead of *knock, knock, knock,* which seemed to make everything go away—the people of Center One, the glaring spray paint, and even that lunatic, Jud.

∽

As Ruby quickly came to discover, escaping Center One was not as simple as she'd hoped.

Day after day, she searched for a plan. She noted every exit, of which there were few, and kept track of the security guards, of which there were many. She watched the members of Center One like a detective, waiting for something—*anything*. But all she came up with were more roadblocks.

Each day during formal breakfast, Jud welcomed new recruits with job titles like MEMBER MANAGEMENT OFFICER and OPERATIONS INVESTIGATOR, titles that seemed to indicate they were all being watched a little more closely. And it *felt* like they were being watched a little more closely.

Still, she asked each new member if they'd heard of a place called the Horizon—which seemed like a good plan, even if all she got in response was a bunch of headshakes.

Until one day a woman with fiery red hair arrived. Her label read: DISHWASHER, PSYCHOSIS.

Ruby approached her like everyone else, ready to ask the same question as always: *Have you ever heard about a place called the Horizon?*

The woman sat at a table, coloring. She was pressing her crayons so deeply into the paper they broke into pieces. Ruby sat, stared. The woman didn't seem to be scribbling anything in particular, just lines and swirls.

"What are you drawing?" she asked.

"The Horizon."

Ruby almost choked. "What did you say?"

"I'm drawing the Horizon."

"*The Horizon*," she whispered, her insides bubbling like a cup of champagne. "That's a *place*, right?"

"Of course!"

"Where is it? Can you show me?"

The woman set down her crayon and pointed to her head. Her eyes were milky, almost white, like she was blind or close to it.

"I don't understand," Ruby said. "The Horizon is in your head?"

The woman smiled, moving her fingers across the paper like the lines and swirls were telling a story.

"I can see the Horizon in my mind. I've been there many times." She took a moment to chuckle, except it sounded far away, like an echo. "Why, I'm practically there right now. There are children laughing in the trees; some are singing." She swayed back and forth. "And the lake! There's a lake, too! It reflects the sky so perfectly I can't tell up from down or down from up. Will you come? Will you come with me to the Horizon?"

Ruby scooted back her chair; her hands fell somewhere beside her, dangling. Everything was dangling. Her whole body: unhinged, just hanging there in space. She couldn't move. She couldn't breathe.

The Horizon.

Not a real place, but a fantasy created by some mentally ill woman who could barely see. The woman was probably the voice from the radio. And the other voices? People just like her, hoping for an imaginary paradise, convinced by the woman's story.

She wondered what happened to those people since.

Probably dead.

The Horizon isn't real. The Horizon isn't real. The Horizon isn't—

"Are you still there, Ruby?" the woman called to her. "Where are you?"

She didn't respond. Instead, she curled herself in a vacant corner and began to cry.

CHAPTER THIRTY-SIX

～

As the days wore on, Ruby fell into the routine of Center One, just like Matthew. She ate and cleaned and slept. Kept her mouth shut.

Because really, what was the point?

She had nowhere to go, nothing to search for. Dad? *Pfff!* The idea was ridiculous. She saw that now. Like she could just waltz outside and there he'd be, waiting for her. Tabitha too. Finding her was a silly thing to suggest. She could be anywhere—or nowhere.

Probably nowhere.

She pictured Mom, lying on the porch with Dad and Tabitha.

Dead.

Just like everyone else.

She could really use a friend. Except even making friends was pointless. Matthew didn't listen to her (within seconds, he was staring off into space) and the rest of the group was constantly dying off. New members replaced the old as bodies left on stretchers.

Life. Death. Life. Death.

Or as Jud insisted on calling it:

Supply. Demand. Supply. Demand.

Either way, that was the nature of Center One. No use getting attached.

Nowadays, she spent most of her free time sitting in a corner, watching people spray paint—which seemed like a bad idea, being indoors and all. But whatever, she'd come to enjoy it.

The sharp toxic scent.

Growing lightheaded as a balloon.

Traveling to a thoughtless place.

It was a nice break. Otherwise, all she could think about was the garden grave. She imagined what it might feel like to be surrounded by dirt, the world existing above, and she below.

Dead.

Not that she needed to imagine it. She'd be there soon enough. And, to be honest, that was probably for the better.

∽

Lately, whenever Matthew stared at Ruby, his chest began to ache, which didn't make much sense.

He was doing fine—more than fine, actually. All of his basic needs were met. He had food, shelter, hot showers, and tinkering opportunities galore. He had many exciting projects on the go. And for the first time in … ever, the people weren't so bad. Most everyone was older, different in some way or another, and kept to themselves. Best of all, life was proceeding like it had in the good ol' days, before *little computers!* and *quick fixes!* and *LOL!* and *everything made in China!* In truth, he was hardly able to get a good rant going these days; his sails lost wind before the boat even left the harbor.

Plus, he'd become a bit of a triumph at the department of innovation. Jud had called the way he took things apart and reassembled them into unique hybrids both "impressive" and "inspiring." He'd never been associated with words like that before.

So yes, all things considered, he should have felt content. But instead there was a lacking inside of him, like a piece had been taken. And that damn ache in his chest, all because of Ruby.

Something was definitely wrong with the girl. Her big molasses eyes weren't so big anymore. Now they were half open, like weights had been attached to the lids, dragging them down. And her face: no expression—not that he always understood all of those expressions, but she used to have a lot of them. Most noticeably, she wasn't talking like she used to. Not about escaping, or the Horizon, or anything. She just stared at the ground, lips pressed shut, like she was empty.

He couldn't take it anymore, to see her like this. A conversation was in order. Even though he hated conversations, he hated Ruby's sadness even more.

After searching the entirety of Center One, he found her in a corner, curled in a slump.

"I'd like to speak with you," he said, sitting down beside her. "Something's wrong. Correct?"

"Yeah, *correct.*"

He folded his hands together, then separated them. *What are people supposed to do with their hands all the time?*

"Have I done something wrong?"

She shook her head.

He opened his mouth to speak, then closed it, then opened it again. He tapped his fingernails on the concrete. "Look, I'm not good at this, you know that, but can you please tell me what's wrong?"

She sat up straight. "Do you really want to know what's wrong?"

He nodded.

"Fine, you asked for it. Everything is wrong. Every single thing! Jud is pure evil. And we're all trapped here in this *stupid* place. And everyone is constantly dying—and, by the way, the dead people are being buried in a place that's supposed to be a garden. I wasn't allowed to tell you that. But I did. So *there!*"

Matthew was quiet for a moment while he thought of a response. "Well, what about the Horizon?"

"There is no such place as the Horizon. A dishwasher with psychosis told me in a crayon drawing. And I'm pretty sure she's blind. So yeah, we're not going anywhere. I don't even know why you care. You're happy here. *You're* having a *great* time. It's not like you ever cared about the Horizon."

Her eyes glossed with tears.

His chest ached again, a dull, throbbing ache. His own eyes began to water, even though the problems were mostly hers, not his. It was the strangest thing.

"Look," he said, all of the words finally arriving. "I'm sorry the Horizon didn't interest me. I'm not very good with change, or people. But it's not true that I'm having a great time, and I've come to realize that's because of you." He grasped her hand. "I want you to be okay, more than anything. I'll help you escape. I'll follow you wherever you bring me. I'll be your Horizon."

She wiped her eyes and leaned into his chest, which suddenly didn't ache any longer.

"Okay," she whispered.

He waited for something more, but nothing more came.

And even though he swore someone scurried out of the shadows right then, it didn't matter, because when he looked down, the girl, pressed up against him, was smiling a little.

CHAPTER THIRTY-SEVEN

∽

For the first time in weeks, Ruby awoke feeling like her usual self again. Sure, the Horizon wasn't real, but was she just going to keel over and die in Center One because of it? *Absolutely not!* Plus, she knew in her gut that Dad was still out there, Tabitha too. They just needed to find them. It would be hard, yes, but impossible?

Nothing was impossible!

She had Matthew to thank for her change of heart. "I will be your Horizon," he'd said. Not that she knew what being a Horizon meant exactly, but it sounded like a lyric from one of Mom's songs. And when she'd snuggled into his chest, she was reminded of Mom in a number of other ways, too.

His warmth, soft as her favorite yellow sweater.

His voice, sweet and gentle.

His hand, dancing across her back.

It seemed the old man cared for her after all, which was exactly the fuel she needed to get herself back on track.

Except, in the days that followed, getting back on track proved more difficult than she imagined.

First came the rumor about Dr. Harrington and Frank the pharmacist. Apparently, they were both getting sicker, which caused people to bop around with owl eyes, all: "Have you heard?" and "Oh my God," and "What are we going to do?"

And what *were* they going to do?

Ruby had a feeling part of the reason people put up with Jud's nonsense was because Center One had a doctor and pharmacist (it certainly wasn't the "organization" and "infrastructure"). Without Harrington or Frank, would the members of Center One try to leave? Maybe—at least Jud seemed to think so.

Shortly thereafter, he doubled work hours, quoting "busy season." But everyone knew what this really meant: *Less time to socialize and plan.* The department of innovation was suspended, too. "Under construction." Or rather: *Stay inside where we can watch and hear you.*

Jud even had a number of recruiters return not with people, but weapons—sharp knives, baseball bats, guns bigger than Sam. He began parading the recruiters around Center One like a marching band with scary objects instead of instruments. He didn't even try to make an excuse for that one, just smiled and glared.

All of this left a knot in Ruby's throat. Sure, she'd seen a lot of mentally ill people in her lifetime. There were mentally ill people all around her, people with major depressive disorder and bipolar disorder and schizophrenia and psychosis. And then there was Matthew, with his Not Normal (whatever that was). At any rate, she knew mental illness was really just a sickness like any other sickness, even though people thought of it differently.

Stigma.

That was the word.

Jud, though, was an exception. There was something inherently evil about him, a type of evil that couldn't be cured. She could see that evil in his eyes, feel it in her bones. Now, every day, every minute, was starting to feel like a race against time.

Get Jud before Jud gets you.

∽

Matthew sat for formal breakfast with Ruby beside him. His stomach rumbled. What would it be today? A silky quiche? A crispy hash? No matter, the cooks always prepared something delicious.

He waited for the crazy man to step out and vomit another meaningless ramble: "Look at us in Center One, a thriving infrastructure, *blah blah blah.*" By now, he'd heard it all a million times.

Except this time, Jud trotted up to the podium and just stood there, silent. He looked different, cleaner. His hair was combed and slicked with some sort of putty. Instead of scrubs, he wore a turtleneck with a pinstriped bowtie (still the ridiculous suit jacket, though). His lips were flat as a board.

Matthew looked around—at open mouths, at squinted eyes, at the lady across from him shivering.

Today, formal breakfast would be different.

Jud began to pace.

"Fellow comrades," he said. "I must say, I'm rather *pissed.* It's come to my attention that *some* members within our organization are unappreciative to say the least. Why some of you feel this way is beyond me. I mean, you guys, I thought we had a good thing going here, no? Look around and consider the alternative! Without me, you'd be stranded in a wasteland of bodies. Alone. No medical assistance out there, people. No delectable meals. I'm *saving* you—I'm saving all of us. And this is the thanks I get?"

Matthew rubbed his eyes. He swore Jud was staring straight at him.

"Anyway, apparently some of you just don't get it. A great shame, truly, considering an organization is only as strong as its weakest member. You've left me no choice. I've been too lax around here, waiting for *certain* people to change their minds."

There was that stare again. This time, he was sure of it.

"Effective immediately, I will be offering incentives to those who step forward with information, because those who serve to protect the values and integrity of Center One, who strive to rid us of the traitors in our midst, deserve only the best. That is all. Cooks!"

Matthew wasn't sure what all that was about, but his mouth began to water as the cooks moved forward with a full tray of food. Except something was off; they weren't smiling like usual. A bowl dropped in front of him with a *thud*. He inspected its contents: gray sludge the consistency of vomit. He smelled it. *Smells like vomit.* After licking the tiniest bit from the end of his spoon, he turned to Ruby.

"Indeed, tastes like vomit." He pushed the bowl as far away as possible.

More cooks returned with a second platter. Thankfully, this one smelled like some type of dessert. He sat straight up. Obviously, the sludge was a mistake, soon to be rectified. His mouth watered all over again as the platter neared.

Cherry pie.

Piping hot.

But the cooks kept walking—wouldn't even look him in the eye. Instead, they distributed the pie to others, not him. His shoulders drooped.

Ruby leaned over. "Spies," she whispered. "The people with pie are spies. Do you recognize any of them?"

He stared at the lucky pie eaters, some swallowing so fast they were practically choking. Others were looking away, no doubt mortified by the exposure. But there weren't many of them and no one looked familiar.

That is, until the kid with the cane, Joshua, tapped him on the foot from under the table. "Thanks, old man," he said, pie sloshing around in his mouth.

"Thanks for what?"

"For the other day."

The other day? What was the boy talking about? Then it hit him, the conversation with Ruby, the shuffle in the shadows. His own words: "I will help you escape."

He stared back at Joshua, who simply smiled, his teeth smeared with cherry syrup—except, in the moment, it looked less like cherry syrup.

And more like human blood.

CHAPTER THIRTY-EIGHT

~

Matthew couldn't stop thinking about food. All day, every day, tasty concoctions swirled around in his mind: hearty stews and freshly baked breads, mysterious curries with aromatic spices, boiled ham with mustard sauce, cheese plates with nuts and pickles. And the desserts.

Oh Lord, the desserts.

Fruitcakes with vanilla frosting, bitter chocolate trifles, whipped puddings with peaches and cherries.

But instead of all *those* tasty delights.

Slop.

Cold, noxious slop.

Following the cherry pie reveal, he and Ruby were in the majority. Nearly everyone was eating slop—at least at first. But with each meal the percentage of slop-eaters declined. Lately, it seemed, there was only a handful of them left.

Initially, Matthew wasn't sure what people were disclosing to earn themselves a delicious dinner. After all, Center One was awfully quiet. Members tiptoed around with shifty eyes and tightly pressed lips, unwilling to become a piece of evidence. And yet, at the very next meal they were stuffing their faces full of chicken pot pie. It didn't make much sense. *Who were they talking about?*

And then he realized.

Him.

He and the girl had become targets, partly because of their continued slop schedule, and partly because the flailing one with the cane, Joshua, had singled them out in the first place.

Matthew decided it was far too dangerous for Ruby to be running around like a renegade, plotting an escape. The timing was off. Instead, they needed to wait patiently for everything to settle—which she'd agreed to, reluctantly.

In the meantime, there was nothing they could do—nothing besides eat slop and keep quiet. Of course, they could *lie for pie* like everyone else. At least they would get something tasty out of the deal.

Hearty stews with freshly baked breads. Bitter chocolate trifles …

But no.

It simply wasn't right. No matter how weak Matthew got, no matter how much he hated the taste of that smelly, gray sludge, lying wasn't an option. They were going to do things the right way, even if it meant the hard way.

∽

"Keep quiet," Ruby whispered to Matthew. "I got this."

They'd been summoned to Jud's office.

She knocked on the door to an old storage closet; her hands were shaking.

A few seconds later, it opened a crack. "Come in."

She edged into the dark, dreary space. As her eyes began to adjust, this *thing* emerged: a wall so bizarre she couldn't look away. In some ways, it reminded her of a bulletin board in a detective's office, where photographs and places were connected with string. This wall, however, was plastered with documents from old books and magazines, photographs of people she didn't recognize, plus dried up bodies of insects—butterflies, bees, a spider curled into itself like a leaf. She stared at one corner in particular. Was that a fingernail? There were words everywhere, too, written in big, bold letters.

BUILD.

GROW.

EXPAND.

And then came a series of photographs that made her stomach curdle. Buildings and towers and pyramids, each with a label.

CENTER TWO.

CENTER THREE.

CENTER FOUR.

He wants want to make more centers?

Everything—words, pictures, documents, insects, possible fingernail—was connected with yarn like a giant constellation.

Besides the terrifying wall, books were piled all over the place: *Business Management for Industry Volume 5*, and *Asserting Yourself: How to Reach Your Potential*. Around these books—none of which were on shelves, for some reason, even though there were plenty of shelves—sat fat stacks of paper, still covered with plastic. More paper than any single person could use in a lifetime, surely, and it didn't seem Jud was using any of it.

For a minute, she just stood in the middle of everything, pressing her lips together, trying not to say it, despite very much wanting to.

This is insane.

Beside her, Matthew glared directly at the ground. She swore he was counting under his breath.

Meanwhile, Jud sipped a coffee with a strong odor. She recognized that odor from across the room. *Alcohol.*

She waited for him to say something, but he only clicked his fingernails on the desk. An uncomfortable amount of time later, he pulled out two binders and tossed them down with a *thud.* The covers read:

JANITOR, CANCER.

JANITOR, HEINZ 57.

"Performance reviews!" he said with a big smile. "*Man* do I love performance reviews." He took a sip of his not-so-secret alcohol-coffee. "Let's start with you, kid. I'm sure this will strike you as no surprise, but your performance, quite frankly, sucks a big one."

She tried to keep her mouth from falling open. *Sucks a big one?* Sure, there were some accusations floating around, but performance, as related to being a janitor at least, hadn't much concerned her. Lately, she'd been trying extra hard.

"I've been doing my job," she said.

"You silly kid. Your inexperience is showing. Surely you must know that performance is many things. Like, for example, attitude. Shall we start with your attitude, Ruby?"

She stared at Jud, trying *really* hard not to roll her eyes. "Okay."

"Well, as you know, we here at Center One expect a certain level of enthusiasm. And then there's acceptance and loyalty and all that. Needless to say, you have displayed exactly zero of these qualities. Let me point out a few examples from your fellow comrades."

He cleared his throat and began to read from the binder with a squeaky, mimicking voice. "She's far too quiet! She's far too loud! She carries about her an air of mistrust! I've never heard her talk about the values of Center One! She spends too much time with that old man and his headphones! She's—"

"This isn't fair," Ruby said. "You've forced people to tell you lies by dangling pie, and—"

"Is it? Is it *unfair*? Obviously, I'm able to sort out fact from fiction. I mean, come on, did you really think I was going to punish you for being too quiet? That's ridiculous. However, if you hadn't so rudely interrupted me, I was about to read a comment that does concern me. And I'll have you know it was brought forward before I was dangling pies. Where were we? *Ahh yes*, 'I overheard her talking to the old man with the headphones. They were discussing an escape.' Escape! Now, I'd say that's something, wouldn't you?"

A twinge pinched her gut. It was true—she couldn't deny it. She carefully considered her response, remembering what Mom always said about honesty.

"Are we not allowed to talk about that?"

Jud slammed his mug on the table and let out a gigantic, "Are you serious?"

She waited for him to go on about loyalty or acceptance or whatever, but instead he flipped through a binder marked RULES, then pulled out a fat stack of orientation documents. After looking through each, he bit his lip.

"You know what, I may not have written it down anywhere, but it's *clearly* implied. And I don't need to explain myself. I make the rules, I call the shots, and I don't think you're fitting in here, which makes me question whether you should be terminated. Fired! Sayonara! Buh-bye!"

∾

As far as being quiet was concerned, Matthew was doing it nobly. The place was textbook LOUDNESS, first of all, and required full headphone concentration—not that he had much to say anyway. He'd barely been listening, primarily waiting for Ruby to wrap things up. But when "terminated" made its way into the conversation, his ears perked.

His cheeks were suddenly aflame. Boiling. He cupped his cheeks to contain the warmth, but, strangely, it began spreading to other parts of his body, slithering up his spine, down his arms, like a lit fuse growing wider, faster, hotter still, until he could no longer feel distinct parts of himself. An uncontrollable fire, blazing on.

He found himself hollering at the top of his lungs, something like, "Nooo!" Then his hands flailed across the desk like a tornado, causing papers to fly into the air then float to the floor. "I don't think so!"

For a moment, Jud and Ruby just stared, eyes humungous, until Matthew slumped back into his chair, unable to piece together what came over him.

"Thanks for that," Jud said. "That was quite the performance. You know, the two of you together ..."

Matthew looked up to find Jud frozen in pause, staring at that god-awful wall. The only thing about him that wasn't frozen were his eyebrows, moving up and down, up and down. After a moment, a crooked smile met Jud's lips. He pushed Ruby's binder off to the side.

"You know what, I think we're done here."

CHAPTER THIRTY-NINE

～

I f Center One were a ladder, Matthew was well aware that he and Ruby had officially become the bottom rung—which, apparently, was something they needed to fix. "We need a low profile," the girl had said, and he was fine with this, until she followed up with, "So act happy, okay?"

Act happy? How the hell was he supposed to act happy? Her answer to this question—"smile at people"—had caused a growl in his throat.

Smile at people? He *never* smiled at people. But she'd given him those jiggly Jell-O eyes, so the least he could do was try.

And so, he curled his mouth upwards and flashed his teeth, again and again, which at first seemed cumbersome, until he realized it was much easier on his facial muscles to simply hold the position steady, aiming it at people as they passed. Sometimes, he even managed to hiss out the word "hi," like a verbally inclined snake, which led to a few wide stares, and a few abrupt departures, but whatever. He was trying.

"How am I doing?" he asked Ruby one night on the way to formal dinner. He flashed his smile at her.

She bit her lip. He swore she was laughing from somewhere.

"Umm ... you're doing great."

He sat at his usual place, Ruby beside him. Like every other formal dinner, place cards were positioned, flowers were fluffed, candles were lit. He awaited the crazy man's speech, but cooks flowed from the kitchen instead—no crazy man.

His stomach turned over.

Slop landed with a *thud* and he forced some down, trying to ignore the other bowls being passed about. Still, a sweet and spicy aroma wafted. A noodle dish, perhaps?

No matter. Because.

Slop.

He turned to Ruby and was about to say, "Plug your nose; it helps," when he caught a glance of Jud standing in the corner. His shoulder was turned and he was staring at the cane-ridden boy, Joshua. Then Jud made some sort of hand signal and Joshua cupped his ears.

Something was definitely ... off.

Suddenly, Joshua screeched, followed by an "OUCH!" so loud it echoed through Center One.

Jud ran to his side, hands flapping like a bird. "What's wrong, buddy?"

Joshua flailed around for a moment, per usual, then moaned like a dying cat. Everyone stared.

"The noise," Joshua said. "My ears are buzzing like crazy. Can anyone else hear that terrible noise?"

Jud looked around like he was searching for something in the air, then he cupped his ears—exactly as Joshua had done.

"Sweet Jesus, yes! It's terrible! People, can you hear it? You *must* be able to hear that awful sound! Something is buzzing, squeaking, squawking."

A lady beside Matthew let out a shrill cry. "Where's it coming from?"

A man across the room began yelping like a dog.

A moment later everyone, it seemed, was complaining about a sound Matthew couldn't hear. Moans, groans, and growls were coming from every direction.

He turned to Ruby. "Do you hear anything?"

She shook her head.

Just then, Joshua pointed straight at him. "It's coming from those headphones! They're making us sick!"

Before Matthew had time to think, let alone speak, people were already yelling, "Stop, make it stop!" So many voices. So many fingers.

He pressed his thumbs into his temples. "No more! Please!"

Jud ran over and yanked the headphones from his ears.

Instantly, a monsoon of LOUDNESS flooded in, hard and fast. Without those headphones, voices and fingers and giant staring eyeballs swirled together. In less than a second, a ring of darkness eclipsed his vision and there was nothing but pain, electric and pounding, as though his brain was being fried in a pan. He couldn't see, couldn't hear, couldn't think. All he could do was yell.

∾

Ruby clutched Matthew's hand as hard as she could. Still he was yelling. Around him: complete silence, not even a movement. It was just Matthew, in the middle of it all, screaming.

"It's okay," she kept saying, even though he didn't seem to hear her.

Joshua stepped forward and hung his head. He patted at his eye with a napkin.

"Looks like the noise has infected his brain," he said.

Ruby wanted to scream. It was all fake, clearly—just an old tape player, nothing more!—but a security guard was already yanking Matthew from her grip. A moment later, he was being dragged across the center. His whole body was shaking—arms, legs, and, worst of all, his eyes, like he was looking for something but couldn't find it.

A fiery warmth blasted up her chest. "Stop!" she cried out. "Can't you see it's just an old tape player?"

She ran toward him, but before she was even half way there, Lance snatched her up and held her tight.

"Relax, miss," he said.

But she couldn't relax. She kicked and scratched and flared her arms, but it hardly mattered. Lance was wrapped around her like a straitjacket.

"Matthew!" She peeked over Lance's boulder-like shoulder. "*Matthew?*"

But Matthew was already gone.

Jud walked over, shaking his head. "I'm truly sorry, kid, but he needs to be quarantined."

Quarantined? She tried once again to pry herself free, smashing her hands against Lance's rock-solid chest.

His grip tightened. "Calm down, miss. You's only making things worse."

She didn't care. All she could picture was Matthew, calling out her name in some small, dark room, shaking all over like a caged animal.

"Look," Jud said, addressing the crowd. "I don't *want* to quarantine the old fella, but we have to. Trust me, I'm here to save us."

A barky laugh flew from Ruby's mouth. "*Save us?* How are you saving us?" She pointed towards the hospital, where sick people were practically piled on top of each other. "We're still dying all the same."

For a second, Jud's face went blank, then his cheeks turned a deep, deep red. He stomped towards her until he was looming above, his neck twisted down like a swan.

"*I'm* the one who predicted all of this! *I'm* the one who saw the light! And *I'm* the one who knows what's best! Okay?"

His pupils shook and his grip on Sam tightened. Ruby was certain he'd shoot her right then and there, in front of everyone. But instead he laughed and took a few steps back. "Silly kid."

He gave the members a wave. "All right people, carry on."

And so they did, until it was just her, standing in the middle of the room, all alone.

CHAPTER FORTY

～

Matthew blinked—probably.

Are my eyes open or closed? He wasn't sure anymore, because his world was now darkness. They'd tossed him into a closet of some sort, but that was ages ago. Since then: darkness—darkness so black he had to periodically pat his arms and legs to make sure they were still there. Was he part of the darkness now? Had he been swallowed up by it? Perhaps.

For a while, he'd called out for Ruby. He'd tugged at the door, scratched his nails against the wood, but that was all useless. Now, he simply sat in that darkness, trying to calm his racing thoughts.

Racing Thought Number One:

Tabitha.

Without the quiet knocking of his headphones, which he'd begun to imagine as *Matty, Matty, Matty* instead of *knock, knock, knock*, he was very much without her. Not that she was physically there before, but she'd felt close in spirit. He could picture her beside him: her curvy body in a purple, cotton dress (her favorite), hair all over the place, lips smelling of the same cherry Chapstick she'd worn every day since eleventh grade.

And, best of all, her honeysuckle voice, whispering throughout the day.

Matty dear, what are you tinkering with?

Matty dear, you missed a spot!

Matty dear, how are you managing without your cherished chicken noodle soup?

Such imaginations had led him to believe it was really only a matter of time before Tabitha waltzed into Center One for real. It would be a miracle, sure, but a miracle didn't feel *that* unlikely—not in his heart. He seldom listened to his heart, believing such types to be granola-crunching, yoga-posing chumps, unable to sort up from down and fact from fiction. But this time, listening to his heart felt right—or *had* felt right, anyway.

Now, though, with darkness all around him, he couldn't feel Tabitha at all. Not the dainty arches of her fingers, or the warmth of her smile. Not even the tingle in his stomach after "Matty."

He rubbed the locket beneath his shirt like a genie might a bottle, trying to enliven her.

Nothing.

Instead came a message from his head, not his heart. And this voice had something very different to say.

Tabitha is gone.

She's never coming back.

Then came Racing Thought Number Two:

Ruby.

What was happening to her out there without him? Was she in danger? Probably. But he couldn't know for certain—and that was the worst part. She was just a small, innocent girl, surrounded by sick people, and crazy people, and men with statues for bodies. Without his eye on her, something was bound to go wrong.

It made him want to scratch apart his skin.

He crawled to the door and pulled with all his might. Nothing. He slouched against the wall.

Time passed. Over and over he would think of Tabitha, and everything inside would stretch like a piece of chewing gum.

"Tabitha," he'd moan, barely even realizing it.

He'd scratch at the door, the walls, ignoring the shooting pain in the tips of his fingers.

"Ruby!" he'd cry, his voice echoing off the walls. But there was nothing to do—nothing besides sit and wait, sulk and stress, moan and shout.

So that's what he did, his sanity dangling by a thread.

∽

Ruby paced toward Jud's office. Even though she'd barely slept, her mind spun. It had taken twenty-four hours of straight thinking, but she'd *finally* come up with a plan. A real plan with actual components.

Now came the true challenge.

Pulling it off.

She knocked on Jud's door; everyone else was asleep.

He yanked it open, still in a robe.

"Great." He chugged the rest of his coffee—alcohol again. "What do you want, kid?"

She smiled, remembering a token of advice that was now incredibly useful: *Play along with his game.*

She handed him the Book of Smart Stuff, trying not to make a sound, even though a cry rose in her throat. She hated giving away all she had left of Dad.

Jud grimaced. "And this is … ?"

"It's my dad's notebook of ideas, his Book of Smart Stuff. I'm not sure what any of it means. But you're smart. I thought maybe you would. "

"*Pfff!*" he said, even though a grin spread across his face.

As he skimmed through the pages, his chin lifted. Every so often he nodded like, *Ahh, yes, brain science.* And even though Ruby wanted to slap the notebook out of his hands, she didn't.

"If you turn to the last page," she said. "I've written some things down for you. You know, stuff you might find useful."

He flipped to the back of the book. "Go on."

"Well, firstly, there's no security guard posted at the back entrance for a couple of minutes every morning." She'd known about this for a while. Unfortunately, it was never long enough to actually *escape.* "That one security guard, the bald one, takes a pee and nobody replaces him. They're all eating breakfast. Maybe it would be helpful to have a rotating officer or something?"

Jud tugged at his chin. "Hmm. Rotating officer. Nice title."

"Also, in the third shower, there's a big fat hole that gets bigger every day. I think someone's trying to maybe ... probably ... escape through it?"

"Good eye," Jud said. "Anything else?"

"Actually," she said, pointing to a chair. "May I?"

Jud shrugged. "Sure."

"What you said the other night, about knowing what's best? I guess it just ... *resonated* with me." She smiled, hoping she'd used the word *resonated* correctly.

Jud grinned. "Well good. It's sort of like ... you know that book, with that guy—three guys, actually. There's a father, his son, a ghost."

Ruby blinked a few times. "Umm, the Bible?"

"*Yes,* that's it. Anyways, at one point, the main guy—God, I'm pretty sure—is straight-up drowning people. Everyone, actually, besides some fella and his ark. Which sounds terrible, but he was drowning people for their own good—for the good of humanity, even though they couldn't see it. Do you get what I'm saying? *I'm like God.* I always know what's best."

She forced a smile, staring at the cluttered (and terrifying) wall. "And this is your plan?"

He laughed. "*Our* plan. It's for all of us. One day— soon, hopefully—there will be more than just a Center One. We'll have a Center Two, and a Center Three, and so forth. A whole world full of centers! Pretty cool, huh?"

A whole world full of centers? Her stomach swirled. She couldn't let that happen.

Still, she nodded. Jud kinked an eyebrow. "Anything else?"

"Actually, yes. I guess … I just wanted to say I'm really sorry. I've been taking things for granted."

For a while, Jud just stood there with his mouth gaped open, like he was in the middle of a yawn and someone had pressed pause. She wanted to physically close it for him, but, instead, she smiled.

"Anyway, I should probably get going. Thanks for your time."

And with that, she stood and left.

∽

That evening during formal dinner, Ruby wasn't surprised to discover a bowl of chowder placed before her, plus fresh bread and whipped butter. To her right, Joshua stared at a heap of stinky slop. His lips drooped into a pout.

"Lucky!" he said.

Ruby leaned in for a whiff. *Cream. Garlic.* She hadn't eaten anything but slop in days. Her mouth watered as she imagined that cream swirling over her tongue, the odd chunk of flaky potato and sweet carrot. And the bread: how *soft* it would be, like a pillow with crusty edges—even better with that fluffy, whipped butter melting on top.

But no, before she could change her mind, she glanced at Jud to make sure he was looking, then she pushed the bowl toward Joshua. "Here."

He coughed. "Are you … serious?"

She forced a nod and he dove right in. He didn't even say thank you, just slurped up the chowder so fast it spilled down his chin. She couldn't bear to watch. That was *her* chowder, and she wanted it *so* bad. But it was all part of the plan. And for now, at least, it seemed to be working.

Jud's mouth was wider than a puppet's.

CHAPTER FORTY-ONE

～

Jud stood before his desk, not exactly sure what to do. The kid—Ruby—had thrown him out of sorts, and he was *seldom* out of sorts. First, she'd brought him that little book with all kinds of tips and tricks. Then she'd apologized.

Ruby.

Apologized.

And *then* she'd given her reward to Joshua. That was very *what the hell.* Nobody liked Joshua. He was a snitch—an excellent one, at that. Easily pleased. Morally ambivalent. He was sort of the crème de la crème of sidekicks. The Robin to his Batman. The Watson to his Sherlock. The flappy kid with chorea to his super mastermind geniusness.

Ruby, on the other hand, was a pain in the ass—or she used to be. But with these new developments, was it possible she'd ... *changed?*

Obviously, a few days ago, the answer was NO. Absolutely. Positively. Resounding.

But now?

He stared at the wall, scratched his neck.

Clearly, the girl had a knack for observation, detecting the cracks in Center One even *he'd* failed to see. Assigning her the role of janitor was a waste of resources. So it seemed, without Headphones, she'd gained a new perspective on Center One, just as he'd hoped. *Pat on the back for that one!*

He picked up the Book of Smart Whatever—he had work to do.

He lit a candle en route to a fine bottle of whiskey, then he poured himself a glass. After a few sips, he stared into the candle light, the way it flickered up the wall.

His wall.

It was, unarguably, the most extravagant creation in the history of mankind. It reminded him of all he'd been through, starting with the Institution.

Fucking institution.

Locked away in a cell like some goddamn stray. The world a cloudy haze of drug-induced nothingness. No feelings to feel, like somehow that was better.

"Lunacy," they'd said, with their pressed blazers and fancy medical degrees. *Tainted by delusion.* And then *whaddya know*, one of those delusions had turned out correct.

He'd been right all along; he *was* connected to something greater—of course he was. Still, what he'd give to see the look on their faces: bile climbing up their throats, minds slipping away. Their last thoughts about lost dreams and loved ones and all that, but somewhere in that sentimental pile, another: *That lunatic was right.*

He was right. And look at him now. A triumph. A leader. Saving the goddamn world, one center at a time.

He opened the notebook.

New information.

He loved new information.

He skipped across the room. A page here, a page there. Then, he reached for a ball of yarn. His favorite part: linking it all together. Because afterwards, everything made sense. All of it.

It was sort of amazing how that happened.

On he went. *Unstoppable. Stupendous.* Until he stood back, skin tingling, mind racing.

It was breathtaking.

Fucking breathtaking.

As beautiful as a sky full of stars.

CHAPTER FORTY-TWO

～

Ruby needed more of something she couldn't have. *Time.* Lately, it seemed like all she could do was pace. Pace. Pace. Pace. Even her *fingers* were pacing, constantly clicking against themselves.

Some questions:

Where was Matthew being kept? Did he have food and water? Would Jud ever let him out?

No one seemed to know—or care. People wanted to pretend the whole incident never happened, as if the old man with the headphones never existed. When she asked around, all she got were shrugs. *What? Who? Headphones?*

More pacing.

Nighttime was the worst, when all those questions— *Where's Matthew? Does he have food? Water? Will Jud ever let him out?*—swirled around her mind on a loop. After several nights of this looping, she could hardly stand it.

To think, she'd almost left Matthew lying in the dust not long ago. That memory felt like it belonged to a different person. Because now, she hated being without him. She missed his quiet company, his grumbly voice, and his old, wrinkly hands. But mostly she missed the feeling in the pit of her stomach when he was around: like the impossible felt possible, like she was invincible with him beside her.

"I'm coming, Matthew," she whispered, willing her words to find him wherever he was. "I haven't forgotten you."

∽

Matthew wanted more of something he couldn't find.

Hope.

He had less and less of it by the day, like a faucet running dry. Speaking of days, he had no idea how many of *those* had passed. Time seemed to stretch, endless, each minute like an hour, each hour like a day. Just darkness. More darkness.

Most of the time, he was certain Ruby had abandoned him. Then sometimes a spark flickered in his chest, and it seemed like there was a stroke of light in that terribly dark room.

Ruby will come.

Right?

He just wanted to know. Was she coming, or wasn't she? Because it made a very big difference. If she wasn't coming, he intended to slip away.

Finally, he could close the hole in his chest.

Say goodbye to Tabitha.

Disappear inside himself like an anchor into water.

But if she *was* coming, he'd try to find the one thing—hope—he'd all but lost. And Tabitha: he'd keep the memory of her alive as best he could, even if he was starting to forget her. Or, rather, forget how to remember her. Actually, he was starting to forget how to remember everything, as if staring into the darkness of that room for so long had turned his thoughts into a sticky, black tangle. He couldn't pull apart one from the other. He couldn't seem to find any facts.

Is this what Alzheimer's was like for Tabitha?

A sound fell from his mouth and he almost choked on it, something like a gasp and a moan mixed together. To think, the person he loved more than anything had been trapped in her mind, in the darkness. He'd never known what that felt like—until now. He leaned into the elbow of his sweater and began to cry, arms folded atop his knees.

Worst of all, there was a cruel ring of justice to the tears and darkness and quarantine, like maybe ... he deserved it? Not only had he lost the person he loved, but day after day he'd wished for nothing and no one. For the world to leave him alone. For young people to screw off. For technology to break apart. For industry to crumble. For the world to get a clue.

Now, most of those things had come true, and he was all by himself, in blackness and silence. People had a word for such a circumstance, didn't they? He tried to push through the sticky, black mass. Oh yes.

Karma.

∽

The next morning, Jud called Ruby to his office.

For a moment, she stood at the door, summoning all her energy.

Finally, after many sleepless nights: progress.

Jud waved her inside, a giant cup of coffee in his hands. He smiled at her with his piss-yellow teeth and she smiled back—until she noticed a few new additions on the wall.

Dad.

Every morsel of oxygen fled from her lungs.

"What do you think, kid?"

Her teeth gritted together. *Stop it teeth!* "Looks great," she managed.

"I thought you'd like it," he said. "Really adds something, you know? Anyways, I wanted to thank you for your service the other day. You were right about the security guard at the back entrance. I appointed a rotating officer—again, great title. And the shower? Gaping hole, like you said. Consider it patched. Any idea who was chiseling away at that sucker?"

"No, but I've been keeping an eye out."

"Good, good." He looked at the wall, a giant smile pushing against his cheeks. "It's just so … *impressive,* wouldn't you say? Distractingly so."

"Kind of like artwork."

"Artwork," he said. "I've never thought of it that way."

"Well, you're very talented."

"Why thank you!" He beamed. "Anyways, it dawned on me that you're a young woman beyond your current rank. Anyone can be a janitor. No offence, but you know …"

She nodded so fast her head almost tilted off.

"So, I'm going to ask you again. What is it you want to do here at Center One?"

She looked at the ceiling, bit her lip. "Oh, I know! This morning, Frank—you know, the pharmacist with Alzheimer's—gave me the wrong pill. The pill I got was yellow, but normally it's blue." She tried to keep her face steady; it was a big fat lie. But Frank *could* have mixed up the pills.

"Well, that's no good. He should probably be fired."

"No!" She nearly jumped. "I mean, you're the boss. But he *is* a real pharmacist. The only one we have. Maybe he just needs some help." She searched for a term she thought Jud might enjoy. "Umm, *inventory control?*"

He nodded.

"He could really use an assistant," she said. "Plus, Frank *will* get worse. At some point, he won't be able to …" she trailed off.

"And *then* we'll fire him."

She looked away. As far as she knew, no one had *actually* been fired. Unless all those people in the garden, supposedly dead from sickness, were actually dead because …

Sam.

A shudder rattled her bones.

Jud removed a fresh label from his desk and wrote PHARMACY ASSISTANT.

Ruby wanted to kick up her heels and shout. Her plan was finally sliding into place—and she was almost done; only a few more questions. But these next ones were tricky and would require a … delicate touch.

Don't blow it, Ruby. Just be calm, professional. Not that she had any idea what *be professional* really meant, besides saying *sir* a lot.

"Sir?"

"Yup?"

"What happened to the headphones?"

Jud knocked on the desk drawer.

Top right. That's where the headphones are.

"And Matthew, still sick?"

Jud was staring at the wall again, a drifty look in his eyes. What was it with him and that wall?

"Sir?" she asked again. "Matthew?"

"Damn it, kid! I don't know. I let my head of security handle the matter. Now, if you'll excuse me, I have a lot to do today."

She grabbed her new label and turned toward the door. Right before she left, she glanced back. And it all seemed easier then, with his stillness and distant eyes. Like he was already halfway gone.

Maybe killing him wouldn't be so hard after all.

CHAPTER FORTY-THREE

～

A s it turned out, being the pharmacy assistant came with a few unanticipated perks. Ruby had a clear sightline of the main hallway, for one— where all the storage closets were—so it wasn't long before she discovered Matthew's whereabouts: the second door from the main entrance. Much to her relief, Lance *was* bringing food and water, once every morning, and the key was in his left breast pocket.

Frank the pharmacist was super friendly—another perk. He reminded her of a chipmunk with his puffy cheeks and constantly wiggling nose. His thick, black glasses were always fidgeting because of it. He also had an accent she'd never heard before. *English? Scottish?* Something like that. But what she liked about him most was his smile, big and toothy and constant. He was possibly the happiest person she'd ever met.

Even though she'd suggested becoming a pharmacy assistant as part of her plan, Frank actually *needed* her help. Before long, she was popping pills into medicine containers, slapping labels on bottles. When there was a break in the line of customers (which was seldom) he'd show her all kinds of other processes, like a medication binder that recorded people's prescriptions. Not that he needed it. He had them all memorized.

She quickly realized the rumors about Frank were just that: rumors. He was sharp as a tack. If he wasn't wearing the word ALZHEIMER'S across his chest, she never would have guessed. This meant she couldn't pull a fast one on him—which she'd been counting on.

Luckily, he occasionally left Center One to accompany recruiters when supplies were running low. Not that he thought them idiots, but how were they supposed to know the difference between *dactino*mycin and *dapto*mycin when they couldn't pronounce either? Frank said this as if it was some hilarious joke, and she'd chuckled along, even though she hadn't the slightest clue what he was talking about.

She considered asking him, but didn't have time. Customers kept coming and coming, no end in sight.

"Is it usually this busy?" she asked.

Momentarily, his smile disappeared. "Lately." There was a drag in his voice when he said it.

"Why?"

He didn't speak, just subtly pointed ahead. Ruby gasped—she couldn't help it. As she stared at the end of the line, a familiar figure emerged.

Back in the hospital, she used to picture death as a person ("helps them process it better," she'd overheard a nurse tell Dad). In her imagination, death was sort of like Santa Clause, except he was skinny, pale faced, and dressed in black.

And instead of presents, he brought things like CANCER.

Now, of course, she knew this was factually incorrect. Death wasn't a person, but an irreversible cascade of biological dominoes. Still, Santa Death, being a prominent character in her imagination for years, sometimes surfaced. And as she stared at the long line

of customers, she swore she saw him. Then she squinted, refocusing. Not Santa Death.

Dr. Harrington.

He was practically a different man. The last time she'd
seen him, his face was round as a peach. Now, it was more
like a skeleton; his bone-colored skin stretched over the
angles of his face like a sheet. And his eyes had sunken so
deep into his skull they seemed lost.

When he neared the front of the line, with his
bony cheeks and dark, inward eyes, Ruby tried not to
shiver. She tried not to stare. She tried, unsuccessfully,
to think of something besides Santa Death.

"Doctor!" Frank shook his hand—his bony, disappearing hand. "How are you today?"

He seemed to smile. "Not well, I'm afraid." His face
looked hard as plaster.

He went on to apologize for his poor health, the
burden it placed on Frank, patients seeking medical
knowledge and assistance well beyond the scope of a
practiced pharmacist. Ruby understood now why the
pharmacy was so busy.

Santa Death. Santa Death. Santa Death.

Frank responded with an ear-to-ear grin. "Don't be
preposterous, Doc! I'm happy to help. I only hope you
get better ..."

He slid over a container of pills and they stared at
each other for a while.

"Sorry," Frank said.

Because there was no getting better.

∽

Later, after formal dinner, when the constant line of
customers was finally gone, Ruby seized the chance
she needed for her plan to move forward.

"I was hoping you could teach me more about how things work around here," she said to Frank. "Starting with these pills." She pointed to the endless row of shelves along the far wall.

"Sure thing. Where shall we start?"

"There are so many bottles, labels, colors. Are they organized somehow?"

"Oh absolutely! They're organized alphabetically by class. Antihistamines, benzodiazepines, decongestants ..."

He proceeded to list these so-called classes as though they were common colors. After a few more, Ruby wasn't even sure he was saying real words anymore. She loved impressive words and all, but these were *way* too impressive for her.

"I'm sorry," she said. "It's just ... I'm not really sure what you're talking about."

He stared at her for a second then laughed. "Oh my! How ridiculous of me to expect those names would make any sense to you. A pile of jargon, surely. Perhaps we'll take a different approach." He picked up a bottle and pointed at the label.

"As you see, I've also labeled each bottle according to the ailment it treats. For example, this one is formally titled *memantine,* an N-methyl-D-aspartate or NMDA antagonist. Gosh—here I go again. Jargon! Forget I said that. Just pay attention to this section right here." He pointed toward the bottom of the label, *Alzheimer's.*

She inspected a few more bottles and noted they were labeled similarly, which seemed unnecessary given Frank's familiarity with the subject.

"Why did you label them?" she asked.

"Memory cues, naturally, and clarity for my replacement when I ..." He trailed off for a moment, eyes growing foggy. "But that's neither here nor there. And now that you're here, I must say, I'm quite relieved. I'll have plenty of time to educate you, or educate you enough to carry on without me when the time comes. Even if you are only ... How old are you?"

"Twelve."

"Twelve years old? By golly. Well, it looks like we have our work cut out for us, don't we?"

She nodded, but couldn't bear to look him in the eye. Frank believed her to be his successor, to help the people of Center One when he was no longer able. And here she was, taking advantage of his generosity, planning to flip the whole place on its head. Even still, she wasn't sure which situation was worse: that members of Center One would be without a pharmacist, or that a twelve-year-old girl would *be* their pharmacist.

She forced up her chin. No time for such feelings.

"The labels help, for sure. Next question: I know it's bad to mix medications. My doctor used to be really careful about that. But are there really bad ones to accidentally mix? Ones that might even ... kill someone? I don't want to hurt people."

She only wanted to hurt *one* person.

"Indeed, there are some combinations you'll certainly want to avoid. Opioids or painkillers—especially the strong ones, which can be found here"—he pointed toward the bottom shelf–"can interact with a number of other medications. For example, benzodiazepines, or anti-anxiety meds, and muscle relaxers do not fare well with opioids. The combination of all three can be especially problematic."

She tried to commit these names to memory, but they were far too long and complicated. "Could you write that down please?"

"There I go again—jargon! I seem to keep forgetting you're a child. A smart child! But a child nonetheless."

He scribbled onto a fresh sheet of paper, which she snatched up before it could make its way into the binder. "If it's okay with you, I'd like to keep this. You know, traitors and such."

He nodded, eyebrows coming together. "Oh absolutely. Keep that safe. In the wrong hands, such information could be very, *very* dangerous."

CHAPTER FORTY-FOUR

～

Jud stood in his office sipping whiskey by candle-light. Ideas and words swirled all around him. Their product was rather ...

Colorful!

Yes, if colors were feelings, the whole rainbow was there: the forceful thunder of a dark red, the dramatic glow of a bright yellow, the theatrical allure of a dazzling purple, and so forth, each expanding before him, within him.

Mania.

At times, it was rather fun.

He stretched out his arms, wishing they could envelope the entire Center—the entire world—in one gigantic embrace. Then he stared at his constellation, groin tingling.

The future: he could picture it so easily. Jud. Just Jud. A celebrated artist, like Picasso, remembered in a world of Center Ones and Twos and Threes and Tens and Thousands. And the wall—his wall—entirely preserved, displayed at the center of an exhibition.

He could almost see people mingling around it, could almost hear a lady whispering to the man beside her, "*To think, this is all we have left of the man who saved the world.*" Then of course the man would whisper back, very hushed and enchanted, *"But what does it mean?"* The two would stare, puzzled, enraptured.

He took a step back and yelled it, "Puzzled! Enraptured!"

And they *should* stare, obviously. His wall was the most spectacular display of human ingenuity and creativity yet to grace the earth. He ran his fingers across it, wishing he could somehow crawl inside of it. Become it.

And then he stopped, stared at the new additions—pages from the Book of Smart Stuff, or whatever the kid had called it. He'd hardly glanced at those pages before. But now, as the formulas and notations and diagrams danced before his eyes, their complexity settling, his stomach did a few loops.

Smart Stuff.

Yeah, the kid was fucking right.

He stood back, paranoia itching up his spine. Clearly, Ruby's dad was a genius. Some sort of brainiac mastermind. His nose twitched. Then his finger. Then his toe. *Is that sort of thing inheritable?*

Of course it was.

He began to pace. Why did he have that book again? A gift? Or ... was it some sort of ploy? He downed the glass of whisky, poured another. The voices were coming, riling up inside of him. All of those colors? Gone in an instant.

He fell into his chair and gripped it for dear life, waiting. Then, all at once, the voices washed over him like a wave, shaking the ground, the walls, the sky.

She's playing you for a fool! You should have fired her long ago! Now, you will fail! Are you listening? You will fail! And then there were other voices, simultaneously. *No, Ruby is your ally! Don't listen! You're just being paranoid!*

"One at a time!" he said, trying to herd the voices like a mob of cattle. But he couldn't. They were rogue, feral, running in all directions.

He sipped on his whiskey, pulled out his hair. Sip. Pull. Sip. Pull.

Until:

"ENOUGH! ENOUGH ALREADY!"

When this didn't work, he gulped straight from the bottle, drowning the voices into submission.

At last he could think clearly, or somewhat clearly, considering a drunken haze had settled over his thoughts. But that was nice, at least. He stumbled back toward the wall, took a deep breath.

Chill.

No matter, suspicion coiled around him, tighter and tighter, choking the air from his lungs. He couldn't shake the feeling that something wasn't right. After all, Ruby had always been a problem, and she'd changed her mind about Center One so quickly.

Too quickly?

Sounds screeched out of him. Not words. Just noises.

He had a few options:

1. Burn Center One to the ground and start again. Fuck it.
2. Cry like a little girl.
3. Just fire her.

That last one—*fire her*—had a certain appeal to it.

He tugged his chin, stared at the wall. At the end of the day, he couldn't trust anyone—except Sam. He glanced at the gun and smiled.

Maybe next time Ruby paid him a visit, there would be a little interrogating.

CHAPTER FORTY-FIVE

～

Ruby clasped the items in her pocket as if they might disappear without her constant touch. She ran her shaking fingers across the smooth surface of each pill. Also in her pocket: the key to Matthew's storage closet. She'd gotten lucky with that one, seized the opportunity when Lance removed his clothing for a medical evaluation. Unfortunately, this meant he was bound to notice soon. How soon? Definitely by tomorrow morning. Before then? Possibly.

She slid her hands from her pockets and wiped them on her pants. They were getting sweaty. Now that it was finally time, she tried to move but couldn't. Her feet seemed planted to the ground. She'd spent so much time *planning* the plan, she'd forgotten to imagine the performing part. Until now. Specifically, slipping a lethal combination of medication into the drink of another human being—a terrible human being, but a human being nonetheless.

Murderer.

That's what she'd be: a murderer. Murder was a crime she'd never in a million years commit. It didn't even seem possible. And yet, here she was, about to become a killer. *A killer!* She couldn't tell if the queasy feeling inside was coming from her stomach or her soul.

Both, quite possibly.

She straightened her shoulders and forced her legs to move. There was no turning back. Not now.

She stared at the clock—almost formal dinner—then grabbed the binder and made her way to the kitchen. She slipped two of the green pills from her pocket and cupped them in her hand. With luck, the concoction of powerful sedatives would ensure the nighttime security guard at the front entrance was fast asleep when she and Matthew arrived later that evening.

Even though her heart was fluttering like a strobe light, she took a deep breath. *Relax already! You're just a pharmacy assistant, doing your job. That's all!* And for a second, she almost believed it.

Standing at the edge of the kitchen, she pinpointed the newest cook, Martha, a middle-aged woman with a horrible stutter. Martha didn't like talking very much, which was ideal, because the fewer questions asked the better. Plus, she had cancer, and not that Ruby wanted her to have cancer, but *maybe* they would bond over it, having something similarly terrible in common—she hoped, anyway.

And so Ruby waited, looking busy with her binder until Martha wandered over to grab a pan.

"*Pssst!*" she whispered.

The woman stopped, glared. "C-c-can I h-h-help you?"

Ruby gave her the biggest smile she could manage. "I'm Ruby, the pharmacy assistant." She pointed to her name tag, specifically at the word CANCER, then lowered her voice and continued. "Frank the pharmacist and I need your help. One of our members won't take his pills. You probably know him. He's the security guard for the nighttime shift? He has black hair? His eyebrows look like caterpillars?"

Martha nodded.

"We're really worried about him. We've tried to convince him how important it is to take his pills, but he doesn't seem to care."

"I s-s-see."

"So, we need your help. Can you slip these into his drink? Can you do that for us?"

The woman shrugged, so Ruby passed over the pills. Her hands were shaking; she hoped Martha didn't notice.

After Martha stashed the pills in her pocket, Ruby lowered her voice to a whisper. "Also, can you please keep this a secret? We haven't told Jud or anything. We don't want the security guard to be, you know, *fired* over a problem that's easily solved. I'm sure you understand."

"F-f-fired?"

Ruby leaned in and whispered what fired really meant.

Martha nodded, her eyes now gigantic. "O-k-k-kay."

Ruby looked behind her—*perfect,* not a single set of prying eyes—then she slipped back into the hallway. Finally, her hands stopped shaking for a second, just long enough to toss them in the air. That couldn't have gone better. Martha only needed to stay quiet and follow through.

She looked toward Jud's office. Her chest tightened, followed by a stabbing pain and a vicious nausea—all of which overcame her so quickly she doubled over. She stood, pushed away the panic.

It was nearly time.

CHAPTER FORTY-SIX

Later that evening, Ruby choked down formal dinner, even though her stomach was in knots. She couldn't stop feeling her pockets. Afterwards, she snuck into a washroom stall, took a deep breath, and emptied the contents of each pill onto a sheet of toilet paper. She gently mixed the powder, feeling somewhat like a scientist—a new, inexperienced, terribly nervous scientist. When she was finished, she placed the sachet of toilet paper in her pocket and left.

Cool beads of sweat formed along her brow. Her heart rattled. Each step to Jud's office was like a step across a pirate's plank. Shark-infested waters were waiting. But Matthew needed her. And if that meant facing the shark?

So be it.

A few knocks later, Jud greeted her with an odd smile, crooked, like it had been drawn on by a child. He was holding a glass of alcohol.

"Come in," he said. His voice was flat and his eyes were narrow and something about him was different—something she couldn't place. He sat back down, folded his hands, and stared at her. "To what do I owe the pleasure?"

"Umm ..." She cleared her throat. "I wanted to thank you, again. I like being a pharmacy assistant. I think Frank likes it, too."

He sipped his drink, still staring. "Yes, I know."

She carried on, trying to calm her shaking voice. "I was thinking we could share a toast? Maybe you could tell me more about your plans for the centers?"

"I see."

He was glaring now, his mouth a perfectly straight line. She needed to be careful with her next few words.

"Yes," she said. "I have lots to learn from my mentor."

For a second, he cracked a smile. "Very well then, let's toast." He grabbed a glass and took a bottle from the top drawer.

"Wait. Before you pour me one, can I try some of yours first? I've never tasted alcohol before. I'm not sure if I'll like it."

He slid the drink toward her. "Knock yourself out."

She took a sip and let out a satisfied sigh (even though it tasted like gasoline and she wanted nothing more than to spit it onto the floor). With her free hand, she reached into her pocket and nudged open the sachet of powder. She would have less than a second when the time came.

She forced a smile. "Delicious. May I please have some more?"

"Sure," he replied.

As he began to pour, his gaze wandered to the bottle, at which point …

Go.

As fast as she could manage, she lowered his glass beneath the edge of the desk and sprinkled in the powder, then raised it back up.

Damn it.

She'd missed the edge of the glass by about half. Her stomach dropped as a puff of powder trickled to the ground. And if *that* wasn't bad enough, the drink began to bubble and fizz, catching Jud's attention. She swirled the glass with all her might.

"What the hell are you doing, kid?"

"Aren't you supposed to swirl it for flavor, or something? That's what I've seen other adults do."

He yanked it from her hands and scowled. "That's wine!"

"Oh, sorry. I don't know the difference."

She stared at the glass, finally able to catch her breath. The alcohol looked no different than before, calm and smooth and, importantly, not poisoned. Half of the deadly concoction was elsewhere, though, and there was no telling whether the amount she managed to slip into his drink would be enough.

She lifted her glass and smiled (even though she wanted to cry). "To Center One!"

"To Center One."

Clink!

As she sipped her drink (*disgusting!*), she looked around the cluttered wall, trying to make sense of it— or pretending to. She was sick and tired of looking at that stupid wall. But such was the plan: *play along with his game.*

She pointed toward it. "Can you explain this to me? I think I'm too young to understand something so … *impressive*," she said, hoping this would be enough to spark conversation.

Jud being Jud, it was.

"Yeah, it's a bit above you, I'll admit. But I can try."

On he went, using big words like *representation* and *embodiment*, and then *organization* and *infrastructure* (of course).

Meanwhile, she sipped and smiled, sipped and smiled, pretending to care. But as he rambled on, her mind began to wander, like a cloud floating through the sky. Until, as if waking from a dream, there was suddenly a very real silence.

"You know, kid, silence is a very telling response."

She froze. "What do you mean?"

"Oh, I think you know *exactly* what I mean."

Her body went stiff, cold. She had no idea what he was talking about.

He stood and began to pace. "I'll admit, you had me fooled for a bit. Batting your eyelashes, giving me this book of smart crap, sharing your dinner with Jittery Joshua. Luckily, I happen to be a bit of a prophet. Answers tend to find me."

"I don't know what you're talking about," she managed.

"Save it, kid. I know guilty when I see guilty. Just admit it, you're trying to screw me over."

"I'm not—"

"ADMIT IT!"

He slammed his drink on the desk. A scream flew from her mouth. Her heart was beating so hard it pulsed through her ears. For at least a minute, Jud just stared at her, waiting.

Finally, he swirled his drink and let out a laugh. "You know what, I think the verdict is fairly obvious at this point. Enough evidence for me, anyways. Sam?"

He glanced over at Sam, then nodded.

"Sam agrees."

He reached over and grabbed the gun. "Do you want it in the front, or the back?"

Ruby tried to scream, but couldn't. Her body wasn't working anymore.

As she stared down the barrel of Sam, her blood froze.

"Shooter's choice? *Hmm.* Let's go front."

The cool metal grazed her forehead. Her heartbeat quadrupled.

She imagined the bullet whizzing into her brain, blood pouring out of her. Yet there was no preparing for it, no way to make her death less gruesome, so she shut her eyes and pictured the ones she loved instead.

Mom, not as she'd last seen her, but singing a song. Her voice was sweet and soft and cocooned all around her, in every cell and every crevice. She could feel Mom, from her fingers to her toes, alive inside of her.

And *Dad.* He was there, too, with his strong and all-knowing voice. But mostly his hands were there, holding hers. He was taking her somewhere else—to a place where she could learn about everything from itty bitty cells to infinite galaxies. *I'm sorry I didn't get the chance to find you, Dad.*

And then came Matthew.

Wait, what was he doing there with Mom and Dad? Did she love him? It seemed so, yes. Even if he was the oldest and strangest person she'd ever met, there was so much to love about Matthew. His concern for her safety. His sad, wrinkled-up eyes. The way he made her feel invincible. Even his grumbly voice, pretending not to love her back. Matthew was her only friend. *Of course* she loved him.

Poor Matthew. After she was dead, he'd continue to wait for a rescue that would never arrive.

"I'm sorry," she whispered. "Please forgive me." And then she scrunched up her face muscles, hoping it would all be over soon.

But then came a *clank.*

She opened her eyes to find Sam on the floor. Jud was swaying a little. His eyes were glossy and it looked like his jaw had been yanked from its socket. He couldn't seem to move it properly.

He tried to step forward but his knees buckled. "What the ... W-h-h-h-at have you don-n-n-e?" he slurred, speaking like his mouth was half full. "You little …" Then he crashed to the floor and began to shake.

After a few moments, he was still.

She waited, half-expecting him to pop back up and finish the job. But he didn't. She considered pinching herself. *Did that really happen?*

It had.

She expected to feel something—*anything*—but nothing came. Her entire body was numb.

Finally, she forced her legs to move. She grabbed the tape player from the top drawer and Dad's Book of Smart Stuff, lying open on the desk. Then, she walked out of the office and quietly closed the door without a single look back. It was better that way.

Outside, the entire center was dark. People were asleep. She tiptoed along the edges, staying close to the wall.

Almost there. Almost there. Almost there.

At last, with the main room behind her, she slipped into the hallway, feeling her way. When she reached Matthew's door, she inserted the key. Her hands were shaky again, but a different sort of shaky. It wouldn't be long now. Freedom was so close she could taste it.

She pressed open the door and stepped inside.

Pitch black.

"Matthew?" she whispered, edging her way around. "Matthew, where are you?"

She slid her hands across the cold cement walls, finding one corner, then another, but no Matthew. Suddenly, a burst of light flashed behind her, followed by the very distinct sound of a door closing.

Someone had locked her inside.

CHAPTER FORTY-SEVEN

R uby whipped around, blinded by brightness, like she was staring directly into the sun. Even when her eyes adjusted, a splotch of fuzziness remained: the after light. All she could make out was a shapeless blob, somewhere in front of her.

"Who's there?" she asked.

The shapeless blob let out a grunt—definitely masculine. *Matthew?* But as she squinted into the darkness, a massive figure emerged. There was only one person large enough to fill that enormous shadow: Lance.

"What are you doing here?" his voice boomed.

Her mind flip-flopped. *What are you doing here, Lance?* Wasn't he on day rotation? Everything felt upside down.

"Where's Matthew?" she asked, her voice quivering.

"Moved him last night. Jud told me to."

As the light haloed around Lance, he looked even larger than she remembered, pulsing in the fuzzy afterglow. Jud suspected her escape all along. *Of course* he had. He'd moved Matthew and switched the security guards.

A cry bubbled from her lips. She'd never felt so small in her life. *Stupid! I'm so stupid!* All of that time planning, strategizing, making sure the pieces were in the place—for nothing.

"Sit," Lance said. And so she did, her legs so shaky she could barely move. Maybe he would take it easy on her? She looked into his beady eyes: two piercing black holes, staring down at her like a demon. Everything about him was gigantic and shadowy, menacing and sharp. Sympathy, she realized, wasn't an option.

"What are you going to do with me?"

Without a word, he turned and left.

She raced behind him, chasing the last sliver of light as it disappeared. Then there was only a door, closed and locked.

She buckled to the floor. Lance was probably on his way to tell Jud, who was now dead or close to it. He'd want revenge—brutal revenge—and there was nothing she could do to stop him.

She sat, whimpered. The room was pitch black, save a single streak of door light—hardly light at all. It reminded her of Matthew's shed, like she was there all over again. Fear swirled as she remembered the soot-black floor and rough wooden planks. The smell of stale, musty air: hot and thick and tinged with rust.

After all she'd been through, only to end up exactly how she'd started: alone and afraid, surrounded by four walls.

Perhaps it was the darkness, or the silence, but time seemed to pass exceptionally slowly. She began to wonder whether the storage closet was, in fact, her punishment: a slow, tortured death, confined like a prisoner. And maybe that fate was exactly fitting. She'd killed a man, or tried to. She'd filled his cup with poison and watched him go slack as a slug. In another lifetime, she *would* be confined like a prisoner. Newspaper headlines and bars for walls and *Murderer! Murderer! Murderer!*

Just as she closed her eyes, prepared to accept her fate—alone, in the dark—the door creaked open.

Again, a piercing brightness flooded in, but this time she didn't bother squinting. She knew very well who stood before her: Lance, back for revenge. But as the figure moved closer, the shadow didn't quite fit. It was too small, too thin, and moved with an awkward stumble. Such awkward movements could only be one person.

She raced toward Matthew and fell into his arms.

He smelled stale and his skin was cold as winter.

"Are you okay?" he asked.

"I am now. And you?"

"Same. I'm so glad you're—"

Thump. Thump. Thump. It was Lance, stomping up behind them.

This was it. They were both going to die. She removed the tape player from beneath her shirt and inserted the headphones into Matthew's ears. "I hope this helps."

"Thank you," he whispered.

Lance lugged forward and she closed her eyes, hugging Matthew tighter. She stood there for ten seconds. *Twenty.* But there was only silence. She cracked one eye open. Instead of pummeling them to death, Lance was holding out a flashlight.

"If you wanna leave, go on," he said.

Ruby took the flashlight, stunned. "But you're the head of—"

"Not no more." He pulled off his label and tossed it on the ground.

"The others?" she asked.

"They'll be okay."

"And you?"

He stared off into the distance. "I'll be as okay as everyone."

She hung her head, because "okay as everyone" really meant *not okay*. And it didn't matter where you were, be it Scarborough, Center One, or anywhere. Every person in the entire world was still …

Not okay.

Lance stepped away from the door and pointed toward the exit, at which point Matthew grabbed her hand and took the lead. For a second, she wondered whether all of this was a dream. Considering she expected to be dead a few times over by now, being alive seemed totally unbelievable.

This time, though, as she stood by the door, she *did* look back. She stared at the behemoth-sized shadow. She wanted to run back and give Lance a hug.

"Thank you," she said.

He smiled a clumsy smile. "Don't mention it, miss."

PART 3:

∽

FINDING THE HORIZON

CHAPTER FORTY-EIGHT

〜

Matthew walked down a street called *Therman Circle* in the thick of suburbia. The girl kept smiling at him. He *almost* smiled back. Theoretically, he had a lot of things to smile about.

He was finally free from the awful closet of darkness—and slop.

Ruby was safe and they were together.

He had his tape player back.

Once again, Tabitha's voice flooded into his thoughts. *Matty, Matty, Matty.* And for the first time in a very long while, he couldn't think of much to complain about. Or rather, he didn't *want* to. No place for mumbling or grumbling. At least, not at the moment.

But many moments later, after they'd been wandering for what seemed like hours, guided only by the harrowing light of their dimming flashlight, he turned toward Ruby.

"Where are we going?"

She stopped and scratched her chin. "Do you think if I maybe-probably killed someone, that makes me a bad person?"

"Umm ... was that person a bad person?"

"Very bad."

"Was that person Jud?"

"Maybe."

"Then no, I don't think that makes you a bad person."

She sighed, nodded.

"Good."

They began walking once more, at which point Matthew remembered his original question. "Wait, where are we going?"

Stop. Glare.

"So, if Jud *was* a bad person, does maybe-probably killing him make me a good person?"

He let out a huff. "Perhaps?" How was he supposed to know? And, more importantly, where the hell were they going? His tolerance for aimlessness was drifting fast.

But Ruby just kept walking—marching rather—her chest puffed forward like a rooster. She looked at the passing houses like she knew exactly who lived in them. And at the next street sign, *Oak Avenue*, she nodded. Clearly, she had some sort of plan.

So on he trudged, down *Oak Avenue*, then *Forest Lane*, then *Mulberry Crescent*—and so on and so forth. Each street looked exactly the same, an endless labyrinth of avenues and crescents and lanes and boulevards. The soles of his feet began to ache, but he kept going, trying his best to ignore the pain. It reminded him of his old instructions: *Do not look. Right foot. Left foot. Swing hands back and forth.* Except now he marched to the beat of his headphones, to Tabitha's honeysuckle voice.

Matty, Matty, Matty.

All too soon, daylight bled across the sky. Details emerged: bushy hedges and wooden mailboxes and bodies. Still bodies. Only now, they were rotted dry.

Even though he didn't want to look at them, he couldn't help it. The corpses were stark in the harsh morning light. Skeletons rising from patchy, gray flesh: rib cages and shoulder blades and cheekbones. Faces were hardly recognizable, sunken like craters, eyes long picked away by birds.

Compared to before, though, it all seemed ... softer? Grass grew between fingers and toes. One woman had patches of clovers in place of eyes. Another had ivy climbing up her leg. And the smell: hardly detectable. Mostly, the world smelled of lilies and freshness.

When his feet approached total numbness, he stopped, gave his head a shake, and stared at Ruby.

"Okay. Where the heck are we going? I won't take another step until you tell me." He stood firm, despite her soft Jell-O eyes.

She crossed her arms. "We're looking for Dad and Tabitha."

"No, we're walking in circles."

"Are not."

He glanced up at the nearby street sign, *Therman Circle*, and pointed straight at it. "We passed this street hours ago. We're no closer to your father or Tabitha than the moment we left. You don't have the slightest clue where you're going, do you?"

She blinked.

He stared, waiting for it.

"Okay fine! I don't."

"I know," he mumbled, wanting to be angry—on behalf of his feet, at least. But the girl's face was long and pouty, and he couldn't find a single ounce of anger, try as he might.

"How about we take a break. Then we'll come up with a plan. Does that sound reasonable?"

She agreed, so he extended his hand over the rows of houses. "Pick one."

She pointed to the house directly across from them. Seemed as good as any, considering each place looked impossibly similar, right down to the choice of shrubbery. *Typical.* Everything was made with a cookie cutter these days.

Ruby trudged over and rang the doorbell. When nothing happened, she wiggled the knob. It opened.

"Good to go," she said, waltzing right in.

He, however, was more hesitant. He couldn't remember the last time he was inside a house that wasn't his own. Decades, probably.

Compared to his house, there was a lot of stuff—useless crap, mostly. He blew the dust off numerous artifacts: half-burned candles, glass ornaments, empty bowls with dots and stripes. Nothing served a purpose. He picked up a pillow with a sequin design and scratchy emblem. *Who would lie on something like this?* Then he looked at the wall and almost laughed. There was a phrase written upon it in cursive. *There is no such thing as a home without family.*

A phrase.

Right on the wall.

Not to mention it was blatantly incorrect—yet another example of people's figurative nonsense. If a person lived in a house, and considered said house their home, what did family have to do with anything? And what kind of person plasters words all over their wall? This wasn't a book!

Ultimately, he shook his head, moving on, only to discover an uncanny number of photographs. *Was there something wrong with people that they couldn't form memories anymore?* Needed ten thousand pictures of their kid all over the place to remind them? He picked up a photograph of a couple holding a baby, then another of the same baby as a young boy. His limbs shuddered.

"Do you think they're still … here?"

"I doubt it," Ruby said.

Just in case, she volunteered to check, returning a few moments later with a head shake.

He kept going, until he reached the kitchen, at which point his stomach rumbled louder than a herd of wildebeests. *Food.*

He flung open the pantry door and fell to his knees.

Chicken noodle soup.

Rows and rows and rows of it.

It took a moment for him to realize the girlish squealing wasn't coming from Ruby's mouth, but his own. He didn't care. It was like winning the lottery—a hundred lotteries.

He popped open a can, tipped it into his mouth, and chugged. The noodles slipped right down his throat and nothing had ever felt so good. When he finished, he tossed the can to the floor and reached for another.

Ruby, who now stood at the door to the pantry, simply stared. "You missed your soup, huh?"

He paused, mouth full, a noodle dangling from his lip. "Yes."

"You know, they probably have bowls."

"No need."

As Ruby filtered through the expansive array of foodstuffs, selecting a granola bar here, a fruit cup there, he carried on, chugging and slurping, until a gigantic belch propelled up his throat—which made the girl giggle.

"Excuse me," he said. And then came another, except this one was … off.

He clutched his stomach.

"Are you okay?" she asked.

"I ate too fast. When you're old like me, you can't handle that type of vigorous eating."

"I don't think anyone can handle that type of vigorous eating, no matter their age."

"Well ..." he began, leaving the kitchen to take a seat in the living room.

∽

"Well what?" Ruby turned toward Matthew, now slumped in a recliner. *Oh brother.* The old man might have just broken the Guinness World Record for Fastest Person to Fall Asleep in History.

She stretched out across the couch and nibbled on a package of fruit snacks. She expected to be tired. And she was, sort of. Her entire body was soggy, like a noodle in Matthew's soup. But her thoughts just kept on thinking. She willed herself to rest (*Sleep, Ruby! Sleep!*), but it wasn't working. The image of Dad kept looping through her mind, except he wasn't Dad, but *almost*-Dad—a close version.

She was starting to forget things about Dad she wanted so badly to remember in perfectly crisp detail. Like the angles of his face, or the exact octave of his deep, rumbly voice—all the more reason to find him, immediately.

But Matthew was right. She didn't have the slightest idea where to look. How would they ever find Dad in such a big world without a clue pointing them in the right direction? She didn't even know where *they* were! And then came a terrible question, one she tried not to think, but this time couldn't help it.

Is he even alive?

She pulled out what was left of the Book of Smart Stuff and clutched it to her chest.

"Dad?" she whispered into its pages. "Are you out there?"

Silence.

She gave the notebook a little squeeze.

Dad was the smartest man she knew—one of the smartest in the country. Maybe even the entire world. He was larger than life. And sicknesses were small, right? Smaller than the eye could see? Surely Dad could outsmart something like that.

She had to believe.

CHAPTER FORTY-NINE

~

E arly the next morning, before dawn had broken up the sky, Matthew's eyes shot open, inviting a blanket of darkness. Panic blasted up his spine. He instantly returned to that dreadful closet, being locked away in the darkest darkness, his thoughts a sticky tangle. But then came Ruby's soft, sleepy breaths, and the sensation of his shoulders, wedged between a giant cushion. *Ahh yes, the recliner.*

He bent forward, cracked his shoulder blades, and noticed a flashlight on his lap. The girl must have left it for him. How thoughtful.

He clicked it on and there was Ruby, asleep on the sofa beside him. For a while, he just stared at her. At the hollows around her eyes, like black crescent moons. *Did she always have those?* At the mottled tone of her skin. *Had it always looked like that?*

No, he decided. Then again, perhaps his eyes were playing tricks on him in the shadowy darkness.

He stared out the window, waiting for the sun. A very important question arose, one he hadn't considered for a while.

What time is it?

His stomach pinched. When it came to basic chronology—the month, the date, the time—he knew nothing. Not a single thing. A woozy sensation tumbled through him, like the world had become a handful of marbles, scattering about. No one to collect them.

Structure.

Routine.

He needed them badly

He stood from the chair and rummaged through the house. *Surely, these people have some sort of time-telling device.* He shone the flashlight upon beige wall after beige wall, expecting to find at least one clock.

A grumble shot up his throat. *No use for a good old-fashioned clock anymore?*

Not here, it seemed. There were plenty of other contraptions, ones he suspected contained time-telling features—or did at some point. Little computers with screens as black as night, shiny metal alarm clocks with paper-flat surfaces, a handheld something or other, also paper flat. He tapped on their screens with his finger.

Useless.

He never trusted anything that needed to be plugged into the wall—and this was precisely why. When the power went out and a mysterious disease decided to end mankind, a person was simply ...

Screwed.

He trudged back through each room, trying not to slam the doors. Really, *who the hell doesn't own a clock?* Not a fancy electronic thingamajig that tells time as a hobby, just a clock. One with a minute hand and a second hand. One with batteries. One that goes *tick, tick, tick.* Not that he wanted to think badly of the deceased, but the longer he stayed in this house, the more he disliked these impractical people.

Finally, after rummaging through a bedside table, he discovered a watch. It had a sparkly band and flowers instead of numbers, but it was a watch nonetheless. He shone the flashlight onto its surface: 5:30 a.m.

Full-body *sigh*.

The time.

Finally, the time.

∽

Ruby awoke in a sunbeam, and for a moment she just lay there, remembering the beach. The tangy smell of sunscreen. The sound of waves crashing against the shore. The scorching-hot sand, burning her toes.

She opened her eyes: beige walls, pictures of people she'd never met, the chalky smell of dust.

She definitely wasn't at the beach.

Strange sounds emerged: crinkling and crackling and crunching—all coming from the kitchen. She stood and headed toward the noise, wondering if a stray animal had found its way into the pantry. A raccoon or something. But it was only Matthew, surrounded by pantry items, now strewn across the counter.

She giggled. "I thought you were a raccoon."

"Why on earth would you think that?"

"You sounded like a raccoon."

He kinked his eyebrow. "Are you hungry?"

She sat at the table. "Kind of. What's for breakfast?"

"*This!*"

He plopped down a bowl full of … everything, as far as she could tell. She leaned in for a closer look. At the bottom was a layer of marshmallows, followed by chocolate chips, a puffy sort of cereal, raisins, sprinkles, a thick sludge of peanut butter, some type of fruit jelly, and a cherry on top.

Matthew sat down across from her with a bowl of soup. "What do you think?"

"Well ..." she began. "It's very colorful." She picked up a spoon and took a bite. "And crunchy. Thank you."

He shrugged. "I tried. I don't know what children eat these days. What type of cheesy puff or chocolate huff or what have you."

She noticed a sparkly purple band around his wrist. "I see you found a watch. *Pretty.*"

"Functional, rather."

She held in a laugh. "Yes, functional."

Matthew grabbed his spoon and waved it around like a conductor. "Here's something for you. Did you know these people don't even own a clock? Is that not the most ridiculous thing you've heard in a long while?"

She shrugged. "I don't remember us having a clock."

His mouth flopped open and a noodle slipped out. It landed back in the bowl with a splash. "Why on earth wouldn't you own a clock? *Everyone* should own a proper clock."

She shrugged. "There are clocks on other things now, like cell phones."

He mouthed the words for some reason, like it was the first time he'd heard *cell* and *phone* together.

"Oh, you mean those silly little computers?"

"Is that what you call them?"

He nodded. "Because that's what they are, silly little computers. Good for nothing, far as I'm concerned, besides rotting people's brains."

"That's not true," she replied. "Cell phones are—or were, I guess—very ... *functional.*" She smirked.

"HA! Only function I ever gathered from them was an excuse to ignore people."

"Well ..." she began, trying to come up with a good example. "What about GPS? That was helpful."

"GP-*huh*?"

"GPS. It's a program that tells you how to get anywhere you need to go."

"So can a map."

"Yes, but GPS is different. It tells you the directions out loud. For example, if you were lost, you could find your way back home. The voice would direct you, like, *turn left on this road, then right on this road.*"

For some reason, Matthew only stared into his soup. Had she said something wrong? She swore he repeated, "if you were lost," under his breath, but it was hard to tell. A distant look clouded over his eyes. When he finally spoke, his voice sounded small.

"Tabitha wanted one of those cellular telephones. Said it might help. Something about a memory app."

"And what did you say?"

He shook his head. His eyes were getting watery around the edges, even though he kept looking away. "I said, 'app, more like crap.' And then we never spoke of it again."

"Oh," she replied.

After a minute of silence, Matthew sat a little straighter, batted his eyes with his sleeve.

"Look. She didn't need a device to take care of her. She had *me* to take care of her."

Ruby sifted through her giant bowl of everything. "Well, when we find her, you can tell her you're sorry. How about that?"

He looked her straight in the eye, like he wanted to say something, but when nothing came, she added, "Anyway, we should probably get going soon. Do you have a plan?"

"A plan?"

"Yes. You said you would come up with a plan. For finding Dad and Tabitha, remember?"

For what felt like a very long while, Matthew just stared at her—same as before, like he wanted to say something, but wasn't sure how. Then he blurted, "You must realize this is all a puff of smoke. A needle in a haystack. Finding Tabitha. Finding your father. A couple of pies in the sky."

"Pies in the sky?"

"Yes, it's an expression."

"About pies?"

"About people believing in silly things."

Her gut went rock solid. "Dad and Tabitha aren't silly."

"The idea of finding of them is silly."

Beneath the table, she clenched her fists. "No it isn't. We're going to look for Dad, and we're going to look for Tabitha, and we're going to find them. Okay?" She said this in her most convincing voice, but Matthew only huffed.

"No," he mumbled. "We won't."

She stood from her chair. "You know what, you're just being doubtful. Mom told me *all* about doubt."

Matthew set down his spoon, propped his elbow onto the table, and rested his chin in his palm. "And what did your mother tell you about doubt?"

"That believing is for young people. And doubting is for old people. That everyone starts out believing, but as they get older, they start doubting."

"Well that sounds like a big pile of—"

"See! You're doubting. You're always doubting." She realized she was shouting. "We're going to find Dad! We're going to find Tabitha! We're going to—" A warm body curved around her.

"Ruby," he said softly. "There is no way Tabitha or your father survived this. It just doesn't make any sense. We have to be rational."

She wanted to object, strongly, but instead came a flood of tears. So many tears. *We have to be rational*—that sounded like something Dad would say.

He'd taught her all about being rational. It meant thinking with your head, not your heart. And when it came to the matter of Dad and Tabitha, she'd *definitely* been thinking with her heart. For a moment, she let her head take over.

Tabitha had been missing for over a year. Her belongings were found in a burnt-up old house, along with a human body. Even though the police couldn't identify that body, what was the most rational conclusion?

She knew the answer.

Of course she knew the answer.

And yes, Dad was smart, brilliant, but did it really make sense? That he was the only healthy person in the whole world to survive, when everyone else was sick?

She pulled away from Matthew and wiped her eyes.

He was right. Dad and Tabitha were long gone.

CHAPTER FIFTY

～

Matthew sat in the puffy recliner across from Ruby. It was night and the girl was asleep. Still, she kept moaning. Long, achy moans—sad moans, thanks to him.

His belly tossed into loops and knots. Guilt dragged down his chest.

What have I done?

On the one hand, he was simply being realistic, observant, skeptical. To be blunt, her father was dead, and so was Tabitha. Of course they were—they had to be. He may have pretended otherwise, but that was just denial.

Deny, deny, deny.

He'd been doing it for years.

But in a moment of weakness, he could no longer pretend the world was full of unicorns when the world was full of horses.

Sick, dying horses.

Now, though, with Ruby's sad moans stretching all around, his stomach pulled with regret. Was it really so bad letting the girl believe?

Surely not.

He closed his eyes and tried to think. He didn't know what to do or say to make things better. She'd hardly spoken after breakfast, hardly did much of anything besides drag her feet from room to room. It was like being in Center One all over again, watching her curl into sadness like a human cocoon.

Except this time, it was *his* fault. He'd broken her spirit. The beautiful, bubbly thing inside of her. Stomped it to bits with his *being rational*.

As he stared at her sleepy face—which, even in the midst of slumber, looked terribly sad—he knew he'd done something awful. Something he needed to fix. Somehow.

It was then he spotted a book upturned on the carpet. He leaned over and squinted. It was her father's— what did she call it? *Right.* The Book of Smart Stuff.

The night before, she'd slept with it strewn across her chest, a testament to how much she cherished the old, worn thing.

He plucked it from the ground. It must have slipped.

For a moment, he considered returning it to her chest, but leafed through the pages instead. There were many missing for some reason—not that it mattered; the book was no more than a bunch of jargon. Formulas and strange renderings and words no regular person could comprehend.

But then he stumbled across something that caught his attention. A diagram, of sorts. He leaned in closer, recognizing parts from a medical book he'd once read, *The Basic Principles of Neuroscience.*

Fascination rippled through his veins as he flipped to the beginning. Maybe the book wasn't utter nonsense after all.

In the wavering light of the flashlight, with Ruby asleep beside him, he tried his best to digest the Book of Smart Stuff. It was like tinkering—in his head—and he was determined to solve the puzzle of ideas.

Even if half the pages were missing.

Even if he was old and Not Normal and "filled with doubt."

Time passed imperceptibly. What seemed like only an hour later, at most, he yawned and glanced down at his watch.

It was 5:00 a.m.!

He stood and tiptoed into the kitchen. As he was coming to discover, there was immense knowledge in the Book of Smart Stuff—knowledge that would change everything—but he was quickly losing concentration. Nothing a cup of instant coffee couldn't fix.

He shook out a few spoonfuls into a bottle of water, hoping that would do the trick, then he spread the Book of Smart Stuff across the table and resumed.

As 6:00 a.m. arrived, he rubbed his eyes. His vision was getting spotty. The coffee was helping, certainly, but it wasn't a miracle. He didn't have the mental stamina for these sorts of all-night escapades, stimulants or no stimulants. Not to mention his aching back. It was as though his spine had been replaced by a concrete post.

He flung his arms wide, attempting a stretch. But in a moment of clumsiness, he accidentally elbowed the bottle of coffee-water, tipping it directly onto the notebook.

"Dang," he said, yanking the book from the puddle of muddied water. He dabbed it with a paper towel, then whirled it around like a bird flapping its wings. No matter, the pages were waterlogged and the cover entirely ruined—like it had gone through a washing machine full of burnt, stale-smelling syrup.

His heart dropped. *When Ruby sees this, she's going to—*

"Hey, is that my dad's book?"

He turned around.

Ruby.

Next came a long, hearty gasp—one that made his hair stand on end, followed by a quick snatch. For a while, she only stared at the notebook with watery eyes.

"You … you wrecked it?"

Matthew wasn't sure what to say. "It was an accident," he managed.

"Ha!" For a moment, she sounded a bit like him. "First, you convince me that Dad is dead, and then you destroy the only thing I have left to remember him by? I can't believe you."

"I can explain. You see—"

"No need. Because I'm leaving!" She whipped around and bolted through the door. Matthew lunged behind her, stumbling over a chair and nearly toppling onto his knees.

"Wait!" he yelled. "I have something important to tell you. About the notebook!"

∾

Ruby blasted through the front door and into the early morning sun. She wasn't sure what to do, besides run. So that's what she did. She ran. She dashed down the pavement as fast as she could, until the pitter-patter of Matthew's footsteps was long gone, and his voice yelling, "Wait! Come back!" was just an echo in her memory.

She stopped for a moment and caught her breath. Her lungs ached. Everything ached—especially her heart. She held out the soggy Book of Smart Stuff, drenched in something brown. It smelled like rust.

She pulled it to her chest regardless, letting the smelly, brown sludge ooze onto her T-shirt.

It was the only thing she had left of Dad.

And now it was ruined.

Her jaw clenched as she thought of Matthew. He'd said it was an accident, but was it? Why did he have Dad's book in the first place, if not to destroy it?

Whatever. She was done with Matthew. Done with his mumbling and grumbling and *let's be rational* and *pies in the sky* and *yadda yadda*.

She turned back, a momentary tug pulling in her gut, like it was attached to something, then she whipped around, the soggy notebook limp in her grasp.

I don't need him. I'll be just fine.

She carried on running, her eyes set on a profile of buildings in the distance.

CHAPTER FIFTY-ONE

~

R uby drifted into the city, staring up at the apartment buildings. They reminded her of home. *Where am I?* She looked for a sign, but couldn't find one. *Welcome to ... ?*

She snuck up the sidewalk, keeping close to the buildings, partly hidden in the shadows. At some point, the sun tucked itself away, drenching everything in a dreary gray. A wind swept through the alleyways, cold on her skin. It gave her goosebumps.

Much like the suburbs, crisped-up bodies littered the streets. But unlike the suburbs, there was no grass, no flowers, just concrete and grayness. Bones jutted from piles of old litter that had blown into heaps. She stepped over tiny landfill after tiny landfill, plugging her nose.

As she pressed forward into the stillness, sounds became apparent. Scurrying and scratching and a *pat-pat-pat* that sounded like dripping water, but also like footsteps.

After each new noise, her body froze. She tilted her ear toward the sound—not that it made a difference. The noises could be anything. Human? Animal? Just the wind? At one point, she swore Matthew's voice was calling to her in the distance. "Ruby! Where are you?" But then it was gone.

She considered yelling back, "I'm here!" but was too afraid. She didn't believe in ghosts, but there was something creepy about the vacant city. The hazy fog rising up from the sewers. The shadows scampering up the bricks. The bones piled in the gutters.

On second thought, maybe she did believe in ghosts.

She stopped. Turned around.

What am I doing?

She stared down at the Book of Smart Stuff, now crisp and dry like an antique, waiting for the anger to return. But it didn't. Only a tingling sensation filled her cheeks. It traveled down her spine, landing in her toes.

What if it *was* an accident?

Now that she'd had a while to cool down, it definitely seemed out of character for Matthew to ruin Dad's notebook on purpose. He might be old and grumbly, but he wasn't cruel. He was kind … and thoughtful … and always looked out for her.

Memories drifted in. They'd been through so much together, from that tiny house in Scarborough to Center One.

She began to march forwards—or backwards; she wasn't sure, but she had to find Matthew. Her feet were practically stomping against the pavement. How foolish she'd been, making a hot-headed decision to run away. She loved that grumpy old man, and he loved her back. They were all each other had.

She turned a corner, then another. Each street looked exactly the same: gray and drab and strewn with garbage and bones. She stared up at the signs: *Coffee Corner, Chopstick Palace, Tracy's Treasures.* Were those familiar? She couldn't remember.

Left. Right. Left. Right.

Back. Forth. Back. Forth.

It was like being in the suburbs all over again: walking and walking and walking and getting nowhere. She pictured Matthew sitting in that house, waiting.

And then it hit her, like a piano falling from the sky.

She had no idea where that house was.

Was it on Therman Circle? Forrest Lane? Was it east of the city? West?

Not that it mattered—she barely knew north from south and east from west.

Her head ached, like it had been physically shaken. The world was a giant maze and she was stuck at the center of it. What she would *give* for a GPS, like the one she'd described to Matthew. She imagined holding that little device, pressing a button called GPS, going to *From* and selecting *My Location*. Under *To*, typing: *The house with the old man.*

She could practically hear the pretty-sounding robot, calling out directions.

Except she had no directions.

A while later, as the sun began to disappear completely, panic took over. Soon, she would be in complete darkness.

In a strange, possibly haunted city.

All alone.

She could hardly breathe. What if she never found Matthew again? What if the darkness swallowed her up and spat her out in the gutter with the bones? What if …

A hand rested on her back and a sigh fell from her lips. *Matthew?* But the second she turned around, her body went stiff.

The man before her was covered in hair—so much hair she could only see his eyes: beady and green and practically glowing. He loomed over her with his giant body, smelling of stale tobacco and rot.

"Need some help, little lady?"

His voice was deep and hoarse. The way he said *little lady* made her skin flinch.

"No," she whispered, barely able to speak.

"Huh?" he barked, his yellow teeth jutting forward. He reached out a spindly hand. "Here, let me help you."

Without wasting even one second further, Ruby sprinted down the alleyway. There was *pat-pat-pat* and *stomp-stomp-stomp*. Two different sounds—two sets of feet running? Was the man chasing her? Or was it just her footsteps, echoing off the buildings?

When she reached the end of the street, she dodged left until—WHAM! Something socked her in the waist so hard she gasped for air.

Again.

And again.

At last, she looked down.

It was an old grocery cart filled with rusty cans and yellow-stained rags and rotten rats. Some had bites missing while others were picked dry like chicken wings—nothing more than skeletons with tails.

She gazed up to find a woman, tall and slim with a long, ghoulish face. Her features looked hollow and carved, like a human jack-o'-lantern. Even though her head was partly covered by a shawl, the woman was clearly balding.

Just as the woman's mouth cracked open, Ruby took off in the opposite direction, squinting into the grayness. Soon, it would be pitch black. And then what?

She dodged into the nearest building—a convenience store—and scrambled to find a flashlight.

She dragged her hands across the shelves, starting to go by feel. The darkness was moving in like fog. Cans flowed beneath her fingertips, then bags of chips, then … there was only darkness.

She grabbed a bag of chips and crumpled to the floor, starved and scared and totally blind. The image of the man in the alleyway lingered: his piss-yellow teeth and glowing eyes and ratty facial hair.

Can I help you, little lady?

He could be standing right in front of her, and she wouldn't even know.

She curled into a ball and opened the bag of chips, but the *pop* it made was so abrupt and piercing she couldn't eat a single one—was too afraid of all that crunching, echoing in the darkness.

She froze, listened. The noises were back: scurrying and scratching and howls in the distance. *Wolves?*

Her mouth went dry.

Or people?

She clutched Dad's Book of Smart Stuff and slunk down even further, curling onto the ground. "Oh Dad," she whispered to the notebook, then she propped it beneath her head as a pillow.

Tears streamed down her cheeks, cold in the zippy night air. She closed her eyes.

What seemed like a second later, a blast of light poured through the window, forcing her to squint.

It's morning?

She sat, remembering all that had happened. *Matthew. She* had to find him. But just as she stood, her head began to pound. A familiar pain shot up her neck. Not a head rush, but many, one after the other, except they burned, sharp and fiery, like flaming arrows lodging into her skull.

She sat back down, a shaky weakness settling everywhere. She remembered this feeling—remembered the pain, the pressure, and, above all, the lingering sense of doom.

In a different world, not long ago, there would be plenty of help: pills and people, doctors, nurses, Mom, Dad.

She peered through the windows into the vacant city.

This time, there would be none of that.

CHAPTER FIFTY-TWO

～

Matthew woke on a park bench. A series of coughs burst from his scratchy throat—all of that calling for Ruby, no doubt.

For hours, he'd wandered through the labyrinth of avenues and crescents and lanes and boulevards, calling her name until his lungs would call no more. He'd followed her footprints, traced the earth for rock and vegetative disturbances, squinted at tiny droplets of coffee, combed through tree branches in search of rogue hairs or threads—exactly as he'd read in *A Survivalist's Guide to Tracking*.

All of those clues had led him to the base of a city.

He sat, reached into the small sac of supplies he'd gathered from the house, and took a sip of water. He barely remembered lying on the bench, using Ruby's favorite yellow sweater as a pillow (he'd brought it in case she was cold).

As daylight brightened all around, he recalled sitting in that house alone, waiting for Ruby to return.

But she hadn't.

As the hours ticked by, though, he'd come to understand exactly what that statement on the wall—*There is no such thing as a home without family*—intended to express. After Tabitha had disappeared, their tiny house felt cold, like there was something missing. And being without Ruby brought that same feeling all over again.

Cold.

Something missing.

He originally believed that silly wall sentiment to be a foolish line of poetry strung together by some millennial (*Millennium? Millennia?*). Whoever it was, they were right. There *was* no such thing as a home without family.

Ruby was family—the only family he most likely had.

Ruby was his home.

He catapulted from the park bench and stretched his back. Before him were a number of buildings. Today's agenda: search the city. Every last inch.

He entered the metropolis, calling her name as loud as he could—"Ruby! Ruby! Where are you?"—except his voice sounded like it was coming from one of those throat stomas, strained and crackly.

Still.

"Ruby!"

Again.

And again.

The echoes returned in succession.

Silence.

He wandered further, over piles of garbage and crispy bones, blown together into heaps. Movement caught his eye. A dash or scurry—always nothing.

"Ruby!"

Still, silence.

After a while, he sat on a curb. He wiped his brow; the relentless sun was scorching his forehead. He chugged a bit of water. The warm liquid oozed down his scratchy throat—more like a cylinder of sandpaper, at this point. Then, just as he was screwing on the cap, a loud crackle echoed from above. He jolted.

What the hell was that?

Another pop hit the sky, as if something had been thrown at it. He looked up just in time to see a series of fizzling streaks fading to the ground like stars.

Fireworks?

Typically, he hated fireworks, and had *plenty* to say on the subject. Not only were they a pointless waste of money—a spectacle no responsible adult should ever support—but some of them were louder than bombs; he was sure of it.

At first, he wanted nothing to do with the initiator of these fireworks, but then he began to wonder. What if the initiator was Ruby? What if the fireworks were a clever way of communicating her whereabouts?

Matthew's heart leapt and he began to run.

"Ruby? Is that you?"

He zigzagged between buildings, turned down alleyways, left then right then left again. Fireworks cascaded, one after another, hardly visible in the striking daylight.

"I'm coming, Ruby!"

Finally, he rounded a corner and there she was, sitting in the distance.

"Ruby!" He raced toward her, no longer old or sore or burdened or stiff—all of that vanished.

But as he approached the figure, the fragility of his body returned.

It wasn't Ruby.

It was a man, sitting in a lawn chair.

A cigarette hung from his lips and a scruffy dog stretched across his feet. The man took a long drag from his cigarette. Matthew gave him a once over. He looked *exactly* like the type of man who'd be letting off noisy fireballs in broad daylight.

Still, his body ached with disappointment.

The man cracked open a beer and took a fast swig, then another. He was wearing a black, sleeveless shirt; his giant belly spilled out over his jeans.

"You just gonna STARE at me?" the man asked.

Matthew shifted his eyes. "I'm looking for a girl. Her name is Ruby. Have you seen her?"

The man shrugged. "Don't think so."

Sigh.

"May I ask why you're letting off fireworks in broad daylight?"

The man spat on the ground. It glistened in the sunlight. "Cause it's July fourth."

A burst flickered in Matthew's chest. *Finally,* he knew the date.

"Anything else?" the man asked, curving an eyebrow.

"Actually," Matthew replied—since the man had asked. "Do you happen to have a phonebook?"

The man nodded and took another swig. Beer dribbled down his chin and beaded across his stubble like drops of dew. Without another word, he stood and motioned Matthew to follow—which he did. The scruffy mutt pranced at his heels, even though he kept mumbling, "No thank you, that's enough now."

After a block or so, they reached a large hotel, a former Hilton. The man blasted through the door and yelled, "Honey, I'm home!" Matthew waited for someone to join them, his wife perhaps. But, instead, out galloped a fat orange cat. He lifted the fluff ball into the air and kissed it on the nose. "Daddy missed you!" Then he tossed it to the ground and lit a cigarette.

The man blew a stream of smoke in Matthew's direction. "Home sweet home," he said, plopping down onto a recliner.

The place was hardly a home—hardly even a Hilton any longer, on account of being filled with sofas and videogame machines and boxes stacked like a giant game of Jenga. Not to mention a lifetime's supply of cigarette packages, beer cans galore (some full, some empty), and ten thousand chocolate bars—at least.

"You said you had a phonebook?" Matthew asked. The man glared at him, his eyes drawing closed like it was time for a nap.

He didn't reply. Instead, he walked behind what used to be a reception area (but was now a pile of beer cans) and removed a phonebook. He tossed it over then plopped back into the recliner, lifting his leg to release a giant fart. Afterwards, he laughed.

"Sorry I'm not sorry."

Matthew ignored this and found a seat on the carpet. He began to riffle through the phonebook, starting with the Yellow Pages. Not long later, the mutt sauntered over. Matthew gave it a good eye roll. *Oh, what could you possibly want?* He turned away, trying not to look at the thing, but it kept yanking on his headphones.

"Get," he said.

But instead of get-ing, the smelly mutt licked him straight on the nose.

He practically fell back onto his skull. After he'd gained his bearings, he wiped the slobber away and grunted. "Go on, scram."

Still, the mutt only stared at him. Panting. Smiling. On his beat-up collar, a name tag dangled:

Jim.

Matthew grunted, reverting his eyes to the phonebook. He'd just have to ignore the creature as best he could.

When he'd finished looking through the Yellow Pages, he flipped through the rest of the content.

"Ah *ha*," he said, finally finding what he was searching for.

He stood, dusted off his slacks. They were covered in fur from the mangy fleabag.

"Good to go?" the man asked.

"Yes, thank you."

He set the phonebook on a stack of beer cases, then headed toward the front entrance. He pretended not to notice the wagging tail accompanying him on the way. Beside the door was an amplifying device of some sort, strewn in a pile of other random objects. He lifted it up, inspected it.

He turned back toward the man. "May I take this?"

The man pulled something thin and white from his pocket, sort of like a cigarette but skinnier. He gave it a light, then a grassy smell floated forward, a bit like body odor. Thin lines of smoke curled from his lips, swirling into the air before disappearing.

He half grinned, shutting his eyes.

"Sure. Whatever."

CHAPTER FIFTY-THREE

~

Out on the street, Matthew broadcasted Ruby's name through the loud amplifying machine. His voice was still raspy and hoarse, just ten times louder.

"RUBY! IT'S MATTHEW! WHERE ARE YOU?"

He was certain he'd searched every inch of the city.

It dawned on him, as he continued to yell into the quiet abyss of metal and concrete, that maybe she didn't *want* to be found. Perhaps she had meant what she'd said about leaving. And could he blame her? He'd crushed her hopes, ruined her last cherished possession.

For a fleeting moment, he considered giving up. Maybe he owed her that: the chance to be without him. Then he remembered her father's notebook. What he'd discovered.

She needed to know.

The rest was up to her. If she wanted to leave, so be it. He would bother her no longer.

A jingle jangled behind him. He glanced over his shoulder to find a fuzzy blob bobbling in the distance.

Jim.

Still, Jim.

The mutt had been following him since the hotel. When he stopped, the mutt stopped. When he walked, the mutt walked.

With each block, the gap between them narrowed. The mutt was cautiously approaching. As it moved from *behind him* to *beside him,* Matthew stopped, glared. He'd had about enough of the scruffy companion.

"Don't you have somewhere to be?"

The mutt shook his head (basically) then pawed at his behind. Matthew lifted his foot, prepared to stomp as loudly as possible—teach the creature a lesson about rump prodding, but, as he stood, leg suspended in the air, the eyes of the thing grew softer, or larger, or sadder—somehow. Whichever it was, he lowered his leg in defeat.

He reached into the sac of supplies and pulled out a can of soup. The sweltering heat was starting to recede. Evening was coming.

He popped open the can and tilted it into his mouth, letting the noodles slip down his throat. Three quarters of the way through, he glanced down at the mutt. It was licking its chops.

The creature's ribs were wide and protruding.

He slurped one last noodle and grunted.

"Oh, very well," he said, setting the can on the ground. The mutt licked it clean in less than one second.

On he went, the sun beating down on his leathery skin, one final blast before settling under the earth. He pulled the amplifying device to his lips and called out Ruby's name into the echo of the vast city, again and again.

The creature waltzed at his heels and a flock of birds soared overhead and the pavement pressed against his aching feet.

As he passed an alleyway, a shadowy figure emerged. Not Ruby, but a woman, frail and slight with one eye missing.

He turned toward her. "HAVE YOU SEEN A GIRL NAMED RUBY?"

The abruptness of his voice blasting through the amplifying device caused her to jump. She shook her head and scampered away into the shadows.

He staggered on. It was nearly dark. There was not a single identifiable part of his body that didn't ache. Even his eyes burned as he strained to see in the dusky twilight.

He clicked on a flashlight, panic starting to loom. His heart thumped and hair stood on end—not because of the darkness, but the many *what ifs*, all arising at once.

What if he never found her?

What if he searched and searched and searched, but never found her?

What if he died in the gloomy city, taking with him the knowledge from the notebook?

After thinking these thoughts, the surrounding buildings seemed to press in against him, stealing the air from his lungs. LOUDNESS clawed up his spine, a storm so tremendous he began to spin. Around. And around. Left. Right. He didn't know which way to turn.

"RUBY!" he yelled so loud that an echo pulsed back through him.

He clutched his ears; his head was spinning and throbbing. It was like Tabitha all over again. The world was unfathomably big. And Ruby was missing. And just like Tabitha, she could be anywhere.

Creatures whizzed past his head. *Bats!* Their scratchy voices rang in his ears—in his eyes, like they had invaded his brain and were hanging upside down from his nerve fibers.

He crashed to the ground, his bearings entirely gone.

Dizzily and with great difficulty, he crawled and crawled until he reached a corner, where he burrowed into a pile of old newspapers and bones like a mole, equally as blind. The pain in his temple was relentless.

Just when it seemed the LOUDNESS would send him straight to the grave, a soft crack of light arrived. Something warm oozed across his cheek.

The mutt!

He wiped off the smelly slobber and broke through the pile of newspapers like a mummy from a crypt. Jim sat before him, panting. Daylight was spreading through the city, erasing the terror from the night before.

He stood. His body cracked in all the wrong places. This journey, finding Ruby, might very well break him. But none of that mattered, because he had to find her. He had to apologize for shattering her beautiful spirit. He had to tell her about the notebook—even if his mouth tasted like old coins and standing was possibly an issue. Even if it was the last thing he ever did.

He pressed his face against her yellow sweater. It was terribly ratty and stained, but it still smelled like her: cotton balls and damp air and droplets of dew. He grabbed the amplifying device from the pile of newspapers, shook it free of a lingering bone entwined around the speaker—a rib.

"RUBY!" he called. His voice box sounded like it had gone through a blender.

Time passed and he trudged onward. His body was falling apart, cell by cell, ligament by ligament—not to mention the very real possibility his kneecaps were grinding into themselves like a mortar and pestle. To distract from the aches and pains, he found himself talking to the mutt.

"You know," he said to the creature. "You should be careful associating yourself with a grumbly old fella like me. I will tell you like it is. No sugar coating over here."

The mutt nodded.

"For example, you smell repugnant. Like a swamp. What do you think of that?"

The creature practically shrugged, then gave him a look like, *what else is new?*

At least it agreed.

"Ruby, is her name."

The dog rolled his eyes like, *yeah, I know.*

Matthew chuckled. "I guess you've probably heard that a few times already."

It nodded.

"She's a small girl—a wonderful girl. Very chatty, but very brave."

Matthew stopped, the state of affairs registering. *What am I doing, talking to a useless mutt?* He gave his head a shake, certain he was losing his mind.

"Enough of this," he grunted. "Go on now, get." He waved Ruby's sweater at the loitering creature, hoping to shoo it off, but, just as the garment wisped across its nose, the mutt cocked his head in the air, taking a whiff.

The creature's eyes narrowed, then it dove toward the ground, muzzle leading. Off it went, sniffing along the pavement, hot on a trail. Matthew's heart flapped against his chest as he ran along behind.

They zigzagged through the city, down alleyways and sidewalks and cobblestone paths. And then the mutt stopped so abruptly that Matthew nearly tripped over him. He stared up at a sign: *For You Variety.*

The mutt clawed at the door, whining. Matthew walked over and gave it a thorough petting, accompanied by a few ear scratches.

"Well done," he said. Perhaps the mutt—or Jim, he supposed; he *had* a name—wasn't so useless after all.

He opened the door and slipped inside. After a few steps, he pulled the amplifying device to his lips. But he didn't need to broadcast "RUBY" in his strained, crackly voice, because there she was, at the end of the aisle, lying in a crumple.

"Ruby?" he said.

She didn't answer.

CHAPTER FIFTY-FOUR

～

Ruby awoke to violent shaking, like she'd been tossed in the dryer. An image whizzed across her vision: A man. A dog.

"Huh?" she said, half awake. As the shaking stopped, her eyes began to focus. No ... it couldn't be. Her heart twirled.

Matthew!

She fell into his arms, ignoring the rush of weakness—even though it made her vision fuzzy.

"I can't believe you found me," she said. "I shouldn't have left. I—"

"It's all right," he said, patting away the tears forming in her eyes.

"Mom said if I ever get lost, I should stay in the same place."

"That's very good advice."

Matthew smiled. His skin looked extra crinkly and very red.

Up trotted a dog—a bit rough around the edges, but its eyes were soft and its tail was wagging.

"Who's this?" she asked.

"This here is Jim," Matthew replied, patting the dog on the nose. "He's one of us now."

Jim licked her on the cheek and she giggled.

A rush flashed up her spine, making her hot and dizzy. She closed her eyes for a second and it went away—*phew*. She decided not to tell Matthew about the symptoms she'd been having lately. Instead, she turned to him and said, "I'm really sorry for running away."

"No, *I'm* sorry," he replied, pulling her into his chest. "I'm a crotchety old man who should've listened to you in the first place. There's something I need to show you. May I?"

He pointed toward the Book of Smart Stuff and Ruby nodded. After a few moments of flipping through the water-logged pages, Matthew said, "Look here." She followed his finger and lost her breath.

Plain as day, in blue pen, it said, *The Horizon*, with a phone number.

Matthew kept talking, but she could hardly believe the words coming out of his mouth.

"So," she said when he was finished, still in disbelief. "What you're saying is, after looking through the Book of Smart Stuff, you think Dad knew about the sickness, and was working on a cure?"

He nodded. "Yes, from what I've pieced together, he was definitely working on a cure." He flipped over a few more pages. "The survivors of this illness are all sick, yes?"

Ruby nodded. She had yet to meet a healthy survivor.

"Not sick with just anything, though. We all have brain-based diseases, or neurological conditions, which your father discusses here." Matthew pointed to a page full of diagrams, specifically at the words "neurological origins."

Ruby's jaw fell as she remembered every single survivor she'd met. Matthew was right, they *were* all brain-based sicknesses—her cancer included.

Matthew carried on. "So, from what I've gathered, there's *something*—a cure, perhaps—at the Horizon. Particularly in light of the voices from the radio. It has to be more than a coincidence."

Ruby found herself nodding, still in shock. The Horizon *was* real. And … the words tumbled out of her mouth. "If Dad found a cure, that means he could be … alive?"

"Certainly," Matthew replied.

Her eyes filled with tears—happy tears—then a choke arrived in her throat.

"But how do we find the Horizon?"

Matthew stood and walked a few aisles over. He returned with a map and a highlighter.

"So," he said, unfolding it. "I found a phonebook earlier, and the phone number's area code is somewhere up north—in the Muskokas." He traced the highlighter along a highway and stopped at a place called Huntsville. "I say we head here, then check another phonebook. It will be more specific." Matthew looked her straight in the eye. "That is, if you would like me to be your navigator?"

She smiled and pulled him into a hug.

"Of course."

∽

They walked through the vast, gray city. Matthew led the way. They had a plan: eat, rest, head toward the highway.

When they passed a Foodmart, Ruby pointed. "How about here?" She gave him a wink. "They'll have soup."

He nearly smiled. "Yes, yes they will."

Inside, there was a forceful stench of rot, a bit like a hot dump, but as they passed the produce section, the smell began to clear. The place was dim and dusty and partly ransacked, but not terribly. Weekly sale signs were still positioned in front of aisles, carts were arranged neatly in lanes, cash registers were closed and locked.

He stepped over a heap of cans as Ruby grabbed a cart. She picked up Jim, plunked him inside, then raced out of eyesight. Matthew huffed. *Probably off to find the big, wide junk food aisle.* He, on the other hand, turned up the volume on his headphones and strutted off to the soup section. His mouth began to water; he couldn't wait to pop open a can of salty goodness.

But just as he passed the cereal aisle, Ruby piped up from somewhere in the distance. "Hey, can you come here for a second?"

He looked up—the soup aisle was next. "No, I cannot."

"I have something to show you."

"That's lovely. But I'm in the middle of—"

"M-A-T-T-H-E-W   C-O-M-E   O-N-N-N-N-N!" She dragged the whole thing out, her voice like some sort of untuned instrument. Worse, halfway through her drawn-out yelling, Jim began to *bark, bark, bark.*

He stomped two aisles over, educating her along the way. "I don't know why your generation seems to think you can just demand things. Like no one else has an agenda. Like—"

He stopped. His mouth began to curl upwards, even though he tried very hard to suppress it. He couldn't help it. He was smiling.

Smiling.

Inside the shopping cart, Jim had ripped apart countless rolls of toilet paper, rendering the vehicle nothing more than a fluff-filled container with a black, shiny nose peeking through.

Ruby hopped in beside Jim. "Mind giving us a lift?"

Matthew didn't even bother looking into those wide Jell-O eyes, he just trudged over and gripped the handle.

"Hooray!"

"There will be no more hoorays," he said, pushing the cart slowly down the aisle.

She banged on the sides. "Let's pick up the pace."

"This is a very reasonable pace. I will not—"

"Faster!"

Matthew grunted and picked up the pace, prepared to say something about bossy requests and demands, but before he knew it, they were practically flying down aisles. Ruby was leaning out the front with her hands as wide as wings. Jim was propped up on the side with his tongue flapping out. And he was cruising on the back, riding the thing.

Riding it.

He hadn't ridden anything in so long he'd forgotten what it was like.

Air whooshing through his hair.

Being weightless as an astronaut.

A stomach full of loops and bubbles.

Fun.

The word popped into his head and he almost didn't recognize it. He rolled it around in his mouth, trying to get a feel for it. *Fun. Fun?* That was a word, wasn't it?

When they reached the soup aisle, he brought the cart to a halt. He dug a hole in the toilet-paper mountain and filled it with heaps of chicken noodle soup.

"Do you ever eat other kinds of soup besides chicken noodle?" Ruby asked.

"Why would I?"

"I dunno. What about cream of mushroom?"

He waited to see if the girl was joking, but she didn't appear to be. *Cream of mushroom? Was she insane?* "Why would I try cream of mushroom when I'm perfectly content with chicken noodle?"

"Just because," she said. Then she popped out of the cart, grabbed two cans of cream of mushroom, and tossed them onto the heap.

Before he could advise her against this reckless decision, she stood in the middle of the cart, thrust her arm forward like a commander, and hollered, "To the treats!"

And so, he wheeled them to the treats.

Down the entire cookie aisle, Ruby extended her hand as he pushed her along, causing boxes to cascade into the cart like a waterfall: chocolate chip, oatmeal raisin, a number of other cookies he didn't know existed—rainbow-colored biscuits, cookies shaped like space aliens, ones with icing *and* sprinkles *and* chocolate chips. Finally, they fetched something for Jim: a big fat bone and treats made of chicken liver.

Matthew wheeled up to the checkout and Ruby hopped out.

She marched behind the cash register. "Hello, sir! Welcome to Foodmart. I see you have some soup today!"

"Umm ..."

She winked.

"What are you doing?" he asked.

"Just play along."

"Play along?" He scratched his head. "Yes? I do have some soup?"

She clapped—he'd done something correct. "Well that's great, because soup happens to be on sale."

"How much?"

"Free!"

He snorted a little. "I have cookies as well, are those on sale?"

"Yep! Also free!"

"And these chicken liver treats?"

"Free!"

"And this bone?"

"Oh, that one will be one hundred dollars."

Unexpectedly, a single "HA!" burst out of his mouth while the girl doubled over with laughter.

∽

Ruby rode inside the cart with Jim as Matthew pushed them across the street, toward a Four Seasons.

She'd never been in a Four Seasons before, and once they'd hauled the cart into the lobby, her jaw practically hit the floor.

It was possibly the fanciest place in the world: large white pillars and vases full of toppling vines, tables made entirely from glass. She skipped up to the front bell and gave it a good ring.

"Hello?"

She squinted at the directory and flicked on a light. A loud rumble drummed across the floor, followed by piercing brightness. The whole place was aglow.

"Nice," Matthew said. "Back-up generator."

She resumed staring at the directory, landing on a single word.

Ballroom.

She pointed to it. "Let's eat *here.*"

Matthew nodded. He pushed her and Jim down a white, marble hallway until two giant doors awaited. Above, *Ballroom* was written in a pretty cursive.

She hopped out of the cart, opened the doors, and gasped. The space was even more beautiful than she'd imagined, like a palace from a storybook. High-arched ceiling and rich burgundy carpet, walls carved with flowers and leaves and swirls. In the center of the room, a chandelier sparkled—too many tiers to count. *Welcome Mr. & Mrs. Holloway,* a banner read; the room was clearly decorated for a wedding. Upon each table were place cards and numbers and gigantic red-rose centerpieces—now dried to a crisp. But still, they were lovely.

"This is amazing," she said, edging inside.

Matthew walked up to one of the centerpieces and gave it a flick. Petals fell onto the table. "This is why real flowers are a waste of money," he said.

She crossed her arms, waiting.

"But otherwise, yes, quite nice."

They dragged the cart up to the head table and unloaded their dinner. Afterward, Ruby took her seat in the *Mrs.* spot; Matthew sat in the *Mr.* spot. He poured a can of soup into a china bowl and passed it toward Jim. The dog took one look at the dish and planted his nose straight in. A moment later, he looked up with a noodle dangling from his snout.

Ruby burst out laughing. "Jim likes soup just as much as you do. You two are perfect for each other."

Matthew grinned. In all of their time together, she'd never seen him so happy.

Ruby carefully arranged a selection of cookies into a pyramid. When she was finished, she picked up her fork, noticing the place card beside it: *Mrs. Anna Holloway.* She set the fork back down, imagining what the day might have been like, with guests all over and waiters carrying fancy platters. The bride: dancing down the aisle in a princess dress, eventually sitting in the exact spot Ruby was sitting, her husband beside her, a five-course meal awaiting.

Instead, nothing happened. And the flowers died.

"Do you think we should say a prayer or something?" she asked.

"Why would we do that?"

"I don't know." And she didn't know; it just felt like the right thing to do.

Matthew shrugged.

So she clasped her hands and cleared her throat, unable to remember much about praying, only that it involved a lot of thanking.

"Dear Man in the Sky. Thank you for the soup and cookies and chicken liver treats. And thank you for this fancy hotel ballroom. It's very pretty."

She considered other things she was thankful for, looking toward Matthew and Jim with half-peeped eyes.

"And thank you for bringing us together, even though almost everyone else is dead."

Almost everyone else is dead. For a second, she wanted to flip over the table, let everything smash to bits (an urge she tried to shake away, because: praying). "Anyway, we hope all of those people are in Heaven now. And we thank you in advance for helping us find the Horizon."

She looked at Matthew and whispered, "Anything else?

He shook his head.

"Okay. The end."

So, they ate. Ruby chipped away at her cookie tower, stabbing them one by one with a gold-plated fork, only to nibble away at the sides. Matthew tucked a frilly white napkin into the collar of his shirt, then slurped his soup. He *even* tried cream of mushroom, and, though he refused to say anything more than, "It's okay," Ruby could tell he liked it more than just "okay," considering he helped himself to a second bowl.

For a while, it was only *nibble, slurp, gnaw.* Only the echo of those sounds in such a large space was astounding. More like NIBBLE! SLURP! GNAW! Then, when Ruby was certain she could eat no more, she leaned back and ballooned out her belly.

They agreed it was time to rest and decided on the presidential suite (because *why not?*). Unsurprisingly (considering the rest of the place) it was the fanciest bedroom she'd seen in her entire life. Bed*room* was hardly the word, considering there was a sitting room, a kitchenette, and a dining space with a grand fireplace. Even the bed was gigantic.

Bed.

She hadn't slept in one of those since before the infection. A big, warm comforter. Fluffy white pillows. A *mattress!* Despite being stuffed full of cookies, she jumped on top of that bed and screamed as loud as she could.

"Matthew, a bed! A real bed! Come on, jump with me!"

His eyebrow kinked like a question mark. "Absolutely not."

"Oh, come on, M-A-T-T-H-E-W!" Words sounded strange as she jumped, like they were being suctioned from her mouth. "It's F-U-N! You'll L-I-K-E it!"

"No, I'm fairly confident I won't like it, actually."

"Suit your-S-E-L-F," she replied, stopping for a moment. "But can you come over here at least?"

He trotted over. "Yes?"

She yanked him up onto the mattress and he tumbled into the covers. For a second, he looked a bit dazed, then he stood.

"Well that was—"

"You're N-O-T jumping!" she said.

"Because I'm an old man. Old men don't jump on beds. I'll break my back."

"You will not! That's just an excuse."

He crossed his arms and made a deep rumbling sound, a bit like thunder, then he took a small hop. Another.

"See!" she said.

"No," he replied. But he did, he must have, because before long he was jumping and smiling—especially when they landed at the same time, and the weight of his body caused her knees to buckle.

When her legs had practically turned to rubber, she plopped onto the mattress and Matthew landed beside her. Jim snuck his way between them, at which point she curled into his scruffy fur. Even though he smelled like a barn animal, she was fast asleep before she even had a chance to care.

CHAPTER FIFTY-FIVE

ᘓ

T he next morning, Matthew rolled over onto Jim, who in turn rolled over onto Ruby. Sunlight blared through the window, hot and sticky. He glanced at his watch— 12:00 *noon Good golly*. He *never* slept until 12:00 noon Such exorbitant hibernation habits were generally reserved for bears, young people, and the lazy.

Beside him, Ruby rustled awake. "What time is it?"

"Noon."

"Noon!" She sat straight up, then snuggled back under the covers.

Matthew dragged himself into the washroom. He kinked his back, his knees, then stumbled into the shower. It was larger than his entire washroom—his entire bedroom, even. He wasn't sure where to stand in such a space. No matter, the water was hot against his aching muscles. He fiddled with what appeared to be a floor-to-ceiling jet, deciding upon the third button: *Deep tissue massage*. He pressed himself tight against the jet stream and his back unbuckled.

Ahh.

There was even a button for extra steam, which seemed completely unnecessary. But, after he gave it a press and steam billowed forth, it was, admittedly, sort of brilliant. Of course, the entire contrivance was utterly ridiculous, with its high-tech everything and football-field perimeter. A good old-fashioned shower would have done just fine. But a person would be foolish not to take advantage of such a contraption. It wasn't like *he'd* installed those bells and whistles.

After twenty minutes—the longest shower he'd taken in his entire life—he stepped onto a plush mat, which appeared to have memory foam inside of it. He moved his feet up and down, up and down. It was like stepping onto a cloud.

He slid into a pair of fluffy slippers and a navy blue robe. After making a hot cup of coffee from a machine with one hundred buttons, he seated himself before the fireplace and turned it on with the flick of a switch. It was a perfect moment—perfect except for one thing. He reached inside his robe and clasped the locket.

If only you were here.

Water sputtered in the room beside him. Ruby was running herself a bath. And then came a loud gurgle; she'd turned on the jets. He leaned back into the recliner and closed his eyes. The mutt curled at his feet, keeping them warm. He could get used to this kind of life. But, just as he was about to doze off, a scream came from the washroom, followed by, "HELP!"

He launched from the chair and burst through the door, prepared to see the girl in trouble, but instead the room was only gushing with bubbles—bubbles so high they were stacked to the ceiling. Through the fizzy mist stood a dark, indistinguishable blob, like a person standing in fog.

Silly Ruby.

He parted through the suds until she was visible, standing in a bubble-covered robe.

"Are you all right?"

"Yes," she replied. "In hindsight, I shouldn't have used the whole container of bubble bath."

Matthew nodded. "Agreed."

He was reaching down to pull her from the bubbles when Jim soared through the suds, his jaw parted like a shark. He began snapping at the bubbles, and, as a result of this snapping, bubbles broke off from larger clumps like dandelion petals.

Ruby laughed, gathering them into a ball.

Matthew looked at her *very* seriously.

"Do not."

But she did. She flung the ball of bubbles toward his chin, where it stuck like Kris Kringle's beard. Then came another. And another.

He was about to say, "Stop this immediately," until he got a good look at the girl.

Her mouth: curled into a mammoth-sized grin.

Her lips: iced with bubbles like a moustache.

Her eyes: glossy and bright and unstoppable.

In light of all that, he simply shut his mouth and tossed some back.

After the epic bubble battle concluded, and the giant blob of foam had reduced to only a thin layer of froth, they gave Jim a bath. He was, inarguably, the dirtiest of the three. Not only did he look like some sort of bog creature, he *smelled* like some sort of bog creature: swamp water and soured milk.

Matthew scrubbed while Ruby combed out clumps of dirt. Afterwards, he looked like a brand new dog—certainly not a bog creature anymore.

With all of this out of the way, they prepared to leave. As Ruby stood by the door, Matthew plugged in his headphones. He looked back at the room, at the wonderful amenities: a fluffy comforter, a giant bed, a flickering fireplace. And that shower.

Good golly, that shower.

He thought of what awaited. Concrete, mostly.

Hot, endless concrete.

Could he *really* keep trudging through the world, day in and day out? He seriously doubted the abilities of his own body. His skin was burnt and crusty. His back was less sturdy than a sheet of cardboard (the cheap kind, from China!). And his knees required assistance from his hands to bend.

He glanced back at the bed, wanting to curl beneath the covers instead of wander the hot, sick earth. He was seventy years old, for crying out loud. The physical demands placed on him lately would challenge someone *half* his age.

And yet, as he stared into the jiggly eyes of his determined companion, he found a morsel of strength.

"Matthew, are you ready?" she asked.

He grabbed her hand. It was time to face the concrete.

"Okay, let's go."

CHAPTER FIFTY-SIX

～

Walking. So. Much. Walking. Matthew tried to align his steps with the knocking from his headphones, creating a somewhat tolerable walking rhythm.

Beside him, Ruby munched on ketchup chips. Jim gnawed on a dried pig's ear. Otherwise, the world was dead silent.

He peered into each alleyway, each window, half expecting to see another leftover person, perhaps sitting on a chair like the fireworks man.

But there was no one. Just bones and garbage.

Everything inside of him loosened when, an hour later, they reached the highway and all he could see for miles was a streak of gray pavement. Less human-ness. *Praise Whoever!*

As they continued to wander along the road, cars emerged, stopped dead in their tracks. Matthew gazed into windows, observing half-packed bags, rotten groceries, empty car seats. Partly, he expected to see a dissolving driver or a skeleton passenger, but there was still no one. He wondered where they all were.

But really, he knew exactly where they were.

They'd left their cars.

They'd run for their lives.

And now, they were nothing more than piles of bones.

∾

Ruby stared at the map. She edged along the route with her fingernail, then looked at the sign to her right, an exit for somewhere called *Port Perry*. She stared at the map again. *Really?*

She passed it to Matthew, hoping she was mistaken. "We're only here?"

"Correct," he said. "We're only there."

"Well, let's pick up the pace!"

She opened up another bag of chips, straightened her shoulders, and hustled as fast as her legs could carry her. After a few moments, her head began to throb, but she pushed away the pain and broke into a light jog. Matthew and Jim were somewhere behind her.

She yelled back at them. "We're going to get there!"

When her lungs started to burn, she took a breather and consulted the map once more.

"Ugh!" She flung her hands in the air.

When Matthew and Jim caught up, she flicked her finger at the map.

"Look! We've barely even moved."

"Yes, I know," Matthew said. "It's a long way."

She stomped her foot and crossed her arms; frustration scratched up her chest. Then she noticed a blue car in the distance. *Hmm.*

It was worth a shot.

"Matthew?" She flashed him the largest smile she was physically capable of making.

"Yes?"

"Maybe we should drive?"

He looked at her the way Mom used to when she proposed they eat ice cream for dinner.

"No."

"Why not?"

"*Why not?* I'll tell you why not."

Turns out Matthew had a lot of reasons why not. On he went, all, "Don't you care about fossil fuels?" and "Driving is the most dangerous thing a person can do!" and "Cars these days are quantity over quality, safety last!"

She nodded all the while, and when he was finished, they kept walking. What was she supposed to say to all of that?

But, a minute later, she stopped again. "Oh come on. *Please* can we drive? This is taking forever!"

"Grow a bit of patience."

"But this is exhausting. And it's hot. You must be tired too?"

"That may be. But still, no."

She looked off into the distance then dragged her feet forward, prepared to continue walking—forever—when a sigh came from behind.

"Oh bloody hell. Fine."

She turned around and smiled, then skipped up to the blue car and opened the passenger's side door.

Matthew circled around it like a shark. "Where's the rest of it?"

"It's a smart car," she said. "There's no rest of it."

"HA!" He walked away mumbling. "*Smart car.* Only an idiot would drive that."

She followed him to the next one, and so it went:

"Rustier than a bucket."

"Can't trust the red ones."

"Nope. Made in Japan."

Finally, they walked up to a roomy, brown box that said *Buick*. It looked exactly like the type of car someone Matthew's age should be driving.

"This one!" Ruby said. "This is the one!"

He circled around it, kicking all the hubcaps. When none fell to the ground, he pressed his lips together. She waited for him to agree. But, instead, he knocked on the exterior, the windows, the door handles. Clearly, he was trying to find something wrong with it.

"It's perfect," she said, sliding into shot gun before he could find an excuse. Jim hopped on her lap and let out a long bark.

∽

Matthew stared at the steering wheel. Theoretically, he knew how to drive the automobile. He even knew how driving the automobile worked precisely, thanks to *Auto Mechanics for the Everyman*, a book he'd read from cover to cover. For example, first came the key, which started the ignition and provided the electrical system with power. Then came the starter, which relayed said power to the motor and turned the engine. The turning engine sucked gasoline into cylinders. Spark plugs sparked. Then, finally, once the gasoline was lit and the engine was spinning with gasoline power, one simply had to press on the gas and drive.

He reviewed these facts one at a time. And it all seemed very simple and straightforward. But, as he pressed the key into the ignition, he realized the manual failed to include a number of other components:

Speeding up.

Heart racing.

Going so fast that everything turns blurry.

Heart racing even faster.

Crashing into a tree, because LOUDNESS!

Slowly bleeding to death on the side of a highway.

He looked at Ruby. "Can *you* drive?"

"What? I've never driven before."

"Neither have I."

"But you're a grown up."

"Yes, so?"

"Just try."

He turned the key and the thing roared to life. The rumbling was louder than he'd anticipated—another component the manual failed to mention. He looked at Ruby; she nodded back.

"You're doing great. Just press the gas."

After another few moments of hesitation, he went for it. He pressed his foot on the gas and the car began to move. It jerked forward, then assumed an even, steady pace. Before he knew it, he was driving.

Driving!

And it wasn't nearly as LOUD as he expected. His heart was possibly spasming, sure, but it was a good spasm, like he had accomplished something great. He pressed the gas a little harder and cranked open the window. The wind crawled through his hair; it was a bit ticklish.

They were soaring down the highway now. Just soaring. He turned to Ruby, pushing down a smile.

"I'm driving. Can you believe it?"

She looked at the dashboard. "We're barely moving."

He glanced at the speedometer—twenty miles per hour. *Huh?* It didn't *feel* like twenty miles per hour. He pressed the gas a little harder.

"Better?"

She looked at the dashboard again. "Forty miles per hour?" She shrugged. "Works for me."

As they cruised down the highway, Ruby fiddled with the CD player. Not long after, music began playing—or rather hooting and hollering. When it came to music, Matthew never much cared for the stuff. The girl, on the other hand, began squirming in her seat.

"What are you doing?" he asked. "Do you need to use the washroom?"

"No, silly! I'm dancing."

She belted out the lyrics, something about life being a highway and wanting to drive forever, whatever that meant. She repeated those words for a very long time. Then, *finally*, she began to trace her finger along the yellow-highlighted route.

"I think we're up north now," she said.

And that seemed about right. Unlike before, the highway was narrower, curvier. The trees were bigger and fuller, too, like gigantic broccoli clusters. The air hung with dampness, as though sagging. He took in the scent, letting his hand venture out the window. His fingers swam through the air.

He liked being up north.

Not long later, Ruby shook the map, pointing to Huntsville.

"We're getting close! Let's pull over at the next rest stop and look for a phonebook."

He agreed, pulling off the highway a few minutes later. He parked outside of a Wendy's service center and began to walk toward the adjacent gas station. He found himself thinking about the song—about life being a highway.

"That's one of those damn metaphors, isn't it?" he asked. "But highways are highways. Life is life. I don't get it."

No response.

"Ruby?" He turned around; she was still in the car.

He walked back and opened the door. "You coming?"

She nodded, but her eyes were damp and her lips were trembling.

"What's wrong?"

She wiped her mouth and held out her palm.

Blood.

CHAPTER FIFTY-SEVEN

~

Matthew stared at the stark, red swipe across Ruby's palm. Everything wavered to a pause: the knocking on his headphones, the tick of his watch, the beat of his heart. Then it all surged forward once more. The rush of it was so intense he could barely breathe.

"Ruby, are you okay?"

He crouched beside her, but instead of replying, she pushed him aside and vomited onto the hot pavement.

More blood.

Everything stopped again. He couldn't seem to look away from the splotch of crimson. Out of the corner of his eye, he watched Ruby stand, wipe her mouth.

"Okay, let's go already!" she said. "Let's find a phonebook."

She marched toward the station as if nothing out of the ordinary had occurred—even though she was swaying. Jim trotted over and nudged her side, keeping her upright. Matthew paced behind, only one thing on his mind:

Blood.

On she went, marching ahead. Even though he knew well she needed to stop, he wasn't quite sure what to do. How did people know what to do all the time?

"Ruby, something's wrong," he finally said. "You need to stop."

She pressed on, dragging her feet against the pavement. "Nothing's wrong. I'm fine!"

He rushed up behind her. "Here, let me help you."

"I don't need any help."

He grabbed her by the arm. "It's okay to need help."

"I said I'm fine!"

She whipped around and glared at him so intensely he couldn't find any words. But, as she kept walking, he knew absolutely, despite her conviction, she wasn't fine. Her entire body wavered like it was blowing in the wind.

"Ruby, stop this instant," he said.

∽

Ruby forced her legs to keep moving, even though they were a hundred pounds heavier with each step. *Keep. Going. Keep. Going. Keep. Going.* It suddenly seemed as if the entire world was slanted to the left. Then the right. She leaned onto Jim for balance. An arm latched around her from the other side—*Matthew.* This time, she didn't resist.

"I'm just hot," she said. Her voice was shaky for some reason. "That's all."

"You need to lie down."

"No I don't."

"Yes you do."

"No I don't!"

But she did. She looked at the gas station and it was like walking along the highway all over again: so far away. Everything inside of her was heavy and light at the same time—her fingers, her toes, like she could sink right into the ground, or float away, one of the two.

Still, the Horizon. She tried to keep going, but fell back into Matthew's arms instead.

"It's okay, Ruby," he said, holding her upright. "Let's get you inside for a rest."

She stared up at him; he looked faded, somehow. "Fine. A quick nap. One hour. That's it! Then straight back on the road!"

"Whatever you say."

"One. Hour. Exactly," she repeated.

As Matthew and Jim led her into the service center, she was confident an hour would suffice. A little rest, then back to the Horizon—just a small blip in the road; nothing to fret over.

Inside, the place smelled as rotten as everywhere else. This time, though, it made her stomach slosh. She took a deep breath, trying not to vomit.

Matthew helped her find a seat on a patch of carpet. He told her to wait for a moment, so she did.

Do not puke. Do not puke. Do not puke.

He returned with his arms full of blankets, travel pillows, and sweatshirts.

"Where did you get all that?" she asked.

"Grab'N Go Souvenirs," he said, fluffing the stuff around her like a nest. She leaned back against a mountain of pillows. Almost instantly, her eyelids were shutting. She forced them open.

"Remember, wake me up in an hour. And not a minute later!"

～

Matthew nodded. He opened his mouth to say "okay," but she was already fast asleep.

During the first hour, he decided to clear away the disgusting trash, the smell of which had turned Ruby a sickly shade of green.

He checked the place for bodies (none, thankfully), then found a janitor's closet. He snapped on a pair of plastic gloves and cleared away the revolting bags, each crawling with maggots. Onto the pavement they went, one by one, until a small garbage dump stood before him.

For whatever reason, he wanted to kick it. And so he did. He booted that garbage like he'd never kicked anything before, cursing at it. Hamburger wrappers flew into the air. Rotten meat splattered across the pavement. Plastic cups rolled across the parking lot. He only kicked harder.

Finally, he stopped and caught his breath. There was garbage everywhere. A fairly offensive display. He wasn't sure why he'd done such a thing, in hindsight, until he saw the sticky pile of Ruby's blood, hardening into a stain.

That's why.

Back inside, he watched the rise and fall of Ruby's chest with Jim. It had been exactly one hour.

"What do you think?" he whispered to Jim. "Should we wake her?"

Jim stared back like, *nah, she needs her sleep.*

Matthew nodded. The mutt knew best.

He collected some more items: water bottles, the map, a few packages of trail mix, a can of soda, a teddy bear from the Grab'N Go, and a phonebook from the gas station. He placed these things around her like a giant halo. Then, he just stared at her for a while.

He wanted to give her everything.

All the health.

All the happiness.

All the Horizons.

But, instead, all he could give her were some measly offerings from a souvenir shop. If he hadn't already obliterated the garbage bags to smithereens, he would have done so all over again.

He wandered into the back of the Wendy's, the staff only section, and walked up to the cash register. The machine looked complex, intricate.

Tinkering.

Oddly, the word did nothing, not even a twitch of excitement. He pulled off the plastic surface and peered at the naked buttons. Then he covered them back up. *Maybe later.*

Jim stood on the other side of the register, panting. He began to bark.

"What would you like, Jim? Some chicken nuggets?"

Jim stared back like, *yes please, twenty.* So Matthew punched 20 *chicken nuggets* into the blank register, then looked over at Ruby.

"And what would you like, Ruby? A cheeseburger with a sprite?" He punched this into the register, too. But Ruby was still asleep. "It's okay, we're out of cheeseburgers anyway …"

As the fourth hour passed, Matthew grabbed a book from the Grab'N Go, *What Happens at Dawn,* and read beside Ruby.

By the time he was forty pages in, Alexandria had met a man named Pedro with "bursting muscles," and "tan skin thicker than horse hide." He wasn't sure why Alexandria was so interested in this burly horse man, but he kept going.

"Alexandria looked at Pedro with a lusty grin. She clutched his arm while her other hand slid down—"

His mouth fell open. He stopped reading out loud.

"Matthew, keep reading!" Ruby said. "What happens next?"

He threw the book on the ground. "You're awake? How are you feeling?"

"Okay." She glanced around the room. "What's all this?"

"Oh, just some items from me and Jim, to help you feel better."

Jim pushed his way through the pillows and blankets and curled onto her lap, then Ruby picked up the phonebook and smiled. As she opened to page one, her mouth curved into a yawn. She leaned onto Matthew's shoulder.

"You know what, let's do this tomorrow."

"Good idea."

He took the phonebook from her grasp, but just as he'd scanned the first few numbers, she sprung up and shot him a glare.

"Hey, don't look without me! We're going to find the Horizon together, okay?"

He gave her a kinked eyebrow. It seemed like a waste of time.

"Please?" she whispered. "Promise me."

Matthew leaned into her curly hair. He'd never done this to anyone besides Tabitha, but he kissed her softly on the forehead.

"Okay, Ruby, I promise."

CHAPTER FIFTY-EIGHT

⌒

Each night for many nights, Ruby discussed *to-morrow*. As in: "We'll find the Horizon tomor-row."

"Tomorrow, we'll leave."

"By tomorrow, I'll be feeling much better."

And even though she looked paler and weaker every day, she said *tomorrow* with such conviction that Matthew believed her. In many ways, it was like Tabitha all over again: watching a person he loved fade away. And, just like Tabitha, he couldn't accept it, refused to face it head on.

Just like Tabitha, he thought he had more time.

Inside of that dank, old service center, the days simply passed. They played checkers and "What Would I Order at Wendy's" and read novels much different than *What Happens at Dawn*. Most afternoons, they played fetch with Jim, who eagerly ran laps of the entire establishment. They fed him beef jerky, eating power bars and nacho chips themselves. Sometimes, they glanced through the phonebook, but Ruby always fell asleep, and Matthew always set it down.

A promise is a promise.

Then one day, as Ruby curled in her nest, Matthew pulled out a calendar he'd taken from the Grab'N

Go. Beside the date, July 17th, he marked an "X." Ruby stared at the number, looking worn.

"What day is it today?" she asked.

"July seventeenth."

"Hey, today's my birthday."

"It's your birthday today?" Matthew asked, but Ruby was already asleep.

He stopped what he was doing and gave Jim a nod. He didn't need to explain himself; the mutt understood.

The two raced off to the Grab'N Go and scoured the shelves for suitable gifts, like a shot glass that read *I'll be sober tomorrow.* He scribbled out "sober" with a black sharpie and wrote "better." *Perfect.*

Next: a flowery key chain, a sparkly candle, a lighter with a rainbow on it. He pulled out a sweater from a pile that read I *cottage,* with a picture of a cottage. He didn't know if Ruby "cottaged," or what that even meant, so he added "at the Horizon." I *cottage at the Horizon.* Sufficient.

For the first time in his entire life, he was glad such useless crap existed. He wrapped the gifts in old newspapers and put them into Wendy's takeout bags. Jim watched, tongue flapping.

"What else is at birthday parties?" he asked.

Jim let out a single bark.

"Yes, of course, cake. How could I have forgotten *that?"*

He rounded up every single Oreo he could salvage and smashed them all together, forming one large Oreo that somewhat resembled a cake (*sort of*?). No matter—Ruby would love it. He covered the mound in peanut butter and plopped a big candle in the middle.

"Balloons," he said to Jim. "We need balloons."

The mutt agreed.

But, after scouring the shelves, he realized there were no balloons. So instead he drew them onto pieces of paper. One hundred balloons in total. As Ruby slept, he taped them all around her. He considered putting one on top of her head, but refrained.

Lastly, he placed the presents before her, set the cake on the nearest table, and waited with Jim. His entire stomach was fluttering.

Wake up, Ruby. Wake up, Ruby. Wake up, Ruby.

Finally, Ruby opened her eyes and he leapt from his chair.

"Happy Birthday!"

He sprinkled her with pieces of confetti made from *What Happens at Dawn*. Jim howled, bouncing up and down.

At first, she just screamed, so he quickly quieted Jim and took a seat. Then she looked around: at the lump of peanut butter with a candle on top, at the presents in takeout bags, at the balloons drawn onto pieces of paper—red ones, yellow ones, green ones.

"You did all this for me?" she whispered.

"Yes. Happy Birthday."

Her eyes began to water; his did too.

"Here." He pushed over the takeout bags. "For you."

She opened them one by one, gasping each time. "A lighter! A shot glass! A candle! A key chain! A sweater!" She read the shot glass, "I will be better tomorrow," and the sweater, "I cottage at the Horizon."

"I love everything! Thank you."

His cheeks grew warm as he helped her put on the sweater. Then he pulled out two plastic forks. "Shall we?"

She picked up the cake and turned it around, staring at it from every angle. "What is it?"

"It's a cake, obviously."

"Really?"

He lit the candle. "Yes, but first, it's time for you to make a wish."

She stared at the ceiling for a while, letting out a long *hmm*. "Oh! I know," she said before giving the flame a good puff.

"What did you wish for?" he asked.

"I can't tell you or it won't come true!"

"Very well then."

"Okay fine, I wished for the Horizon, and Tabitha, and Dad."

He was about to say, "That's not one wish, it's three," but instead he just tousled her hair. "Good wish."

He fed her big mouthfuls of Oreo-cake while she fed him equally big mouthfuls. Their forks and arms crossed, and every so often she would *accidentally* push some onto his cheek, and he would *accidentally* shove a bit onto her nose. She would laugh. And he would laugh.

He would laugh.

At first, it was just a quiet laugh, like a "ha!" here and there. But then it evolved into a gigantic rumbling thing he couldn't contain. It spewed out of his mouth, straight from his belly, and once he started he couldn't stop.

There they were, in an abandoned service center, with cake all over them—in their hair, on their faces— lips smacking while eating a feast made predominantly of peanut butter. He was old. And she was young. And they were opposite people that had somehow become less opposite, even though that wouldn't have happened in the real world.

But to hell with the real world. There wasn't much left of it anyway.

∽

Later, as the sun drained into the horizon, Ruby snuggled into Matthew's shoulder. Her breath grew softer and softer and Matthew swore she was asleep, but then her tiny, faded voice croaked beside him.

"Can we go outside and watch the sunset?"

"Of course," he said.

She sat; he rushed to hold the front door open.

A few seconds passed. He waited, but as Ruby stood from her nest, her legs began shaking. She looked at him with her big, glossy eyes, sagging at the edges, and she didn't have to say it—not out loud. Those eyes said it all.

Help me.

His heart oozed open, like those eyes had caused a leak. Then he raced back, scooped her up, and carried her outside, astonished by how light she was.

The sky was lit with a soft lilac, accompanied by a few streaks of plum. It was brightest along the horizon, where the sun was scarcely visible.

"It's very beautiful," she said, still in his arms. He agreed.

He set her on a picnic table and took a seat. Jim nuzzled between them.

For a while, they stared at the sky, speechless, until it was completely dark and a new sort of beauty emerged. Stars twinkled in every corner of the sky, slowly at first, then all at once. It was the most dazzling thing Matthew had ever seen.

"I didn't know this many stars existed in real life," Ruby said.

"There are one hundred billion, actually. I read it in a book called *Astronomy for the Layperson.*"

"Of course you did." She chuckled. "Can we name some?"

"My dear, you can name as many as you like."

She pointed to the middle of the sky. "That big one! I shall call it, Fred."

Matthew couldn't help but smirk. What she pointed toward wasn't actually a star, but a planet (Venus), though he didn't plan on telling her this. Instead, he pointed to the prettiest one he could find, a small, glimmering star. "Ruby. That one is Ruby."

She looked into the vastness, taking her time. "That one!" she said at last. "That blinking one, on the outskirts. That's Matthew."

It was a satellite.

He held back a laugh. It was almost impressive that in a sky full of stars Ruby had yet to find one.

They stared into the sky; nothing to see but stars twinkling in the blackness. After a while, Ruby snuggled into his shoulder. He pulled her close, letting the heat from his body trickle over to hers.

"Matthew," she said. "What's it like to be in love?"

He turned, a bit surprised. "What kind of love?"

"Romantic love, like you had with Tabitha."

"Why do you ask?"

"I've just always wanted to know."

"Well," he began, unsure how to describe it.

He thought back to those very first moments long ago, of Tabitha racing through the hallways, her wild hair springing all over the place. And that big, silly grin. She was beautiful in the most unusual way. Breathtaking—literally. He'd just stood there for a while, trying to catch his breath.

Her bottomless, chocolate eyes.

Her cherry-glossed lips.

Her quirky expression—possibly in response to him staring at her for so long.

"Hi, Matty!" she'd said.

And so erupted the twinkling tingle, right in the pit of his stomach. He'd known right then and there that she was the one. He'd known it like he'd never known anything before—or since. In a world full of confusion and LOUDNESS and uncertainty, loving Tabitha was the only thing he'd ever been certain about.

He stared into the sky, at the twinkling stars.

God, I miss you.

"Being in love feels like stars twinkling inside of you," he finally said.

Ruby snuggled deeper into his shoulder.

"That sounds really nice."

"It is."

They lay in the darkness and stillness of night, not saying much, until Ruby began to shiver.

"Let's get you back inside," Matthew said, standing up. He placed his hands under her bony shoulders and began to lift. Simultaneously, her mouth cracked open, and he waited for it, the same thing she continued to say in her sturdiest voice: *tomorrow.* But, instead, she looked at him with a milky stare—looking at him, but not at him. Like he was someone else, someone she didn't like, and her awareness of the world was slipping away.

Her voice crackled as she said it.

"Santa Death?"

CHAPTER FIFTY-NINE

～

Matthew sat in a corner beside Jim, staring at the phonebook. He opened it to page one, then moved his finger down each number. No, no, no. He proceeded to page two, and then page three, carrying on. Logically, he knew the number for the Horizon wouldn't be found on a page with numbers unlike it. But he hardly cared, because what if some arbitrary typo occurred in the process of making *this* phonebook? What if the Horizon was on page seventeen instead of eighty-three by mistake? What if his failure to dutifully scan each number was the reason they'd never make it?

Either way, he preferred this line of thinking to the alternative.

The alternative being.

Ruby is dying.

And so, he committed to the search no matter how long it took—promise or no promise—as if finding the Horizon wasn't a miracle, but a matter of will and dedication. He collected himself a tower of energy drinks. Even though they appeared radioactive and tasted dully unfit for human consumption, he chugged them in succession, optimism spiraling (or was it him who was spiraling?). Either way, by the time he was halfway through, it *seemed* he was closing in on something and it was only a matter of time.

On he went, concentrating with such intensity that even Jim couldn't distract him. Jim's afternoon game of fetch was due, and he very much wanted to play, but Matthew had no time.

"Sorry, fella, not now," he said.

Finally, as he reached the last page, his heart sank. He shook his head at the book—it should know how disappointed he was.

Eight entire hours.

For nothing.

He rustled from his spot on the floor, plucked up a lighter, and walked into the thick heat of summer. He peered into the distance. The sky was full of billowy, white clouds. Cumulus clouds—the puffy ones.

Nice day for a fire.

He lit the corner of the worthless, good-for-nothing phonebook and tossed it to the ground where it blazed and blazed. He yelled at the thing—"Useless!"—realizing that was precisely how he felt.

Useless.

For a few moments, he idled on the pavement. His whole body was sweating and quivering—he couldn't contain it any longer. The rage widened inside him, a series of outbursts that needed to erupt, starting with the phonebook.

He stomped out the fire until every page was nothing more than disintegrated ash. And then he yelled, but it didn't sound like his usual yell. It was more like a dry howl releasing from his throat. Still, the inadmissible facts remained.

Ruby was dying, and there was nothing he could do about it.

Tabitha was gone, and she was never coming back.

He would soon be completely alone.

These thoughts made him want to destroy ... everything—starting with the gas station. He burst inside and knocked over a rack of chocolate bars. Then he squeezed every single one until chocolate sludge oozed from the wrapper. Even though his hands were brown and sticky, he kept going.

Next came the bags of chips, all popped, crushed, crumbled into dust. He recited every single swear word he knew in a loud stream. And when all the snacks had been demolished, he looked at the cash register.

"You," he said.

He heaved it to the ground and the whole thing smashed apart. Then he stomped and stomped—stomped until his feet were numb, and then some. Finally, he tipped the counter upright and it all came crashing down.

When there was nothing left to destroy, he slid down the wall and began to cry. Tears flowed from his eyes with such vigor he could hardly see. Jim curled into his lap and licked up his tears.

"She's dying, fella," he said. "I don't know what to do."

Never had he been so alone in his life, so utterly lost.

He wiped his eyes on his shirt, then glanced around for a tissue.

"Look at the mess I've made."

And that's when he spotted it: a little plastic donation box, strewn on its side. He rubbed his eyes, surely mistaken.

He read it again.

There had been no mistake.

CHAPTER SIXTY

～

R uby woke to the sound of a car engine and a song blaring in the background. Jim lay curled on her lap and Matthew sat to her left, driving—eighty miles per hour to be exact. She cleared her throat, or tried to. Her mouth was so pasty it tasted like glue.

"Matthew, where are we going?"

"A surprise."

She looked out the window, at the trees hurtling past her. Her stomach started doing loops, so she rested her head on the door. She wanted to ask why they were driving so fast, but she could barely talk. All that came out was, "fast."

"Yes, I'm driving fast this time."

She tried to remember the past few days, but it was all a blur. She was looking for something? A place?

They were going somewhere important?

～

Matthew could see it up ahead: a wooden sign on the side of the road.

The Horizon.

Based on the donation box, the Horizon was a camp for sick and disabled children. He wasn't sure what Ruby's father or the cure had to do with this camp, but he didn't much care. They were running out of time.

He touched Ruby's shoulder. "Look where we are!"

She barely lifted her head. "Huh?"

"The Horizon! We made it."

She snuggled back into the door. "Later, okay?"

As he tore down the long laneway, people began to emerge: a woman tending to a garden, a man adjusting a solar panel. The woman motioned Matthew to roll down his window, which he did.

She rushed up, all smiles. "Oh my goodness! Welcome! How did you find—"

He pointed toward Ruby. "She's dying. Please."

The woman's eyes doubled in size. "Absolutely. Follow me."

Inside a small clinic, two women hoisted Ruby onto a bed. They pricked and poked her with needles and tubes. Matthew stood back, his stomach whirring. When Jim began to howl, he lifted him into his arms.

"It's okay, fella," he whispered. "She's going to be okay."

But he had no idea if this was true. Her skin was even paler than he remembered, and every so often her inward eyes rolled around in their sockets like a marionette.

It took him a moment to realize, but tears were streaming down his face and landing onto Jim. Even though a bunch of strangers were around, he couldn't have stopped crying if he tried—and he didn't care.

"Oh, you poor thing!" the woman from outside said. "Come with me." She led him to a chair and handed him a tissue.

"What are they doing to her?" he asked.

"They're giving her fluids and nutrients. She's very dehydrated."

He looked away—eyes fogging up again. "Is she going to make it?"

The woman sighed. "I sure hope so." She extended her hand. "Stella. Nice to meet you."

He stared at that hand, wondering if it was stuck like that, all kinked out in front of her.

"Not into shaking hands? Got it. I've always thought it was a strange thing as well. *Shake hands.* Let's transmit some bacteria!" She chuckled. "Can I get your name at least?"

"Matthew."

"And your furry friend?"

"Jim."

"Well, Matthew and Jim, welcome to the Horizon."

"Thanks," he replied, and then he pulled out the Book of Smart Stuff. "Now, if you don't mind, I have a few questions."

He proceeded to tell Stella about Ruby's brilliant father and the possible cure. When he showed her the page with the Horizon's phone number, her eyes went especially wide. Afterwards, she just stared at him for a while.

"So you're telling me that little girl is Ruby Sterling?"

He nodded.

"A true miracle," she said, mostly to herself. "We must find Doctor Bradley. He's working on the other side of the camp. Would you like to accompany me? I'll give you a tour on the way."

Matthew nodded, then he followed Stella out of the clinic and through the camp. The place was surprisingly extensive, equipped with all kinds of nooks and crannies and never-ending buildings. Mostly, there were many cottages. They seemed to be fitted with various types of specialty equipment: lifts, ramps, pulleys, levers, buttons.

"These," Stella said, "are our main resident cottages. Behind them, we have greenhouses and a garden, past that a mess hall. And past *that,* is our community lodge. That's where we're headed."

Matthew nodded. The Horizon was fascinating. Wide solar panels flanked the sides of each building and giant metal satellite dishes spun and spun.

"I see you have a lot of contraptions," he said.

Stella chuckled. "*Contraptions.* Indeed. We really invested in the green technologies these past few years. Being a remote location and all, it keeps the place self-sustainable—one of the reasons we're all here."

"Wait," Matthew said. "Are you the woman from the radio?"

"The radio?" She bit her lip. "Oh, right! The radio. No, that was Betsy. She passed last month. Her granddaughter, Matilda, is still here though." She pointed to a group of children in the distance.

Matthew had so many questions he wasn't even sure where to start. "How did you all get here?"

"After my colleague, Doctor Bradley, told us about the infection—about how people with brain illnesses were immune—we got to work informing as many specialty-care centers as we could. You know, developmental, mental health, elderly. From there, they did some recruiting—radio mostly—and voila. A small community formed."

She motioned toward a group of people up ahead. As they approached a picnic table of mostly women eating lunch, Stella called out their names.

"Ladies, this here is Matthew. Matthew, meet Brenda, Carolyn, Jennifer, Linda, Charlie, Dora, and Tabitha."

Tabitha?

His eyes zoomed in.

Tabitha?

His heart stopped completely.

It was Tabitha. *His* Tabitha.

The entire world dissolved in an instant and it was only her, at the center of the universe—his universe. Every cell inside electrified, like one thousand twinkling tingles popping all over his body. His eyes filled with tears as he buckled to his knees, hands reaching to the sky. He didn't know why they were reaching to the sky, but they were, and he couldn't stop them.

It was her.

It was *really* her.

"Tabitha, my love. You're ... here." Tears streamed down his cheeks, his neck, his chest. Everyone was looking at him—everyone except for her, for some reason—but he didn't care. He needed to go to her. He needed it more than he'd ever needed anything.

Stella helped him up.

"How ... how ..." He could barely form words. "How did she get here?"

"She came to us with a group from Memory Lane. Looks like you know her?"

"My wife," he said. "She's my wife. She's been lost for over a year."

He ran to her side and cupped her soft, bony fingers in his. She turned toward him, those dark eyes melting his soul into sludge.

"Sweet love, I'm so sorry. You have no idea how much I've missed you. I thought ... the fire ... never mind. You're here now and I love you. I have so much to tell you."

For a long moment, she just stared at him, her eyes hazier than he remembered.

"Tabitha, darling," Matthew whispered. "Please say something."

Her hand slowly drifted from his.

"I'm sorry. Have we met?"

CHAPTER SIXTY-ONE

Approximately one year earlier.

Tabitha Werner stepped outside and whipped back around. "See you in a jiffy!" She shut the door behind her, and, for a brief moment, wafted in the sweet spring air. Lately, she'd been trying to exercise an increasing appreciation for life. And really, how could a person not revel in such a season? Everything fresh and new. Why her husband disliked being outdoors was beyond her. Then again, they were opposites when it came to that sort of thing—most things.

But she wouldn't have it any other way.

She strolled down the sidewalk, smiling at people as she passed. "Good morning, sir!"

The stranger nodded. "Ma'am."

"Morning, Tabitha," her neighbor, Mrs. Able, said. "Where are you off to today?"

"Bookstore."

"Lovely. Well, enjoy!"

Everyone, it seemed, was out and about, tending to gardens or straightening the hedges, sweeping the front stairs or spraying off the pavement. She liked the busyness, even if it was distracting.

A gust of wind swirled and she shivered. On second thought, a shawl would be nice. She marched herself around, heading back home.

A moment later, unfamiliarity encroached.

A man tossed her a smile. "Hello again, ma'am."

Again? Why again?

A woman waved. "Back from the bookstore so soon?"

Right! The bookstore! That's where she was going. The woman was Mrs. Able—of course.

"Silly me!" Tabitha said, shaking her head.

She turned around. *Bookstore. Bookstore. Bookstore.* Repetition helped. But a few moments later, it faded all the same. *Where am I going?*

She shivered.

Oh right! Shawl!

She looked around. Except this time, nothing looked familiar. Not the people on the street, not even the streets themselves. It was as if she'd been plucked up and moved to an entirely new community.

Where am I? How did I get here?

She kept walking, waiting for the fog to clear. In the meantime, she turned left, then right, then left again. She'd walked these streets for years. Even though they appeared unfamiliar at the moment, she knew they *were* familiar, on some level.

I know where I'm going.

Her memory would return.

It always did.

But an hour later, it still hadn't. She ducked into a coffee shop and ordered a sandwich. "Ham on rye, please and thank you."

"Not the usual today, ma'am?"

She wrinkled her nose. "Usual?"

"You always order egg salad."

"Oh. Well then, yes, egg salad please."

The waiter smiled and the tension building in her shoulders faded. She was in a usual place with a usual order. She couldn't be *that* far from home, even if she didn't remember. So she ate her sandwich, read the paper, and afterwards asked the waiter for a bit of assistance.

"Sorry to bother you, but can you point me in the direction of ..."

Her mind drew a blank. *Bookstore. Bookstore. Bookstore.*

"Ah yes, the bookstore."

"Certainly. You're going to take a left at the next crossroads, then head down ..." He stopped, scratched his chin. "You know what, how about I write this down for you."

⌣

She glanced at the paper. *Keep walking, it will be on your left.*

But it wasn't on her left. Nor had it been on her left for quite some time. *Maybe I missed a turn?*

Nothing looked familiar. She was buried in the thick of suburbia, no commercial buildings in sight. An odd place to plop a—

Wait?

What am I looking for again?

She tried to focus.

Home? Yes, of course!

A few steps later, her mind turned over like a page in a book. She couldn't remember what she was supposed to remember. Every house looked more or less the same. *Am I looking for a house?* She stared at the sky, vast and perfectly cloudless, like still water.

It was a nice day for a walk, at least.

In what seemed like an instant, the houses were replaced by apartment buildings and store fronts and traffic whizzing past, at which point it all came rushing back.

I'm lost.

How could she have wandered for such a long time?

She tapped a woman on the shoulder. "Excuse me, I seem to be lost. Can you help me find my house?"

"Sure," the lady replied, pulling out her cell phone. "What's your address?"

"It's … it's …" But she couldn't remember.

"Ma'am?"

Address. Address. Address. She looked around for a clue, a street sign. And then she spotted it. *A bookstore!*

"Never mind," she said to the woman. "I just found what I've been looking for!"

Inside, she selected a bestselling title, then slumped into a chair.

A barista wandered over. "Can I get you anything, miss?"

"Hello, Jeffery! I'll have the usual peppermint tea."

Jeffery curled his brow. "Excuse me?"

"You're Jeffery, from Pages on Main. Right?"

He pointed to his name tag. "No, I'm Declan. And this isn't Pages on Main. This is South Street Reads. Would you still like that tea, though?"

She looked away, her cheeks getting hot. "Yes please."

She wanted to bury her head in a cushion. But by the time he returned, the ordeal was all but forgotten. She abandoned her worries in a book, sipping one tea, then another, until Declan returned.

"Sorry, but we're closing in ten minutes."

"Already?"

"Yes, ma'am, it's 9:00 p.m."

"9:00 p.m.!"

She set down the book and raced outside, the world now dark.

35 Tremblant Street West! That's my address!

She turned around to ask Declan for directions, but the door was already closed and locked. The night air was cold, practically winter again, and she didn't have a coat. She burrowed herself as best she could, edging into the darkness.

Her teeth chattered and bones chattered and she could hardly feel her fingers. An abandoned house sat up ahead, so she wandered toward it, desperate for shelter. The windows were barricaded, but the door was open.

She crept inside to find a mattress, a shopping cart, and a scattering of needles. *What is this place?* She kept going. Room after room there was nothing but junk, until, finally, a blanket. Beside it: a candle and a lighter.

The place was stale, filthy, disgusting, but she was so cold and tired it didn't matter. She lit the candle, spread out the blanket, and curled into a ball. Right before she closed her eyes, she removed the locket, just as she did every night, and placed it beside the burning candle.

∽

Tabitha's eyes shot open as a mouse scurried over her fingertips.

Oh. God.

She bolted straight up and dashed into the hallway. Sunlight flooded through cracks in the wall.

Where am I?

She kept walking. Trash was everywhere. The floor was rotting out. A dead rat, half flattened like a board, curled itself over a vent. And a person! The body lay face down on a mattress, something hanging from its vein.

Nothing made any sense. Why was she here? It was as if her mind had become a labyrinth of sludge, each path a sticky trap.

Who am I?

She wandered the streets, then ordered a peppermint tea from a place called Starbucks. She knew that name from somewhere. *Jeffery from Starbucks? Declan from Starbucks?* No, that wasn't quite right.

And then she saw it: *Memory Lane.*

That's where I'm supposed to be!

She walked through the front doors, and there it was: a sweet, musky scent—which she definitely remembered. And wide, peach floor tiles: she remembered those, too. And *Nurse Belinda!*

"Hi, Belinda!" she said. "I'm back!"

Nurse Belinda gave her a puzzled look. "So you are. Here for another visit?"

"No, this is my home now, I think."

"*Hmm.*" She slipped behind the reception desk. "We're not expecting you for a while yet. You and your husband."

"Husband?" she said. Something about that sounded equally correct and incorrect. "I don't have a husband."

Nurse Belinda brought her hand to her mouth. "Oh, Tabitha, I'm so sorry. My condolences."

"Thank you," she said, not exactly sure what there was to be sorry about.

Belinda passed a stack of papers toward her, then shuffled them back in. "You know what, we'll figure out the paperwork later. Here, come with me."

And so she did.

CHAPTER SIXTY-TWO

～

Matthew woke to a thick coating of slobber sloshed across his cheek.

Jim.

Of course.

He sat up straight and bumped his head on something. He'd forgotten where he was for a moment: a cabin fitted with numerous bunk beds. He rubbed his forehead as a giggle chirped beside him. He swiveled toward it.

"Ruby!"

The pain in his forehead vanished. There she was, alive and looking decent. Her eyes were bright and jiggly, per usual, and her skin was only very pale (instead very, *very* pale).

As he pulled her into his arms, it all came rushing back. Seeing Tabitha—*Tabitha!* Wrapping his fingers around hers.

But then he remembered that milky, forgotten stare. Her saying, "I'm sorry, have we met?" Followed by weakness, then more weakness, until Stella led him into a cabin and told him to rest.

"Matthew, why are you crying?" Ruby asked.

He patted away the tears and told her about Tabitha. When he'd finished, she held his hand, leaned into his chest. "I'm sorry she doesn't remember you."

"Me too."

The door creaked open, followed by a single knock.

"Yes?" Matthew said.

In stepped a tall, lanky man in a lab coat. Nearly everything about him was long and stretched and large. He was holding a tray.

"Hi, I'm Doctor Nicholas Bradley," he said. "I've brought you some tea."

He passed a mug to Matthew, then one to Ruby.

"May I?" he asked, motioning toward the opposite bunk.

Matthew nodded and the man sat. For a while, he just stared at Ruby with extra-wide eyes.

"I can't believe you're here," he said finally. "How did you find us?"

"The Book of Smart Stuff," Ruby replied.

"Pardon?"

Matthew pulled the notebook from his pocket. "This. It was her father's. It's missing quite a few pages, but we have reason to believe he was working on a cure."

Doctor Bradley nodded. "He was, yes."

Ruby skidded to the edge of the bed. "Dad *was* working on a cure? And he found one? And he was able to save himself? And he's here?"

Doctor Bradley's mouth went flat. He stared into his mug for a while.

"You know, your father and I were colleagues, but we were also friends. He talked about you all the time, about how smart and pretty and lovely you were. You were his motivation—the reason for all of his research."

Ruby smiled. "I was?"

"Absolutely. Indeed, your father *was* working on a cure ... a cure for your cancer. Or that's how it started. A few years ago he made some very important discoveries about the principles of synaptic nerve transmission—particularly in the realm of synaptic binding protein complexes. You see—"

Matthew gave the man a sideways look. "Synaptic *huh?*"

Doctor Bradley half grinned. "Right. Audience. In sum, Richard and I were working on a microchip that could essentially rewire the human brain from within. A cure, not only for Ruby's cancer, but for all neurological and neurodegenerative diseases."

"Even Alzheimer's?" Matthew asked.

He nodded. "All of them. When the infection hit, Richard and a few others were able to identify the odd pattern of immunity. He called me immediately, on account of my multiple sclerosis, and told me to move what I could of the lab here, to the Horizon. It was the only location he knew of that was both self-sustainable and could accommodate the ill."

"How did he know about this place?" Ruby asked.

Doctor Bradley frowned. "He was planning to send you here this summer."

"Oh … so that's why it was written down in the notebook." She stared at Matthew, her eyes a bit shaky, then she looked back at Doctor Bradley. "Where's Dad now?"

Again, the man looked at his mug, gave it a few swirls. "He called me on the way home. That was the last time I heard from him."

∽

Ruby stared at the ground, the words replaying in her mind.

He called me on the way home. That was the last time I heard from him.

Even though she knew exactly what this meant, it took a minute to register. First there was only numbness, but then her body began to jerk, followed by a tidal wave of tears. She fell into Matthew's chest and cried.

Dad was gone.

After all this time.

Gone.

"Doc," Matthew said. "Can we have a minute?"

Ruby couldn't make out his reply—couldn't hear anything over the sobs launching from her throat. She was crying so hard she could barely breathe. When she finally sat, pulling away from Matthew's chest, Doctor Bradley had left.

"It's all right," Matthew said, resting his hand on her cheek. His eyes were wrinkly and soft.

"Dad's gone," she whispered. "He's really gone."

Matthew combed his hands through her hair and wiped her wet face with a blanket. "You know, I'm not sure anyone is ever really *gone.*"

She sniffed. "What do you mean?"

He pulled out the locket from beneath his shirt and gave it a little rub. "The ones we love are always alive in our thoughts—and our hearts. When Tabitha first started losing her memory, this locket always brought her back."

He unclamped the locket and placed it around Ruby's neck. "How about this: anytime you miss your father, you hold this locket. I bet you'll find him."

Matthew winked. She touched the cold, smooth silver. *Dad?* At first, nothing happened. She waited for his booming voice, or for a vision of Dad to beam before her like a mirage. But then she closed her eyes, looking deep inside.

"I'm right here, Ruby," Dad whispered. "I always will be."

When she opened her eyes, Matthew was grinning.

"Did you find him?"

She nodded, choking back tears.

The front door creaked open and Doctor Bradley's face popped in.

"Is there anything else I can get you?"

"Actually, Doc," Matthew said, "I have a question, if you don't mind."

"Yes of course. What would you like to know?"

"How close are you to finding this cure?"

The man sighed. "Well, it's hard to say. I'm working solo now. I'd be lying if I said things aren't challenging without Richard's brilliant insight."

Matthew leaned into Ruby's ear and whispered, "Is it okay if I give him the notebook? It might help."

She took one last look at Dad's Book of Smart Stuff and nodded. She didn't need it anymore. He wasn't in that book anyway; he was in her heart and memories.

Matthew passed over the notebook. "Here. It's a bit rough, and some pages are missing, but it's worth a look."

For the next few minutes, Doctor Bradley thumbed through the Book of Smart Stuff, mumbling under his breath. Ruby could only make out some of what he was saying. Like, "Interesting use of theta waves," and "Hmm, implant the device more proximal to the dorsolateral prefrontal cortex?" Finally, he looked up. His eyes were brighter—less saggy than before.

"Yes, I think this notebook will help immensely."

CHAPTER SIXTY-THREE

~

Matthew walked down a dusty path with Ruby to his left and Stella to his right. Up ahead, Jim streaked across the property like a bolt of lightning. Every so often he'd stop and wiggle in the dew-covered grass, tail wagging something fierce.

The sight made Matthew crack a smile.

They were on their way to see Tabitha. Remembering the look in her eyes, muddled and blank, sliced through his chest like a gash. Still, he wanted—needed—to see her, even if she'd forgotten him. They didn't have to talk, or hold hands, or any of that. Her closeness was enough.

Tabitha was standing in the garden picking bumbleberries. She was beautiful as ever: dark, bottomless eyes; hair still wild and uncontainable. Despite everything that had happened, she was smiling that big, wacky smile.

As they approached, he stared at the nape of her neck—creamy, soft—and fought the urge to kiss it. Instead, he smiled the same smile he'd given her decades earlier, during that first day in the hallway. She stared at him for a while, then looked away. Was she blushing? A little, he was sure of it.

"We have some new friends for you to meet," Stella said. "This here is Ruby."

Tabitha leaned over and shook her hand. "Why hello, Ruby!"

Ruby smiled. "Hi, nice to meet you, Tabitha."

"And this is Matthew," Stella said.

Matthew extended his hand and stared into Tabitha's dark eyes, waiting for them to move, or soften, or pull him, or push him. But they didn't do anything. Not even a speck of recognition.

"Hello, Matthew! Pleasure to meet you," she said.

He pulled her hand upwards and gave it a kiss. She was blushing again.

He wanted to say a thousand things. Like, "I love you more than life itself," and "I've missed you with all of my soul," and "May I kiss your neck?" But all he could say was "Hello."

"Great!" Stella said. "Now that we're all acquainted, Matthew and Ruby will be spending some time with you this afternoon. Is that okay, Tabitha?"

"Of course. Happy to spend time with new friends."

Matthew straightened his shoulders and kinked out his elbow. "Ma'am, if it's okay with you, it would be my pleasure to escort you."

"A true gentlemen," Tabitha replied. "Yes, you may."

As she latched onto his elbow, Matthew adjusted her shawl. He stomped his foot, just to make sure he wasn't floating into the sky.

Ruby gave him a thumbs up as they walked toward the lake.

Moments later, they sat on a bench by the water's edge. The breeze was earthy and soulful. Perfectly calm water extended in every direction, so grand and imposing and beautiful. Matthew stared at the sky full of clouds. *Cumulus clouds. The puffy ones.* Beneath the heaven-bound fir trees, it was easy to forget about all that had happened.

No bodies, hardening to a crisp or dissolving to bone.

No societal aftermath, as if the world had been placed on pause.

No Center Ones or pale, gray cities or soul-rattling silence.

"It's really something, isn't it?" Tabitha said, staring out at the lake. She looked at Matthew and smiled. He stared into her dark, consuming eyes.

One.

Twinkling.

Tingle.

Maybe he was a stranger. And maybe he was too old for this. But it felt like old love, and new love. And *so what* if she didn't remember—could never remember.

He would remember for the both of them.

Jim galloped over and curled at their feet. He arched his back on the bright, green grass, soaking it all in. Ruby leaned into Matthew's shoulder.

Despite it all—the Not Normal and the world ending and the sickness and the unknown—he was momentarily thankful.

He loved, and was loved.

What more could an old man ask for?

Acknowledgments

First, thanks to you—yes you, dearest reader. Whether you found this book terrific, meh, or a steaming pile of rubbish, I'm immensely grateful you took the time to read it. Stories are nothing without an audience, so thanks for being a part of mine.

A very special thanks to my editor, Lou Aronica at The Story Plant, whose insight, vision, and publishing expertise brought Matthew and Ruby's journey to life. Many thanks to the rest of The Story Plant crew, in particular Allison Maretti, Stacy Mathewson (copyeditor), and Philip Newey (proofreader). I greatly appreciate your assistance and attention to detail.

Endless gratitude for my wonderful agent, Travis Pennington at The Knight Agency. I count my lucky stars for you. Your literary clairvoyance, kindness, and patience are beyond appreciated. Thank you for believing in this story. And thank you for believing in me.

As you know, I made all of this up. However, I'd be remiss not to acknowledge a few nuggets of science that perked my imagination years ago. Specifically, online coverage of the Frankenvirus (it's real)[1]; this paper[2], and this paper[3], on the topics of parasitic and stress-induced viral reactivation; and this case study[4], documenting a prospective case of rabies with a 25-year incubation period.

My journey as a writer has been shaped by so many fabulous people. Notable mentions include my high school English teacher, Cindy McDowell, who adopted one of my kittens, but more importantly taught me the beauty of creative writing. Thanks also to my master's supervisor, Dr. Ken McRae, for saying, "Hey, you're a really good writer," and for encouraging (forcing) me to step outside of my comfort zone on a number of occasions (one of which included teaching statistics, shudder). The skills I acquired under your supervision have greatly served me in life, and I look forward to our next beer at the Grad Club.

To the many remarkable friends and colleagues whose support on this journey has left me feeling warm and fuzzy: you know who you are, and I thank you. Special mention to my dear friend, Amanda Lyons, for being a continual burst of confidence throughout this admittedly terrifying process. Your text-based counseling sessions were (are) very appreciated.

I'm tremendously grateful for the loving encouragement of my wonderful in-laws: Gerbert, Dorothy, Tracy, Paul, Tyson, Max, Sam, Abby, Josh, and Nik. Your support means the world. I also must pay tribute to the love, wisdom, and appreciation for a good story that my grandparents Betty and Robert King conveyed over the years. Grandpa, we miss you dearly. I hope you're able to snag a copy up there (and thanks for passing on the "writing gene").

Lastly, there exists a small tribe of people for whom I am especially grateful. While each of you deserves an entire chapter of gratitude, you'll have to settle for the following.

To my sisters, Emily and Sarah: I'm delighted (particularly after years of stealing your stuff), that you not only volunteer to read every word that I write, but seem to enjoy it. Your encouragement has greatly contributed to the publication of this book, which may have otherwise remained a half-wit idea, taking up space on my hard drive. You're extraordinary sisters, extraordinary people, and my very best friends.

To Mom and Dad: You have awarded me with a lifetime of love and support that was often undeserved (during all years ending with teen, specifically). I'm at a loss when it comes to properly articulating how blessed I am to be your daughter—which says a lot, given that I'm a writer. I'm continually inspired by your selflessness, dedication, and honest-to-God kindness. The world needs more of you two.

To my husband, Dave: I love you oodles. That's probably a cheesy thing to publicly profess in an acknowledgement section, but I do. Thanks for reading my work with integrity, loving me despite my flaws, and being my partner in crime (but mostly just everydayness—like dishwashing. Thanks for being my partner in dishwashing). You make me the happiest.

Lastly, to my daughter, Andi: You can't read this, on account of being two, but you're the most wonderful thing that's ever happened. Even though your nap regressions majorly contributed to the amount of time it took to edit this damn book, that's perfectly all right, because I love you. I hope you read this story one day, and I hope you enjoy it.

References

~

[1] Morelle, R. (2014, March 4). BBC News. 30,000-year-old giant virus 'comes back to life'. Retrieved from: http://www.bbc.com/news/science-environment-26387276.

[2] Reese, T. A., Wakeman, B. S., Choi, H.S., et al. (2014). Helminth infection reactivates latent γ-herpesvirus via cytokine competition at a viral promotor. Science, 345, 573-577.

[3] Padgett, D. A., Sheridan, J. F., Dorne, J., Berntson, G. G., Candelora, J., & Glaser, R. (1998). Social stress and the reactivation of latent herpes simplex virus type 1. PNAS, 95, 7231-7235.

[4] Shankar, S. K., Mahadevan, A., Sapico, S. D., Ghodkirekar, M. S. G., Pinto, R. G. W., & Madhusudana, S.N. (2012). Rabies viral encephalitis with probable 25 year incubation period! Annual Indian Academic Neurology, 15, 221-223.

ABOUT THE AUTHOR

Lisa King is a fiction author and researcher whose work has been published in numerous academic journals. She holds degrees in psychology and neuroscience from Western University. In her spare time, Lisa enjoys family outings, ample coffee, and unapologetic napping.

She lives in London, Ontario with her husband and daughter, and can be found online at www.Author-LisaKing.com.

Vanishing Hour is her debut novel.